ANNIE H⧸
THE BLUE DIAMOND

Annie Haynes was born in 1865, the daughter of an ironmonger.

By the first decade of the twentieth century she lived in London and moved in literary and early feminist circles. Her first crime novel, *The Bungalow Mystery*, appeared in 1923, and another nine mysteries were published before her untimely death in 1929.

Who Killed Charmian Karslake? appeared posthumously, and a further partially-finished work, *The Crystal Beads Murder*, was completed with the assistance of an unknown fellow writer, and published in 1930.

Also by Annie Haynes

ANNIE HAYNES

THE BLUE DIAMOND

With an introduction
by Curtis Evans

DEAN STREET PRESS

Published by Dean Street Press 2016

All Rights Reserved

First published in 1925 by The Bodley Head

Cover by DSP

Introduction © Curtis Evans 2016

ISBN 978 1 911095 25 5

www.deanstreetpress.co.uk

The Mystery of The Missing Author
Annie Haynes and Her Golden Age Detective Fiction

The psychological enigma of Agatha Christie's notorious 1926 vanishing has continued to intrigue Golden Age mystery fans to the present day. The Queen of Crime's eleven-day disappearing act is nothing, however, compared to the decades-long disappearance, in terms of public awareness, of between-the-wars mystery writer Annie Haynes (1865-1929), author of a series of detective novels published between 1923 and 1930 by Agatha Christie's original English publisher, The Bodley Head. Haynes's books went out of print in the early Thirties, not long after her death in 1929, and her reputation among classic detective fiction readers, high in her lifetime, did not so much decline as dematerialize. When, in 2013, I first wrote a piece about Annie Haynes' work, I knew of only two other living persons besides myself who had read any of her books. Happily, Dean Street Press once again has come to the rescue of classic mystery fans seeking genre gems from the Golden Age, and is republishing all Haynes' mystery novels. Now that her crime fiction is coming back into print, the question naturally arises: Who Was Annie Haynes? Solving the mystery of this forgotten author's lost life has taken leg work by literary sleuths on two continents (my thanks for their assistance to Carl Woodings and Peter Harris).

Until recent research uncovered new information about Annie Haynes, almost nothing about her was publicly known besides the fact of her authorship of twelve mysteries during the Golden Age of detective fiction. Now we know that she led an altogether intriguing life, too soon cut short by disability and death, which took her from the isolation of the rural English Midlands in the nineteenth century to the cultural high life of Edwardian London. Haynes was born in 1865 in the Leicestershire town of Ashby-de-la-Zouch, the first child of ironmonger Edwin Haynes and Jane (Henderson) Haynes, daughter of Montgomery Henderson, longtime superintendent of the gardens at nearby Coleorton Hall, seat of the Beaumont baronets. After her father left his family, young Annie resided with her grandparents at the gardener's cottage at Coleorton Hall, along with her mother and younger brother. Here Annie doubtlessly obtained an acquaintance with the ways of the country gentry that would serve her well in her career as a genre fiction writer.

We currently know nothing else of Annie Haynes' life in Leicestershire, where she still resided (with her mother) in 1901, but by 1908, when Haynes was in her early forties, she was living in London with Ada Heather-Bigg (1855-1944) at the Heather-Bigg family home, located halfway between Paddington Station and Hyde Park at 14 Radnor Place, London. One of three daughters of Henry Heather-Bigg, a noted pioneer in the development of orthopedics and artificial limbs, Ada Heather-Bigg was a prominent Victorian and Edwardian era feminist and social reformer. In the 1911 British census entry for 14 Radnor Place, Heather-Bigg, a "philanthropist and journalist," is listed as the head of the household and Annie Haynes, a "novelist," as a "visitor," but in fact Haynes would remain there with Ada Heather-Bigg until Haynes' death in 1929.

Haynes' relationship with Ada Heather-Bigg introduced the aspiring author to important social sets in England's great metropolis. Though not a novelist herself, Heather-Bigg was an important figure in the city's intellectual milieu, a well-connected feminist activist of great energy and passion who believed strongly in the idea of women attaining economic independence through remunerative employment. With Ada Heather-Bigg behind her, Annie Haynes's writing career had powerful backing indeed. Although in the 1911 census Heather-Bigg listed Haynes' occupation as "novelist," it appears that Haynes did not publish any novels in book form prior to 1923, the year that saw the appearance of *The Bungalow Mystery*, which Haynes dedicated to Heather-Bigg. However, Haynes was a prolific producer of newspaper serial novels during the second decade of the twentieth century, penning such works as *Lady Carew's Secret*, *Footprints of Fate*, *A Pawn of Chance*, *The Manor Tragedy* and many others.

Haynes' twelve Golden Age mystery novels, which appeared in a tremendous burst of creative endeavor between 1923 and 1930, like the author's serial novels retain, in stripped-down form, the emotionally heady air of the nineteenth-century triple-decker sensation novel, with genteel settings, shocking secrets, stormy passions and eternal love all at the fore, yet they also have the fleetness of Jazz Age detective fiction. Both in their social milieu and narrative pace Annie Haynes' detective novels bear considerable resemblance to contemporary works by Agatha Christie; and it is interesting to note in this regard that Annie Haynes and Agatha Christie were the only female mystery writers published by The Bodley Head, one of the more notable English mystery imprints in the early Golden Age. "A very remarkable feature of recent detective fiction," observed the *Illustrated London News* in 1923, "is the skill displayed by women in this branch of story-telling. Isabel Ostrander, Carolyn Wells, Annie Haynes and last, but very far from least, Agatha Christie, are contesting the laurels of Sherlock Holmes' creator with a great spirit, ingenuity and success." Since Ostrander and Wells were American authors, this left Annie Haynes, in the estimation of the *Illustrated London News*, as the main British female competitor to Agatha Christie. (Dorothy L. Sayers, who, like Haynes, published her debut mystery novel in 1923, goes unmentioned.) Similarly, in 1925 *The Sketch* wryly noted that "[t]ired men, trotting home at the end of an imperfect day, have been known to pop into the library and ask for an Annie Haynes. They have not made a mistake in the street number. It is not a cocktail they are asking for..."

Twenties critical opinion adjudged that Annie Haynes' criminous concoctions held appeal not only for puzzle fiends impressed with the "considerable craftsmanship" of their plots (quoting from the *Sunday Times* review of *The Bungalow Mystery*), but also for more general readers attracted to their purely literary qualities. "Not only a crime story of merit, but also a novel which will interest readers to whom mystery for its own sake has little appeal," avowed

The Nation of Haynes' *The Secret of Greylands*, while the *New Statesman* declared of *The Witness on the Roof* that "Miss Haynes has a sense of character; her people are vivid and not the usual puppets of detective fiction." Similarly, the *Bookman* deemed the characters in Haynes' *The Abbey Court Murder* "much truer to life than is the case in many sensational stories" and *The Spectator* concluded of *The Crime at Tattenham Corner*, "Excellent as a detective tale, the book also is a charming novel."

Sadly, Haynes' triumph as a detective novelist proved short lived. Around 1914, about the time of the outbreak of the Great War, Haynes had been stricken with debilitating rheumatoid arthritis that left her in constant pain and hastened her death from heart failure in 1929, when she was only 63. Haynes wrote several of her detective novels on fine days in Kensington Gardens, where she was wheeled from 14 Radnor Place in a bath chair, but in her last years she was able only to travel from her bedroom to her study. All of this was an especially hard blow for a woman who had once been intensely energetic and quite physically active.

In a foreword to *The Crystal Beads Murder*, the second of Haynes' two posthumously published mysteries, Ada Heather-Bigg noted that Haynes' difficult daily physical struggle "was materially lightened by the warmth of friendships" with other authors and by the "sympathetic and friendly relations between her and her publishers." In this latter instance Haynes' experience rather differed from that of her sister Bodleian, Agatha Christie, who left The Bodley Head on account of what she deemed an iniquitous contract that took unjust advantage of a naive young author. Christie moved, along with her landmark detective novel *The Murder of Roger Ackroyd* (1926), to Collins and never looked back, enjoying ever greater success with the passing years.

At the time Christie crossed over to Collins, Annie Haynes had only a few years of life left. After she died at 14 Radnor Place on 30 March 1929, it was reported in the press that "many people well-known in the literary world" attended the author's funeral at St.

Michaels and All Angels Church, Paddington, where her sermon was delivered by the eloquent vicar, Paul Nichols, brother of the writer Beverley Nichols and dedicatee of Haynes' mystery novel *The Master of the Priory*; yet by the time of her companion Ada Heather-Bigg's death in 1944, Haynes and her once highly-praised mysteries were forgotten. (Contrastingly, Ada Heather-Bigg's name survives today in the University College of London's Ada Heather-Bigg Prize in Economics.) Only three of Haynes' novels were ever published in the United States, and she passed away less than a year before the formation of the Detection Club, missing any chance of being invited to join this august body of distinguished British detective novelists. Fortunately, we have today entered, when it comes to classic mystery, a period of rediscovery and revival, giving a reading audience a chance once again, after over eighty years, to savor the detective fiction fare of Annie Haynes. *Bon appétit!*

Curtis Evans

Chapter One

"THERE! I think that will about do! No, stay—the tail of that 'M' is not quite right, and I will make it all a bit deeper while I am about it. Our initials must last as long as anybody's, eh, Minnie?"

The girl blushed and smiled as she glanced at the tall, well-set-up figure.

"I think they look beautiful," she said shyly, as after putting a few finishing touches the man stepped back to her side and surveyed his handiwork with pride: J.G. and M.S.

"May it soon be M.G.," he said as he slipped his arm round her waist. "What a lot of initials there are! The old tree will soon be full."

"All the lovers that have been in Lockford for years have carved their initials there," the girl observed, looking up at the wide, hoary trunk. "See here, Jim, these new ones—G.D. and M.H. That will be Mr. Garth Davenant and Miss Mavis."

"Then it is all right that Miss Mavis's maid should be the next," the man responded, implanting a kiss upon her half-averted cheek. "Never mind, Minnie"—with a careless laugh—"there's nobody here to see!"

"How you do go on!" said Minnie, releasing herself and turning her hot cheeks away. "I have to be back at six to dress Miss Mavis for this dinner at Davenant Court, and we haven't drunk the water at the Wishing Well yet."

"That is the next thing, is it?" the man said absently. He was gazing intently up at the grand old oak, under the wide-spreading branches of which they were standing. "Minnie, I believe that is a grey crow's nest up there! Wait a minute, I must have an egg if it is. This old fellow won't be difficult to climb, I fancy."

"Oh, Jim, Jim! Indeed you mustn't!" the girl began. But her protest went unheeded. He had already thrown off his coat and was climbing up the tree before the words had left her mouth, and she could only watch his ascent in a sort of terrified fascination.

Half-way up, however, he halted with, as it seemed to her, a sharp exclamation, then after a moment's pause he turned and began his downward journey.

"'Twasn't a crow's after all!" he said as he slid rapidly to the ground. "It was nothing but some old rubbish, and the game wasn't worth the candle."

"It will bring us bad luck, though," Minnie wailed. "Whatever made you climb the Lovers' Oak, Jim? It shows right well you are a foreigner. If you'd been a Devonshire man you wouldn't have tried it on, not for twenty nests."

Her lips were quivering, big tears were standing in her eyes. The man glanced at her with some compunction; quite evidently the ill-luck of which she spoke, and which his hasty action had braved, was a very real thing to her.

"Cheer up, Minnie!" he said with a rough attempt at consolation. "I promise you I will let the Lovers' Oak alone in the future. And come along now, I'll drink gallons of water at the Wishing Well to make up!"

"It is dreadfully unlucky"—Minnie sighed—"but maybe it'll be taken into account that you are a foreigner. Now the Wishing Well—do be careful there, Jim."

"I won't move a step till you give me leave," he assured her as they turned aside down a narrow rugged path and picked their way over stones worn smooth by the feet of countless lovers. "You wish while you drink, that's it, isn't it, Minnie?"

"Yes. They say in olden times a man who went out to the wars—Crusades they called them then—was wounded and reported dead. When after long years he made his way back to Lockford he found his wife, believing him dead, had married again. So for love of her he would claim neither title nor estate lest he should shame her, but made himself a hut here under the oak so that, all unknown, he could watch over her. They called him the hermit of Lockford, and only when he died was it found out who he really was."

"Umph! I fancy I have heard something like that before," said Jim slowly.

Minnie was too much in earnest to heed the scepticism in his tone.

"He lived on berries and things from the woods, and he got his drink from the Wishing Well. See"—as they came in sight of the clear, limpid water, with tiny, wild maidenhair-fern growing in every niche and cranny of the old grey rock above it—"this was his cup," picking up a curious-looking hollowed stone that stood on the wide ledge beside, "so they say, but Miss Mavis doesn't believe it; she says she's sure it can't be so old."

The man took it from her and looked at it.

"Um! Queer sort of thing, I should say. Now you must tell me what to do, Minnie, or I shall be making a mistake again. You have to drink out of this, don't you?

"Drink and wish," she said solemnly. "Wish for something you want very much, Jim, for a man can only have three wishes granted in his lifetime."

Jim stooped and filled the cup.

"Well, here goes, then! I wish—"

With a cry Minnie stopped him.

"You mustn't say what it is. You mustn't tell anyone, or you won't get it," she said, with real distress. "Oh, do be careful, Jim! Let me drink first."

"Right you are!" and with affected contrition he handed the cup to her.

Minnie stood silent a moment as if lost in thought, then she raised the cup to her lips and sipped the water slowly.

"Now, Jim!" she said as she passed it back.

Apparently Jim was in no uncertainty as to his wish; he emptied the cup with great celerity.

"That is soon done, then. Now if our wishes come true we shall be happy enough, Minnie."

He tucked his arm in hers as they turned back.

"Yes, unless climbing the oak has brought us bad luck," Minnie rejoined, unable to forget her grievance. "What made you stop when you got so far, Jim?" she went on curiously. "I heard you call out as if you were surprised." The man hesitated a moment.

"I was surprised it wasn't a nest, after all. As for why I came back, I could see you didn't want me to go on and that's enough for me any day, Minnie."

Minnie rewarded him with a glance and a smile.

"Why, Jim—" The sound of a clock striking the hour interrupted her. "Six! Why, I ought to be at the Manor!" she cried in consternation. "How we must have dawdled! Come, Jim," quickening her steps, "we must make all the haste we can or I shall be late and Miss Mavis will be waiting."

"Tell her you have been to the Lovers' Oak and the Wishing Well and she will understand," suggested Jim as they hurried along. "I dare say she took her time with Mr. Davenant the other day. You won't be so very late, after all; we are getting to the edge of the wood, and it won't take you a minute to run across the Park. Oh, confound it all, here's that fellow Greyson!"

Minnie's pretty pink colour deepened a little as she caught sight of the tall figure in corduroy shooting-coat and knickerbockers coming round the corner of the path; and as the new-comer stepped a little aside to allow them to pass she glanced up into his moody face wistfully.

"Good evening, Tom!" she said, with a little hesitation and a half movement as if to hold out her hand.

But the man's face did not relax; he affected not to see her pause.

"Good evening, Minnie!" he said stiffly as he went by.

Minnie glanced round after him with an uneasy look upon her pretty face.

Three months ago all Lockford had looked upon Tom Greyson and Minnie Spencer as lovers. They had been the best of friends from their childish days, when their fathers had lived side by side in the row of cottages standing on the bank of the little stream that ran through the village; and when in due time Tom was second gamekeeper at the Manor, and Minnie became Miss Mavis Hargreave's own maid, it seemed only natural that they should walk out together on Sunday evenings, and that Tom should fondly dream of a day when he should bring his old playfellow to the little cottage in the Home Wood which he found at present so lonely. But with the advent of Jim Gregory as under-gardener at the Manor everything was changed—from the moment when the glance of Gregory's dark eyes had lighted upon pretty Minnie Spencer sitting demurely with the head servants in the house-keeper's pew at church the very first Sunday he came to Lockford he had attached himself to her, and very soon poor Tom Greyson was rudely awakened from his blissful dreams of the sweet young wife who was coming to share his little home.

From the first Jim Gregory had fascinated Miss Hargreave's susceptible little maid with his tales of life under other conditions and the fact that he was a "foreigner,"-—i.e. not Devonshire born and bred—while it caused the other inhabitants of Lockford to look at him askance, apparently only increased his fascination for her.

Gregory laughed openly now as he opened the wicket leading into the Park, and saw the stalwart form of his discarded rival striding away through the wood.

"Tom Greyson looks pretty bad, eh, Minnie?" he observed teasingly.

Minnie was not to be drawn. She took no notice of his remark; her rosy mouth was pursed up ominously.

"You must walk quicker than this, Jim, or I shall be too late to dress Miss Mavis."

Gregory's long strides soon caught her up.

"What is Miss Hargreave going to wear—the diamonds, the 'Luck of the Hargreaves'?"

"The 'Luck of the Hargreaves'!" Minnie echoed contemptuously. "That shows how much you know about such things, Jim.

Miss Mavis will never wear the 'Luck'—nor her ladyship either. It is kept for Sir Arthur's wife."

"Oh, I didn't know!" Gregory said humbly. "I thought as it was such a grand occasion, the first time Miss Mavis has been to the Court since she was engaged to Mr. Davenant, maybe she would wear them—that Sir Arthur would lend them to her, like."

Minnie shook her head decidedly.

"They will never be worn until Sir Arthur's bride wears them on her wedding-day. Miss Mavis was telling me the other day that they say the heir's bride must wear the great Blue Diamond then if it is to bring them good luck."

"Luck! Luck!" Gregory repeated impatiently. "What people you Devonshire folk are for talking about luck, to be sure! I should say it was luck enough to have those diamonds to wear at all. Why, how many thousands of pounds are they worth?"

"Oh, I don't know! Ever so many," Minnie replied at random." I have heard Granny say, when they sent them to the London Exhibition in 1854, that they had a special case with iron bars outside for them and a policeman to watch them night and day!"

"My word! And have you ever seen them, Minnie?"

"Once," Minnie replied, pleased at the effect her words were producing. "When I was a little child, and Sir Noel was High Sheriff, he gave a big ball to the county and Mother and I came up to see her ladyship, Miss Dorothy's mother, dressed. She had the diamonds on them. They looked like—like a string of fire!" concluded Minnie, somewhat at a loss for a suitable simile.

"My!" said Jim in an awestruck tone. "Where do they keep them, Minnie, and the gold plate? Mr. Briggs was telling me about that the other night. It must be a rare sight."

"They are all safe in the strong-room," replied Minnie importantly. "And I have heard that even Mr. Jenkins can't get at them, nor anybody—only Sir Arthur himself. Miss Dorothy is more likely to wear the diamonds than Miss Mavis, I'm thinking," she concluded with a little laugh.

Jim glanced at her curiously.

"What! You think Sir Arthur—"

"Hush! Hush! Somebody might hear us," the girl said apprehensively as they entered the dark belt of shrubbery which immediately surrounded the Manor. "I really must make haste now, Jim."

"You will be in time enough," the man said, detaining her. "Miss Mavis was sitting with Mr. Davenant when we came out. I'll warrant she won't be thinking about the time. What is the story about Mr. Davenant's brother, Minnie? I have heard there is queer talk about him, that he daren't come back to the country."

"It is years since it happened," Minnie said slowly, "and I don't rightly understand it. But I believe he had a quarrel with somebody over cards, and it ended in Mr. Walter Davenant shooting the other. They say he would have to stand his trial for murder if he came home. Folk said her ladyship wouldn't think Mr. Garth good enough for Miss Mavis because he was only the younger son, but if Mr. Walter can't come back Mr. Garth is as good as the eldest, I say."

"Just as good," Mr. Gregory acquiesced. "And they seem to be very fond of one another—he and Miss Mavis—though he is so much older. But I haven't heard half I wanted, Minnie; you'll be at the same place as last night about nine o'clock?"

The girl hesitated.

"Oh, I don't think I dare."

"There will be no one at home to-night," urged Jim. "And I must see you again. Say you will come, Minnie?" coaxingly.

"Well, if I can," Minnie conceded. "Oh, Jim, there is Sir Arthur— he wants you!"

She tore herself away and ran down the path leading to the back of the house.

Jim touched his hat as he went towards the tall, fair young man who beckoned to him.

"Yes, Sir Arthur."

"I have been round to the houses just now," Sir Arthur said with a frown, "and I scarcely think there is enough ventilation in the first. I shall send for Slater in the morning. And the renanthera want sponging; the sphagnum was quite dry. You must be more careful, my man, or—"

Jim touched his hat again.

"I will go at once, Sir Arthur," he said.

Sir Arthur turned back to the Manor with a nod. His orchid-houses were his latest hobby—a very expensive one, as he was finding—and his frown deepened as he recalled the cost of some of his failures.

Hargreave Manor was a low, rambling house, built for the most part of grey stone; the centre and main portion were gener-ally ascribed to the early Stuart or late Tudor period, though local tradition assigned it an even earlier date. Since that time succes-sive Hargreaves had added a story there, a room here, until they had succeeded in producing a structure which, delightful as it was to its possessors, was the despair of archaeologists. To its archi-tectural deficiencies, however, Time had been very kind, throwing over them a rich veil of jasmine and clematis, of ivy and Virginia creeper, until in mellow autumn the hoary walls were covered with a crimson glory. But to-day, in the cool spring twilight, the tender green leaves were unfolding themselves, the tiny clinging tendrils catching at the rough old stones.

The front-door stood hospitably open; it was a fancy of Lady Laura Hargreave, who acted as chatelaine for her son, to make a sit-ting-room of the wide, low hall, and in winter tea was always served there, by the big open hearth.

Sir Arthur's face brightened as he stepped in and saw a tall, slight girl playing with two great wolf-hounds which were leaping up and caressing her boisterously.

"Why, Dorothy!" he began, as he crossed quickly to her. "This is an unexpected pleasure. How did you get here? Down, Hero! Down, Lion!"

"The dears! They knew me directly," Dorothy Hargreave said with a laugh. "And they were so pleased to see me, weren't you,

Hero?" laying her soft cheek against the dog's velvet skin. "You did not ask me how I got here first thing, did you, Lion?"

Sir Arthur looked amused.

"If a certain young lady arrives a week sooner than she promises isn't it likely that her affectionate cousin will inquire how she managed to surmount the two miles from the station?" he demanded jestingly. "You haven't shaken hands with me yet, Dorothy!"

"Oh, haven't I?" his cousin said carelessly, though her colour deepened perceptibly, and her soft brown eyes drooped as she laid her hand in his.

Dorothy Hargreave was the orphan daughter of Sir Arthur's uncle and predecessor, the Sir Noel who had been High Sheriff in his year. Though she was the child of the elder brother she was several years the baronet's junior, and her spirit and vivacity, with her lonely position, had combined to make her since her mother's death the pet and plaything of her cousins. Sir Arthur had with the title inherited the entailed estates, but Dorothy's father had naturally left his daughter everything that was in his power; and as a consequence his successor had found himself considerably crippled as regards money affairs. His long minority however—for the unwritten family law of the Hargreaves enforced by Sir Noel delayed the coming of age of the heir until he was five-and-twenty—gave the estates time to recover themselves. The Lockford gossips, moreover, had long since made up their minds that matters would eventually be straightened out in the old time-honoured fashion—the heiress would marry her cousin, Sir Arthur, and title and money would come together again.

The cousins were excellent friends, though of late Dorothy's gaiety had given way to a curious embarrassment when Sir Arthur was in the room. Hargreave himself had known ever since his accession to the title that it had been his uncle's great wish that he should marry Dorothy, and he had always held himself, to a certain extent, bound by it; but so far he had shown no disposition in any way to place the affair on a different footing. Dorothy was very young, he told himself; it was only fair that she should see more of the world before she pledged herself, and he was by no means anxious to resign his bachelor liberty. But to-night his eyes softened as he watched the girl, as she stood alternately caressing and teasing the two hounds.

"I am very glad to see you too, Dorothy," he said softly.

"Are you?" Dorothy's ready tongue for once seemed to have deserted her. "I am afraid I have upset Aunt Laura's plans a little by my unexpected appearance, though," she went on, with an effort, "but Mrs. Danver's infant developed measles, and we all had to leave at a moment's notice. I really had no choice but to take you by storm. Besides, I wanted to congratulate Mr. Davenant."

Hargreave smiled at her.

"And incidentally Mavis?"

"I must wait and see what he is like in his new character first."

"Were you surprised to hear the news?"

She shrugged her shoulders.

"They always seemed to be quarrelling."

"A sure sign, I am told," Hargreave said quietly.

"A sign of what?" wilfully.

"Of love. Come and sit down, Dorothy. I want to hear what you have been doing."

He drew forward one of the big oak chairs.

"The Manor will be dull without Mavis. We shall have to persuade you to stay with us, Dorothy."

The girl made no reply; her face was turned away. Hargreave could not guess at the sudden shy consciousness that was sending the blood in one glad tumultuous wave over cheeks and temples and forehead right up to the roots of her curly brown hair.

He leaned forward.

"Well, will you, Dorothy?" he said.

"I dare say you will soon be tired of me," the girl said in a muffled tone.

"I don't think so," her cousin said meaningly. "Will you let us try, Dorothy?"

"I don't know—perhaps—"

Before the girl had time for more the sound of footsteps on the wide oaken staircase made them both start.

"Why, Arthur, Dorothy, what are you dreaming of? You will certainly never be ready in time to start. Be off, both of you!"

And Lady Laura Hargreave, drawing on her gloves, came slowly across the hall to them, little guessing how inopportune her entrance was, or how she was thereby retarding the fulfilment of her favourite scheme.

Chapter Two

"You will come over early to-morrow, Garth?" Garth Davenant wrapped Mavis's cloak more closely round her.

"At the very earliest moment that I can get away. My father wants me to go over McDonnell's estimates for the drainage first thing, but that will not take me long. Will you come and meet me, Mavis?"

"Where?" Mavis Hargreave glanced up shyly into the dark rugged face, with its look of latent strength and power and the grey eyes fixed on hers so lovingly.

Her love for Garth Davenant had become so entirely a part of her being that, though she had in no degree realized its strength until his words and caresses had called it into active life, the very intensity of her happiness now almost frightened her. She told herself that it was too full, too complete, something would surely happen to mar it; and to-night her vague fears shadowed her big brown eyes and gave a touch of pathos to the curves of her mobile mouth.

Garth Davenant thought that never had she looked fairer, more altogether desirable in his eyes, than now, when under pretence of arranging her wraps, he detained her for a few last words in the corridor.

"I fancy you don't look quite happy to-night, dearest," he went on, "and I feel as if in some way it must be our fault. You mustn't let the trouble that lies over this unhappy house shadow your life too, Mavis."

The girl's lips quivered a little as she glanced up at him.

"It is so dreadful for poor Lady Davenant, Garth! She looks so sad, always. I am so sorry for you all!" with a touch light as a feather upon his arm.

Garth stooped and put his lips upon the ungloved fingers.

The shadow that lay over Davenant Court sometimes seemed to him almost too heavy to be borne, since the dread was a never-ending one. Poor Walter Davenant had been but a boy when the tragedy occurred that wrecked his life. He had become involved with some card swindlers and discovered that his great friend, a man whom he trusted implicitly, was deceiving him. In his anger he accused him openly of unfair dealing, and in the hubbub that followed the man was shot, and Walter Davenant fled from the country with the mark of Cain on his brow.

One of the saddest things about the whole affair was the fact that if he had remained and stood his trial the verdict would almost certainly have been one of acquittal, or at the most the sentence would have been merely a nominal one, since there was no doubt as to St. Leger's guilt, and his reputation was thoroughly bad. Young Davenant's flight put a different complexion on the matter; a warrant was issued for his arrest, and if he should be brought to trial, after the lapse of years, things might go hard with him.

Small wonder was it that Garth spoke of the trouble overhanging them, or that Sir John Davenant should look years older than his actual age, while a terrible dread haunted his wife's eyes.

Entertaining at Davenant Court had been for years a thing of the past, and this dinner party in honour of their son's engagement had been somewhat of a strain on both Sir John and Lady Davenant.

Garth feared that the effort had been apparent to Mavis, and his thoughts grew very tender.

"Under the big beech by the park gates at eleven to-morrow," he whispered. "Will you be there, darling? I will bring those poems you wanted to hear, and try to coax the smiles back somehow."

"Then you will read to me? Yes, I will come."

Garth lowered his tall head a little nearer.

"You will have a smile ready for me, Mavis? I cannot help fancying that there have been tears very near the surface to-night."

Mavis's lips quivered, the clasp of her slender fingers upon his arm tightened.

"Sometimes I am afraid we are too happy, Garth—that something will come and spoil everything."

Garth's look was very tender as he gazed into the dewy eyes upraised timidly to his.

"What a silly child it is!" he said fondly. "Nothing could spoil our happiness as long as we care for one another. Come, shake off your fears and give me one smile before we part!"

Mavis did her best to obey him, but her lips were trembling when he placed her in the carriage with her mother.

"Courage, Mavis!" he whispered, just touching her hand. "You will laugh at all those fears to-morrow. Are you getting in, Hargreave?"

Dorothy drew her skirt aside. Arthur hesitated a moment, then the obvious anxiety in his mother's glance decided him. He held out his cigar.

"Thanks; I am going outside. It is a shame to miss a night like this. The moon makes it almost like day."

The three ladies in the carriage were unusually silent; each had her own special subject for thought. Lady Laura Hargreave, rejoicing in her daughter's happiness, began also to think that another certain long-cherished desire of hers was about to be fulfilled. Mavis was absorbed in dreams of her lover, and Dorothy lay back in her corner, a pretty tremulous smile flickering round her lips as she thought of the cousin who had been her hero in her childish days.

But as they turned in at the park gates Lady Laura drew herself up and listened.

"I thought I heard a cry! Arthur, what is it?" as the carriage stopped and her son got down from the box.

"I thought I heard something. Surely there is some one sobbing."

"Among the trees over there," Sir Arthur said with a backward jerk of his head. "I must see what it is. You won't mind being left along, mother? Jervis will look after you."

"Oh, my dear boy, don't think about us; we shall be all right," Lady Laura said hurriedly. "Some poor creature must be in trouble, I am afraid."

"A tramp, probably," Sir Arthur remarked as he strode across the grass to the spot whence the sounds appeared to come.

The brilliant moonlight made it easy for him to discern a dark figure crouching at the foot of one of the big beeches as he went forward and heard the sound of piteous weeping and sobbing.

"What is the matter? Can I do anything?" he began awkwardly enough.

At the first sound of his voice the figure started violently; the dark cloak fell back and he caught sight of a white dress beneath. Instinct told him that this was no common tramp or wayfarer. He went forward, raising his hat courteously.

"I beg your pardon. I fear you are in trouble. Can I do anything?" he said.

The woman raised herself slowly to her feet, and he saw that she was above the common height; another glance told even his unpractised masculine eyes that the cloak slipping from her shoulders was a distinctly fashionable garment, and that the white dress underneath was just such a frock as those in which Mavis and Dorothy were wont to appear.

She turned to him with a forlorn gesture.

"What am I to do? I do not know where I am. I have lost my way."

There was a quiver in the clear pathetic tones.

All the chivalry in Arthur's nature was aroused.

"You will allow us to do what we can," he said quickly. "My mother—Lady Laura Hargreave—is waiting in the carriage just below. If you will allow me to take you to her, later on we shall be delighted to see that you arrive safely at your destination."

She gazed at him a moment, then she spread out her hands.

"That is it," she said with an irrepressible sob, "I have forgotten where I was going! I cannot remember—anything!"

She swayed slightly, her voice failed, she staggered and would have fallen. Hargreave sprang forward and caught her in his arms.

"You are ill!" he cried anxiously.

"Oh, I don't know!" she gasped. "I—I think I am dying!"

Sir Arthur felt that she was resting a dead weight against his breast, and all his sympathy was called forth by her evident distress. As he gazed down at the white face with its exquisitely moulded features, at the wealth of golden hair lying across his coat, such a thrill ran through his pulses as he had never experienced in all his mild affection for Dorothy. Gathering the slender form in his arms, he turned back to the carriage.

Lady Laura was leaning out.

"Oh, my dear boy, what is it?" she asked in evident perturbation. "We heard voices, but who—"

"It is a lady—she has lost her way," Sir Arthur said breathlessly as he laid his burden in the carriage. "We must take her to the house, mother. I think she has fainted; when she recovers she will be able to explain matters."

"What could she be doing in the park?" Lady Laura went on helplessly, while Mavis and Dorothy, with ready sympathy, were settling the helpless girl more comfortably and chafing her cold hands.

"She has lost her way; she was too far gone to tell me any more," Arthur said briefly. "Shall I tell Jervis to drive on, mother?"

"Well, I suppose so," Lady Laura said, perforce resigning herself to the inevitable. "Though really—"

"She is well dressed," Dorothy said presently in a puzzled tone. "But what could she be doing wandering about alone at this time of night, Aunt Laura?"

Lady Laura made a gesture as if washing her hands of the whole affair.

"I have no idea indeed, my dear."

"She is better," Mavis said quickly as the carriage drew up at the door of the Manor. "See, she is opening her eyes! Get some brandy, Arthur," as her brother came round. "She will be able to walk in a minute or two."

"I could help her—"

"No, it will be better to wait," Mavis said decidedly. "The brandy, please."

She held it to the girl's lips and saw that a few drops were swallowed and that a tinge of colour was returning to the pale face before she spoke again.

"You are better now, aren't you?" Dorothy said gently as the stranger opened her eyes again and made an ineffectual attempt to rise.

"I—I think so," she said unsteadily. "I should like to—"

"Now we will help you indoors," Mavis interrupted quickly. "You can tell us all about it then."

Sir Arthur held out his arm, and with Mavis's help on the other side the girl managed to walk into the hall, sinking with a pretty gesture of thanks into one of the big oaken chairs.

Lady Laura, looking perplexed and doubtful, waited near the door, the old butler and the footman, discreetly unconscious, hovered around. Dorothy knelt down and rubbed the chilly white fingers.

Presently the girl looked at her in a puzzled fashion and sat up.

"Where am I? I don't understand," she began, gazing around with bewildered eyes.

"This is Hargreave Manor," Mavis said gently. "Were you trying to make your way here when we found you?"

"No, I think not," the girl said unsteadily. "I don't know the name at all. I was under a tree—it was damp and cold—" She looked round in a vague troubled way that went straight to Lady Laura's heart and dispelled certain misgivings as to the wisdom of the course to which she felt committed.

"You are not well, I think, my dear," she said gently. "Will you let us know your name so that we can communicate with your friends? And, —Mavis, tell them to make the pink room ready."

The stranger's big blue eyes filled with tears; she pulled her hands from Dorothy's gentle clasp and thrust back her mass of golden hair.

"My name—" she faltered. "I don't know—I don't seem to remember anything at all, except that I was all alone and cold and tired." Her lips quivered pitifully. "Perhaps," glancing appealingly at Lady Laura, "it will all come back in a little while. I—I don't feel very well just now."

Lady Laura's face as she glanced at Mavis was very grave, but her voice sounded reassuring as she gently touched the shaking hands.

"You will be better after a night's rest, my dear, and be able to tell us all about yourself. For the present don't try to think of anything; just lie back and put your feet on this stool and try to rest."

She laid a thick rug over her and turned aside, drawing her son with her to the other side of the hall.

"Arthur, one of the men must ride over for Dr. Grieve, and then as soon as her room is ready we must get her to bed. Whoever she is she will have to stay the night here."

"Certainly!" Sir Arthur acquiesced warmly. "I will send James off at once."

"Oh, yes. Poor girl!" Lady Laura assented, with a little reserve. "She must be staying at one of the houses round here, but I cannot imagine what has happened to her. However, no doubt Dr. Grieve will be able to enlighten us. She is very pretty, Arthur."

"One of the most beautiful women I ever saw in my life," Sir Arthur agreed warmly.

Lady Laura looked doubtful.

"One can hardly judge of that to-night, I think. Does she remind you of anyone, Arthur?"

"Certainly not!" Hargreave's tone was decisive. "I have never seen anyone in the least like her before."

"When she looked at me I could not help fancying that I saw a faint resemblance to some one, but I cannot place it just now," Lady Laura went on musingly as they turned back.

Suddenly the deep-fringed eyelids were raised.

"How very—very kind you all are to me!" the girl murmured glancing round the little group, her eyes resting for one second on Sir Arthur's troubled face. "So very, very kind!"

Chapter Three

"WELL, IT IS one of the queerest things I ever heard of!" Garth Davenant's dark face looked puzzled. "You say the girl cannot give any account of herself at all?" Mavis shook her head.

"No, she has for the time being entirely lost her memory. Dr. Grieve says she has had some great shock, and that she is in a state of intense nervous prostration."

"Grieve is a muff, in my opinion," remarked Mr. Davenant irreverently. "If the girl is as bad as you say, she ought to have other advice."

"Oh, I don't think so!" Mavis dissented. "Dr. Grieve says that what she needs is absolute rest and careful nursing; then he thinks her memory will come back to her gradually."

"Umph!" said Garth sceptically. "And where is I this rest and nursing to be obtained, may I ask? Lady Laura will hardly wish to keep her indefinitely at the Manor, I conclude?"

"She will stay with us until she is well," Mavis said indignantly. "Don't be so hard-hearted, Garth. I am sure mother will not let her go; she thanked us all so prettily this morning for what we had done for her, and; seemed so distressed to think of the trouble she was giving, and I fell quite in love with her."

Garth pulled his brown moustache moodily as he looked at her flushed face. The two, having met at the park gates, were now walking up to the Manor together, and Garth had been listening with amazement to Mavis's story of the discovery of the unknown girl in the park the preceding evening.

"Was there absolutely no clue to her identity about her clothes?" he asked after a pause.

"Her things were all marked 'Hilda' or with a big 'H' which means the same thing. We think she must have been staying somewhere near and have had some great trouble," Mavis went on speculatively. "We have no idea what it might have been, but I cannot help wondering whether she had quarrelled with the man she loved; perhaps he had played her false in some way or other. I don't think anything could be quite so bad as that, Garth," with a shy, trustful glance. "I—I know it would make me very miserable."

Garth Davenant's eyes were very tender as he looked down at her; he caught her slender fingers in his. "My darling!" he whispered.

Mavis blushed prettily as she drew them away, but she was too thoroughly in earnest to be turned away from her subject.

"So, you see," she went on after a moment, "that is a reason why I feel that I ought to be especially good to this poor girl. Think of all that she may have suffered before her brain gave way under the strain and left everything a blank. I must do what I can for her; if one is very happy oneself one ought to try to help other people. Don't you think so, Garth?"

'Y—es!" Garth hesitated. "Only, Mavis, I cannot help saying that, though things may certainly be capable of a perfectly innocent interpretation the whole affair is so extraordinary that one cannot help regarding it with a certain amount of suspicion. And I cannot bear to think of your being brought into daily contact with a girl who may be little better than an adventuress."

"Garth!" Mavis cried indignantly. "If you had seen her you could never apply such an expression to her. Why, even Arthur says that she is simply one of the prettiest and sweetest-looking girls he has ever met!"

"Don't you think that, as I have not seen her, I may possibly be all the better able to look at matters without prejudice on that very account?" Garth suggested mildly.

"Without prejudice, indeed!" Mavis repeated scornfully. "I think mother and Arthur can quite be trusted to look after our companions—Dorothy's and mine. No, Garth"—as he tried to take her hands again—"I am not pleased with you."

There was no one in sight; the big trees of the avenue screened them from sight of the house. Garth ventured to slip one arm around the girl's waist.

"Aren't you, Mavis? Won't you forgive me, if I promise to take this newly-discovered young woman at your valuation for the future?"

For a moment the girl held back stiffly, but Mavis never bore malice; the next moment she had turned to Davenant with her own sunny smile.

"Certainly I will! And, Garth"—with an effort—"I know I was wrong. I must not expect you always to think as I do, and I know that a barrister must be brought into contact with all sorts of people, and naturally becomes distrustful. We must," smiling bravely, "agree to differ; that is it, isn't it?"

Garth drew the slight form closer to him and bent his head until his dark moustache just brushed the soft cheek.

"Darling, you know I—"

"Hallo! You two—"

The sudden shout discomposed them, and they sprang apart, looking considerably startled as Sir Arthur cantered up behind them.

"Many apologies!" he began, laughing at Mavis's hot cheeks. "I am extremely sorry to disturb you good people, but I have just been over to Chadfield on the chance that they might know something of our mysterious visitor; and I am anxious to get back to hear Dr. Grieve's report. They told me at his house that he had already come up to see the stranger."

"Did they know anything at Chadfield?" Mavis interrogated breathlessly.

"Not a word." Arthur took off his hat and rubbed his forehead. "It's a queer affair altogether. What do you make of it, Davenant?"

"I should prefer to see the young lady before I commit myself to an opinion," Garth replied diplomatically, with a glance at Mavis's averted face.

"Well, I think we have now pretty well exhausted the houses around here," Sir Arthur went on, walking his horse beside them. "Chadfield was really my last hope. How on earth the girl got into the Park I cannot imagine; no one seems to have seen her, and the lodge-keeper is sure that the gate was locked all the evening."

Garth made no reply, but as they walked on to the house together his face was very grave. Fond as he was of Mavis's brother, neither his very real affection for him nor the fact of his relationship to Mavis could disguise from him Arthur's weakness of will and instability of purpose.

Thus he was doubly inclined to mistrust the introduction, in such extraordinary circumstances, of a new inmate amidst the family at Hargreave Manor. Arthur turned to him as they reached the house.

"You will come in, Garth, and hear what the doctor says?"

After a momentary hesitation Davenant assented, and they entered the house together, just as Dr. Grieve came downstairs.

"Oh, Dr. Grieve, she is better, isn't she?" Mavis asked, after shaking hands with him. "Can she remember anything yet? Have you found out her name?"

"One at a time, my dear young lady, one at a time! The patient is not in a very satisfactory state, I regret to say. There is a good deal of cerebral excitement, and the action of the heart is weak—decidedly weak!"

Sir Arthur opened the dining-room door.

"Come in, doctor; you must try a glass of my port, and tell us what is the best thing for your patient."

Jenkins, the butler, produced glasses and a decanter, while the doctor beamed upon them complacently and Mavis fidgeted impatiently.

"Splendid colour, Sir Arthur," Dr. Grieve remarked appreciatively as after a sip or two he held the glass up to the light and regarded it critically. "I remember Sir Noel laying it down before you were born, or Miss Mavis there," with a reminiscent chuckle. "Yes, my memory carries me back a long way! I'm not like our young friend upstairs, who has forgotten her own name, poor young thing—can't even remember where she was yesterday morning! It is a sad case, Sir Arthur."

"She knows no more this morning, then?" Sir Arthur asked concernedly. "My mother said she recognized her at once, and we thought that a good sign."

The doctor put the tips of his fingers together and surveyed him over the top of them.

"I dare say. She remembered seeing me last night, for the matter of that; but up to the time you discovered her in the park her mind is a perfect blank. I did not ask her questions, but I applied a few simple tests."

"And the result?" Sir Arthur's tone was calm, but an under-current of anxiety ran through it which made Garth glance at him keenly.

"Entirely confirmed my diagnosis of last evening, I regret to say," Dr Grieve returned. "The very faculty of memory is for the time being entirely dormant, overclouded by some great shock."

"But she will recover?" Mavis interjected anxiously.

The doctor turned to her with a benign smile.

"Recover her bodily health undoubtedly, my dear Miss Mavis. As for her memory"—after a noticeable pause—"one can but do the best and trust to Time, the great healer. Of one thing you may be assured, absolute rest is the very best thing for her—for some days at any rate—and quite possibly by that time you will have ascertained something definite about her friends. Lady Laura tells me that it is your intention to keep her here for the present."

"Undoubtedly, it is!" Sir Arthur said with decision. "In fact, as it appears to me, we have no choice in the matter."

The doctor shrugged his shoulders. "She could be admitted to the Cottage Hospital at Lockford, you know; and for some reasons I am inclined to think it might be the wiser course."

"Why so?" Sir Arthur's tone was curt. The little line between his straight brows told that the suggestion had displeased him.

Dr Grieve hesitated a moment and drummed his fingers on the table absently.

"Well, there might be complications—the idea of a beautiful young woman such as this wandering about the country by herself naturally suggests that. But quite apart from any such idea"—as Sir Arthur made a hasty gesture of dissent—"the nursing there would be a slight matter, while here—"

"Surely we can look after one girl amongst us?" Mavis said quickly. "Dorothy and I are both going to help, and my maid, Minnie Spencer, is a very good girl."

"A very good girl, I have no doubt, Miss Mavis," the doctor said as he beamed at her over the top of his gold-rimmed spectacles. "But I am afraid our patient requires rather more attention than I could impose upon either of you two young ladies or upon Minnie Spencer. Now at the Cottage Hospital—"

"The Cottage Hospital is out of the question," Sir Arthur interrupted brusquely. "I beg your pardon, doctor. But this young lady is in some sort our guest. We could not entertain such a suggestion for an instant. Still, if you think she requires further care, by all means let her have a trained nurse here. Can you get one for us?"

Dr. Grieve stroked his chin thoughtfully.

"They can't spare one at the Cottage Hospital, I am sure of that. I might telegraph to Exeter, but I doubt our being able to get one from there to-day. I know they are very busy. Well, we must do our best."

Garth Davenant had taken no part in the conversation after the first; he had been looking abstractedly through the window and fidgeting about from one foot to the other, but as the doctor spoke his face lighted up. He turned round.

"Upon my word, I believe I can help you there, doctor. You remember Mary Marston?"

"Yes, I remember Mary—she has been trained at one of the London hospitals. You don't mean—"

"She is at home now, I know—or was yesterday afternoon. She has been nursing on her own account lately—has severed her connection with the hospital, I believe. She has been at home for a holiday, but I heard she was anxious to be at work again. I dare say she would come."

"The very thing!" Dr. Grieve exclaimed. "If you approve, Sir Arthur, you could send for her. She could come up to-day and the worst of our difficulty would be over."

"Certainly," Arthur said heartily. "I remember Mary Marston well; she was always a nice, reliable woman. My mother will like it better than having a stranger."

"I will go down and ask her to come if you like," Garth interposed.

"The very thing!" the doctor said again as he rose.

"Then you will tell her to be here as soon as she can, Mr. Davenant?"

"One moment, doctor," Garth went on, as the little man turned to the door. "Wouldn't you be inclined to suggest a consultation? It seems to me such a strange case!"

Dr. Grieve did not look quite pleased.

"Not the least necessity for that! Any doctor would only tell you, as I do, that rest and quiet are the best things for her. We can do no more at present. Ah, here comes Miss Dorothy! My dear, you are a sight for sore eyes this morning!" as the girl, looking very fresh and sweet in her simple morning-gown, came running down the stairs.

She laughed and blushed.

"You have not forgotten how to pay compliments, I see, Dr. Grieve. Mavis, Aunt Laura wants you for one moment," with a laughing glance at Garth, whose expression at the moment was by no means attractive.

The long morning with Mavis upon which he had been reckoning was out of the question now, and his stay at Lockford was limited. But the cause of his dissatisfaction lay deeper than the mere disappointment; the more he heard of it the more inexplicable did the discovery of last night appear to him, and the less did he relish the idea of this unknown girl being brought into daily contact with Mavis.

Mavis's whispered promise to come down again when he returned from Nurse Marston's house served to dissipate the clouds for the moment, however, and while she ran upstairs he turned to Dr. Grieve, and, chatting with him, turned down the steps.

Arthur was left alone with his cousin; he crossed to her as she stood near the fireplace with Nero lying at her feet, his eyes upturned with an expression of ridiculous devotion.

"Dorothy, I wanted to ask you—"

The girl's eyes glanced round nervously; the pretty faint colour in her cheeks flickered.

"I—I don't think I must stay now, Arthur. I told Aunt Laura I would sit with that poor girl a while this morning. Dr. Grieve says she ought not to be left alone."

"That is very good of you!" Arthur said heartily. Not for a moment did he glance at the girl's downcast face—his eyes were straying absently to the door and watching Dr. Grieve as he bent down from his dog-cart for a last word with Garth Davenant. "It was about her that I wanted to speak to you," he went on. "Have you seen her already? How does she strike you this morning?"

"I hardly know," Dorothy said, vaguely chilled by his manner. "She has not spoken when I have been in the room, and Minnie says that for the most part she lies quite still with her eyes wide open, though every now and then she will moan or cry mournfully to herself."

Her cousin's face looked very pitiful.

"Poor girl! I wish we could do more for her."

"It is very queer that we cannot hear of her friends," Dorothy said thoughtfully. "She is very pretty, Arthur."

"It is the most beautiful face I have ever seen!" he declared enthusiastically. "The features are perfect, and her colouring—did you notice what glorious masses of hair? Just the colour Titian would have loved to paint! One can only imagine what she would be like in health; but even last night—" He broke off suddenly. "Well, I must not keep you from her, Dorothy. If she will only let me paint her later on—"

For in the intervals unoccupied by his different crazes he was wont to devote himself to painting, and was by no means destitute of artistic abilities.

The vague unrest in Dorothy's eyes deepened, her lips quivered a little.

"It—oh, I should think she will!" she said simply. "For the Elaine, you mean, don't you? I—we must all try to persuade her, Arthur."

"Thank you! Hasn't she exactly the ideal face for which I have been waiting? I knew you would understand," he said heartily. "Thank you for all you are doing for her, Dorothy."

Chapter Four

"Minnie, can I speak to her ladyship?" said the nurse.

The maid looked doubtful.

"Her ladyship has just gone downstairs; she told Mrs. Parkyns and me to see that you had all you wanted."

The nurse paused a moment in indecision. She was a pleasant, capable-looking woman, nearly thirty years of age, with dark hair, already beginning to be streaked with grey, drawn back from her face and braided smoothly beneath her cap. "It isn't anything of that kind. I have everything I need, thank you. But I should like to speak to her."

Minnie shook her head as the sound of wheels became audible.

"It is no use now. We have a big dinner-party to-night and the guests are arriving. I couldn't go to her ladyship. If Miss Mavis—"

"Miss Mavis wouldn't do," Nurse Marston said decidedly, frowning as if in perplexity. "I must see her ladyship to-night. It is about my patient."

"Is she worse?" the girl asked in consternation. "We thought she was going on so nicely, and Dr. Grieve said—

"She is doing very well," the nurse said absently. "It wasn't about that I wanted to speak. It—well, I suppose you know how to keep a still tongue in your head, Minnie?"

"I should hope I do," returned Minnie in an affronted tone. "I should hardly have risen from waiting on the schoolroom to being Miss Mavis's own maid if I didn't, let me tell you that, nurse."

"Well, well, I dare say you wouldn't," conceded the nurse in a conciliatory tone. "The fact of the matter is I am so bothered that I hardly know what I am saying or what to do. But I understand that nothing has been found out about my patient, or who she is, since I saw Dr. Grieve this morning?"

"Not a word. I heard Sir Arthur tell Miss Mavis as much not half an hour ago on this very spot," glancing down the corridor and at the door leading into the pink- room, which the nurse had carefully closed behind her when she came out. "None of the people around here know anything of her, and nobody seems to have met her on the way or seen her come into the park. We can't see daylight in it— not Sir Arthur or any of us," concluded Minnie breathlessly.

The nurse bit her lips nervously and glanced at the closed door behind her.

"Minnie, it is in this way—if nobody else has seen that young lady before, I believe I have," she whispered. "Now you know that I must see her ladyship to-night and why."

Minnie's eyes opened to their fullest extent.

"You don't mean it, nurse! Are you sure?"

"Sure enough!" the nurse replied with a significant nod. "We come across many folk, do we nurses, and little think how we shall see them again, some of them."

"But where did you see her? Do you know who she is?" asked Minnie.

"I don't know who she is, any more than you do yourself, but I may know what will lead to its being found out!' the nurse replied enigmatically. "That will do, Minnie—the rest is for her ladyship's ear only. Now, can you get a message to her? Tell her Nurse Marston must speak to her, and alone, to-night."

"I don't quite see how it is to be managed," debated Minnie slowly, "but I will do my best. I'll speak to Mr. Jenkins—or perhaps it would be better if you wrote a bit of a note, nurse, so as to let Mr. Jenkins give it to her ladyship."

Nurse Marston hesitated a moment; then she tore a leaf from the notebook hanging at her side, and, after hastily scribbling a line or two, folded it up and handed it to the girl.

"There, if you can get that to her!" she said.

"I will try. And—and"—Minnie detained her—"won't you tell me a bit more, nurse?" wheedlingly.

"Not a word!" said the nurse positively. "I dare say I've said more than I ought now."

"But—"

With her finger on her lips to enjoin silence, and with a farewell nod, the nurse turned the door-handle and slipped quietly into her patient's room.

Minnie went slowly down the passage, stopping a moment to peep over the banisters and get a glimpse of the gaily-attired ladies who were passing through the hall below before she made her way to the backstairs to perform Nurse Marston's errand.

With the note in her hand she tapped lightly at the door of the housekeeper's room, blushing as she caught the sound of voices and saw a man standing with his back to her when she entered.

"I've come with a message from the nurse to her ladyship. Could you send it to her, do you think, Mrs. Parkyns?" holding it out.

The housekeeper looked important.

"Well, I think I might take it on myself, seeing it is marked 'Immediate.' You wait a minute, Minnie. I will speak to Mr. Jenkins."

She bustled off and Minnie was left *tête-à-tête* with her sweetheart.

Mr. Gregory was distinctly inclined to make the most of his opportunity; he caught hold of Minnie round the waist with both hands before the girl had time to raise any objection.

"Well, and what have you been doing with yourself all day, Minnie?" he said. "Not talking to Mr. Thomas Greyson, I hope?"

Minnie raised her eyes reproachfully.

"Jim, how can you? As if I should! I have been sitting with the poor young lady they found in the park last night for the biggest part of the day."

Gregory held her from him at arm's length.

"That's why your eyes look heavy," he declared. "I can't have you put upon. What is the good of that fine nursing madam that I saw talking for a good half-hour to Mr. Garth Davenant in the avenue this afternoon if she can't look after the lady herself?"

"Oh, I haven't had anything to do since Nurse Marston came—" Minnie was beginning.

Gregory interrupted her, his eyes regarding her keenly from beneath his narrowed lids.

"Nurse—what did you say her name was—Marston?"

"Yes, Marston. She is Mrs. Marston's daughter down at Lockford. Do you know her, Jim? She has been in London."

"Not that I know of," he said carelessly. "Mr. Garth seemed pretty thick with her this afternoon, to my way of thinking. That note you gave Mrs. Parkyns was from her, wasn't it?"

"Yes. She wants to see her ladyship most particular to-night," said Minnie, forgetting her promise. "Something about the young lady—"

Jim glanced obliquely at her a moment.

"What about her? She doesn't know anything of her, this Nurse Marston, does she?"

"She thinks she does, but I don't know what. She said she wouldn't tell anyone but her ladyship," Minnie said carelessly; then in an altered tone, "There! She charged me I wasn't to say a word to anybody and here I am telling you all about it!"

"Don't you fret yourself, I shan't say anything. For the matter of that, telling you is the same thing as telling me, for ain't you and me going to be one, Minnie?" responded Mr. Gregory, his clasp growing tighter. "I have got something better than that to talk about to-night. There's a little cottage down against the common at Lockford to let. How'd that do—Ah, Mrs. Parkyns, you do come into the room quiet! I never so much as heard a step!"

The housekeeper laughed meaningly.

"Ay, maybe I am a bit too quiet for some folks! Bless me, Minnie, there's no need to put yourself about!" for the girl had sprung away from Gregory and thrown up her hands to her flaming face. "We have all of us been young once, my lass. Where are you off to now, may I ask?"

"There's some lace to be put on Miss Mavis's gown for to-morrow," faltered Minnie. "I—I must be off, Mrs. Parkyns."

"And her ladyship's message to the nurse?" remarked the housekeeper, chuckling at the girl's confusion. "There, if I don't believe you have forgot all about it! What can you be thinking of, I wonder!" with a laugh at Gregory. "Her ladyship says if Nurse Marston's business is very important she is to come to her in the small library when all the guests are gone. She does not think they will be very late to-night."

"The small library? I haven't seen that, I think," Gregory remarked, moving a little nearer the girl but keeping his eyes on the housekeeper.

"Well, I dare say you haven't," she remarked a trifle condescendingly. "It hasn't been, so to speak, in general use, though it has been kept aired, since Sir Noel died. He always sat there in the morning when he was indoors. It is that small room that opens into the conservatory to the right of the drawing-room."

"Oh, ah, I think I have seen it," Jim said absently, edging nearer the door through which Minnie had already vanished. "I'll be pleased to do what I can for you at any time, Mrs. Parkyns; but if there is nothing more tonight—"

"I should be sorry to keep you if there was," the housekeeper said with a significant laugh. "You are to let us have the cattleyas for the table to-morrow night, Sir Arthur said."

"Very good, m'm," and Jim made his escape without, more ado.

In the wide stone-flagged passage outside he caught a glimpse of Minnie's black skirt as she hurried round the corner, and gave chase at once.

"Why, Minnie," he said reproachfully as he came up with her, "you are never going off like this without a word? I want to talk to you about that Cottage; but I haven't finished with Mrs. Parkyns yet. However, you come round while they are at dinner and I will tell you all about it."

Minnie looked frightened.

"I don't know as I dare. It would be as much as my place is worth if her ladyship or Mrs. Parkyns got to hear of it."

"You won't need to keep the place much longer if we settle on the cottage," Jim reminded her. "You must come, Minnie; there's the dearest little sitting-room and the regular picture of a kitchen."

Minnie hesitated, but the wish to hear more of her future home overcame her scruples.

"Well, just this once," she conceded. "You won't keep me long, Jim?"

A light gleamed in the man's eyes.

"Not a minute longer than you want to stop, Minnie. Now I must go back to Mrs. Parkyns."

Minnie's face was still flushed as she walked slowly up the back-stairs; half-way down the corridor leading to the sick-room one of the other maids ran after her.

"This parcel has just come up from Lockford for Nurse Marston; will you give it to her, Minnie?"

Minnie took it and tapped at the pink-room door.

"Her ladyship will see you in the small library when the guests have gone, nurse," she announced. "This has come for you."

Nurse Marston stepped into the passage, pulling the door to behind her.

"Ah, my things for the night!" she said as she took the parcel from the girl's hands. "Mother said she would send them; but I don't think I shall go to bed, though they have given me this room," nodding to the door of that next the one occupied by her patient. "However, I can't decide that till I have seen her ladyship. But I will put my things out"—unfastening the parcel—"and here's my knitting. If I do sit up I like a bit of work in my hand, and I am anxious to get mother's stockings done before winter. I knit them all myself, Minnie."

"Do you really?" The girl looked much impressed. "You will ring if you want anything, nurse," she went on. "Wright will bring your supper up; and I will let you know when the folk are going."

"Thank you, Minnie!" the nurse responded as she laid her modest belongings in the big wardrobe and the drawers that looked so ludicrously out of proportion with their contents.

A few minutes later she was back with her patient, who was apparently asleep, and stood regarding her with a puzzled expression.

"I cannot be mistaken," she murmured, "and yet—"

She shrugged her shoulders as she crossed the room and, taking her knitting in her hand, sat down before the fire, watching the flames with absent eyes, while her fingers clicked the steel pins with mechanical regularity.

She had scarcely moved, save to give her patient the required nourishment, when several hours later Mavis tapped at the door.

"You wanted to see mother, nurse," she began. "The people are going now, so if you—"

The nurse came softly across the room.

"I would go at once, Miss Mavis, but Minnie promised to come and sit with the young lady while I went. I hardly care to leave her alone."

Mavis came into the room.

"Oh, I will stay, nurse! I dare say Minnie is busy with the cloaks."

She drew nearer the bed and looked at the fair pale face, at the cloud of golden hair spreading over the pillows.

"How lovely she is," she said with involuntary admiration.

"She is pretty," Nurse Marston admitted, with a kind of grudging reservation.

"Is she unconscious?" Mavis went on. "Does she hear anything we say?"

"It is impossible to tell how much she understands," the nurse said repressively. "She lies for the most part in this kind of stupor, and I must ask you not to talk before her, Miss Mavis. It might do harm."

"Oh, I am so sorry! " Mavis exclaimed penitently. "It was very thoughtless of me. You will be afraid now to trust me with her."

"Well, I am rather anxious to speak to her ladyship, so if you really don't mind staying a few minutes I shall be very grateful to you, Miss Mavis."

"Oh, that will be all right!" Mavis tiptoed across the soft carpet to the nurse's big easy-chair. "Don't hurry yourself at all on my account, nurse," she added pleasantly. "Just tell me, is there anything I ought to give her?"

Nurse Marston considered a little.

"There's her draught, but that is not for half an hour, and I shall be back in plenty of time for that. No, there is nothing now, thank you, Miss Mavis—only just to give an eye to her every now and then."

"I see." And Mavis settled herself comfortably in her chair. "Tell mother not to stay up gossiping too long," she said lightly as, with a half-reluctant backward glance, the nurse left the room.

Mavis's glance lingered a while on the straight white figure lying so still and motionless in the big bed, then her thoughts wandered to Garth, and the little smile which certain memories of the evening evoked was still lingering round her lips when a weak voice spoke from the bed.

"Who is there? Who are you?"

Mavis sprang to her feet and hurried to the bedside, starting as she met the gaze of a brilliant pair of blue eyes.

"Who are you?" the soft voice went on insistently.

"I am Mavis Hargreave. You saw me last night. Don't you remember now?"

The girl pressed her hand over her forehead. "I —I think I have seen you somewhere," she said perplexedly. "But I don't remember. Where am I?"

Moved by a sudden impulse of pity, Mavis took one of the slim trembling hands in hers and held it tenderly.

"You are at Hargreave Manor—we found you in the park last night."

The girl tossed restlessly about.

"I don't seem to remember anything," she said, her mouth trembling pitifully. "But I think you are being very good to me, and I thank you very much." Her fingers closed on Mavis's and her eyelids drooped.

Mavis glanced across the room longingly at the bell. She was uncertain how this interval of consciousness should be treated and felt anxious to summon Nurse Marston back to her duties, but the hold on her hand detained her. She stooped over the invalid gently.

"Hilda—may I call you Hilda?—will you let me go for one moment? I want to call some one who will know just what you ought to have now."

The weak clasp did not slacken.

"No—I want you—to stay with me," the invalid said wilfully. "It—Where was I last night?"

Mavis was uncertain how far the question should be answered; her eyes sought the clock as she hesitated. Already the nurse had been away twenty minutes. Surely she would soon be back now?

"I—When do you mean?" she parried.

Big tears came into the blue eyes.

"Ah, why will you not tell me? I cannot remember, try as I will. All I can recall is a sort of medley, like a bad dream—trouble—and I was all alone—and darkness and difficulties all around me."

There was a low tap at the door, but Mavis was too much interested to notice it.

"Then out of all that was vague and indefinite," the girl continued, "one face seemed to shape itself, looking down at me with pity—a man's face—and I was borne away into light and warmth."

"My brother Arthur found you in the park and carried you to the carriage," Mavis returned prosaically. "We were very glad we heard you; it might have killed you to stay there all night."

The knock at the door was repeated, and a voice called: "Nurse!"

Mavis recognized her mother's voice and tried to draw her hand away.

"It is my mother," she said." I must speak to her."

But the other girl still clung to her.

"You must not go," she said. "I am not strong enough to see anyone else to-night—indeed, I am not. Promise you will not let anyone come in."

Chapter Five

WITH A jerk Mavis freed herself.

"Indeed I must—"

At the same moment the door opened and Lady Laura looked into the room.

"I have been waiting for you for quite a quarter of an hour, nurse," she said in a distinctly aggrieved tone. "If anything prevented your coming you ought at least to have sent me word. I told my daughter—Mavis! You are here still! Where is Nurse?" glancing round in surprise.

"I don't know. She left to come to you, mother. She —Hilda is better; she has been talking to me."

Lady Laura stepped up to the bedside and smiled reassuringly into the eyes raised imploringly to her.

"I am so glad you are better, my dear," she said in a cheery, comfortable fashion. "But you ought to have something now. Mavis, give me that glass. Ah, that is right!" with a confidence born of experience as the girl swallowed a few drops of the champagne. "Now if you can get some sleep, my dear, I think it will be the best thing for you. What is this you say about Nurse Marston, Mavis—that she left here to come to me? Poor thing, she must have gone into the wrong room, and I dare say is abusing me for keeping her from her patient all this time!" with a laugh. She rang the bell. "Oh, Minnie! Find Nurse Marston and tell her that I am here, and ask her to come up. She must have gone into some other room."

Minnie looked puzzled.

"I showed her the small library myself, my lady. I had been helping Lady Davenant with her cloak. I came out as Nurse Marston passed and I went as far as the bend in the passage with her and pointed out the door."

"Then she must have mistaken you," Lady Laura decided easily, "and you will find her in one of the adjoining rooms. Be as quick as you can, Minnie."

"Yes, my lady," and the girl hurried off.

Lady Laura turned to Mavis.

"Now, Mavis, it is time you were in bed, or you will lose your beauty sleep. Come, I will stay with Hilda"—and she smiled at the girl—"until Nurse Marston comes."

Mavis glanced at Hilda's white face, at the suspiciously bright eyes in which there lay no shadow of sleep, and then, moved by some sudden impulse, she leaned over and kissed the girl.

"Good night, dear, and sleep well!"

Outside in the passage she encountered Minnie.

"Oh, Miss Mavis, has the nurse come back?" she began excitedly. "I can't find her anywhere. She isn't anywhere downstairs, as far as I can see."

Mavis looked perplexed for a moment, then her face brightened up.

"I dare say she is in her room. Perhaps she is not well." She tapped at the door, which was left ajar, but there was no response, and a glance was sufficient to show them that the room was untenanted.

Minnie looked troubled.

"I can't think where she can be, Miss Mavis. I have been everywhere downstairs except in the billiard-room and the smoking-room, and not a sign of her can I find. If her lady—"

The door of the invalid's room opened noiselessly, and Lady Laura herself looked out.

"Is Nurse there? I want to—"

"My lady, I can't find her anywhere!" Minnie burst out.

But signing to her to be silent, Lady Laura came into the passage.

"What do you say, Minnie—you cannot find her? Have you looked in the morning-room? She has probably turned in there in mistake for the small library."

"I have been in all those rooms, my lady, and she isn't there. I can't think where she can have got to. And she was that anxious to speak to you, my lady! "

For a moment Lady Laura looked vaguely disturbed, then she smiled at Minnie's evident perturbation.

"Well, I don't suppose she is lost, Minnie," she said cheerfully. "Probably she did not feel well, and is sitting down quietly somewhere; but I think I will just go down and speak to Mrs. Parkyns, and look into the rooms myself, and I think we must turn you into a nurse for the time being, Minnie. Be sure you let me know as soon as Nurse Marston comes back."

"Yes, my lady." But the girl still looked uneasy and worried.

Mavis followed Lady Laura and tucked her hand under her arm.

"I am coming with you, mother dear. Yes, really you must let me," as Lady Laura began to remonstrate. "Indeed, I could not sleep until we have found the nurse and heard what she has to say. Isn't Hilda perfectly lovely, mother? Much prettier than we thought her last night."

"She is very beautiful," Lady Laura said abstractedly. "I fancy that Nurse Marston wished to speak to me about her. Perhaps she has discovered some clue to her identity. Ah, here is Parkyns!" as that functionary appeared, looking portly and important in her rich black silk. "Well, Parkyns, have you seen anything of Nurse Marston yet?"

"No, my lady," the housekeeper replied with dignity. "Where the young woman can have put herself I can't imagine. We have looked all over the bottom part of the house ourselves, me and Mr. Jenkins, as soon as Minnie said she couldn't be found, and one of the maids has been upstairs. It really doesn't seem as if she could be in the house."

Lady Laura felt bewildered.

"It is impossible that she can have gone out at this time of night without telling anyone!" she exclaimed. "You are sure she is not downstairs, you say, Parkyns?"

"Quite sure, my lady! Leastways, we have been in every room except the smoking-room. Sir Arthur is there."

Lady Laura pondered a moment; then she turned down the passage leading to the smoking-room and opened the door. Sir Arthur was lying back on the lounge, his feet on a chair and his head thrown back as he lazily watched the rings of smoke curling up to the ceiling from his cigar.

He sprang up in surprise when he saw his mother, with Mavis clinging to her arm and Mrs. Parkyns bringing up the rear.

"Why, mother, what is it? What has happened? Has there been a change for the worse?"

"No, no! Nothing of that kind," Lady Laura said quickly, with an indefinable feeling of unrest as she noted the trend his anxiety had taken. "It is only that—have you by any chance seen Nurse Marston?"

Arthur stared.

"Seen Nurse Marston? My dear mother, no! Why, what do you mean? Is she lost?"

"Oh, no!" Lady Laura said helplessly. "Only we can't find her."

Arthur laughed.

"Seems much about the same thing, doesn't it? How does it come about? Has she left her patient?"

"She was to come to me—" Lady Laura began.

"She left me with Hilda," Mavis interjected, "and said she should not be away long."

"She was particularly anxious to see her ladyship, Sir Arthur," Parkyns added. "Sent Minnie down to me to get a letter to her ladyship before dinner, she did. We can't see daylight in the matter, me and Mr. Jenkins can't."

Arthur looked from one to the other in utter amazement as they mentioned further particulars; the story appeared to him improbable in the extreme, and he was inclined to ridicule it.

"Oh, well, she can't be far off, that's certain!" he cried in a tone of raillery as he turned to accompany them. "We must have a general search. She wouldn't be likely to take offence at anything and go home in a hurry, I suppose?"

Jenkins joined them now, lamp in hand.

"I have been in some of the rooms as are not in general use, Sir Arthur," he said apologetically, "thinking the young woman might have got in there by mistake, though it don't seem likely. But, begging your pardon, I couldn't help hearing what you were saying to her ladyship, Sir Arthur, and I can answer for it the nurse hasn't gone home, nor nothing of that sort, for all the doors are fastened same as I did them myself before dinner, as her ladyship bade me, all except the big doors, that is to say, and them I fastened as soon as the company was gone, and I was in the hall myself with James seeing after the coats and things till then. No, she is in the house, Sir Arthur, you may take it from me."

"Oh, well, then she will soon be found," Arthur decided cheerfully. "One of us will go in search of her one way and one another. It will be a regular hide-and-seek business. I really think that there ought to be some sort of prize for the one that finds, what do you say to that, mother?"

Lady Laura did not echo his laugh; her face was unwontedly pale, her dark eyes looked frightened.

"I do not know what to think," she said unsteadily. "I don't feel quite comfortable about it really, Arthur!"

"No more do I, my lady," chimed in Parkyns obsequiously. "If the young woman has been taken ill, or—"

"Well, we will soon find her," concluded Arthur, to whom the affair appeared rather a joke. "Here is Dorothy in time to join the search"—as the girl, her white *peignoir* thrown hastily on and her long fair hair floating over her shoulders, came to the top of the staircase, drawing back hastily as she saw the little group below— "or do you bring us news of the runaway, Dorothy?" he went on, raising his voice.

"What runaway?" Dorothy asked. "I don't know what you mean. I thought I heard Aunt Laura's voice and nobody came when I rang. I was so frightened by that shriek that when I heard people moving I came to see what it was all about."

"What shriek? What did you hear?" asked Arthur rapidly, while Lady Laura and Mavis turned pale, and Parkyns, with a murmured "Heaven save us!" threw up her hands.

Dorothy was not inclined to explain.

"Oh, it was nothing! I dare say I fancied it," she murmured as Arthur put his foot on the stairs and she quickened her steps down the corridor. "It—it was silly of me to be frightened, that's all."

"One moment, dear," and, putting her son back with one hand, Lady Laura hurried after the girl. "Wait a moment, Dorothy. What was it you heard exactly, and when?"

Arthur and Mavis were following their mother, and Mrs. Parkyns was pantingly bringing up the rear.

"It was just after I came upstairs, Aunt Laura. You know I was a little early, and I was alone, sitting before my glass thinking over different things, when I heard a cry—a sort of muffled, choking scream, that was all—but it made me feel just a little nervous. I waited some time, thinking that Mavis would be sure to come in on her way up for a chat; but she did not, and at last I rang for Celestine; and then, as she did not answer and I could hear that you were moving about and talking—I heard you speak, Aunt Laura—I came out just to see if there was anything wrong. What is it really?"

"We cannot find Nurse Marston," Lady Laura continued in reply to Dorothy's question. "Arthur, I cannot understand it," as her son joined them and Dorothy entered her room. "What could it have been that Dorothy heard?"

"Where is Dorothy sleeping?" Arthur answered her question by another and his face was grave.

"Over—over the small library," Lady Laura said, with a quiver in her usually clear, full tones. "Arthur, you do not think that any harm has happened to her—to Nurse Marston?"

"In the house? Not likely!" Arthur said reassuringly. "I was thinking—I suppose nobody knows whether Nurse Marston was subject to fits"—raising his voice—"or anything of that kind? I have heard they go off with a scream."

"If she had been, Sir Arthur, she would hardly have been fit for her work at the hospital, I should say," Mrs. Parkyns submitted respectfully.

"Didn't Garth tell us she had severed her connexion with the hospital?" Sir Arthur demanded. "Ah"—as his mother made a gesture of assent—"you may depend upon it that accounts for it! She has had an attack somewhere or other, and is *hors de combat* for the time being. Garth ought not to have sent us such a person, I think."

"Arthur," interposed Mavis, looking by no means reassured by this easy fashion of disposing of things, "supposing that Nurse Marston did have a fit while she was waiting for mother, where is she now? Minnie and Parkyns have looked through all the rooms."

For a moment Arthur was nonplussed.

"It seems to me she must have been trying to avoid them," he decided at last. "It is a queer sort of business altogether. I shall go down to the small library and take a good look round myself."

"That will be no use," Lady Laura said decidedly." My dear Arthur, do you forget that I sat waiting for her in that room for more than a quarter of an hour before I made any inquiry at all? Wherever she may be, it is assuredly not there. I did think it was possible that she had lost her way, but—"

"We will go through to the bottom part of the house," Sir Arthur said after an almost imperceptible pause, "and as soon as we have thoroughly satisfied ourselves that she is not in any one room the door shall be locked. Come, Jenkins! Mother, you and the girls had better go to bed. I will bring you word as soon as we find her."

"My dear, do you think it would be possible for me to rest until we know something more definite?" Lady Laura asked reproachfully. "I am coming with you now."

The green baize door leading to the kitchen part of the house was standing open; contrary to rule, and close to it the servants were assembled in quite a crowd, looking bewildered and mystified as they gossiped over Nurse Marston's disappearance. For once their presence there passed without rebuke from Mrs. Parkyns, whose nerves were, as she phrased it, "quite overset" for the time being.

"Has anyone seen anything of Nurse Marston?" Sir Arthur demanded, pausing.

There was a moment's silence, followed by a medley of negatives, in the midst of which the head housemaid's voice made itself heard:

"We have been in every room on the first and second floor, Sir Arthur, but there isn't as much as a sign of her."

"It is quite evident that I shall have to look for her myself," Sir Arthur said, with an attempt to laugh that ended in a failure. Truth to tell, the affair was beginning to puzzle him more than he would have cared to confess, and his face, as he turned down the passage leading to the small library, wore a distinctly uneasy expression.

There was a general move to follow him, but he held up his hand.

"Not every one, please! You, Jenkins—and Parkyns. Mother, if you could persuade Mavis to go to Dorothy—"

"Yes, Mavis dear, and see how that poor thing is getting on. Take care she suspects nothing of this, or she will be very upset."

Somewhat unwillingly, Mavis obeyed, and Lady Laura joined her son.

"The morning-room first, Arthur. You have not turned the lights off, I hope, Jenkins? Really, this search is making me feel quite creepy."

"No, my lady," the butler responded. "As soon as Minnie told me the nurse couldn't be found, and that it was your ladyship's wish that she should be looked for, I concluded that it would be better that the lights should be left on."

"Quite right, Jenkins," Sir Arthur assented as he threw open the door of the morning-room and looked in.

Certainly there was no trace of the missing nurse to be seen in the cheerful, modern-looking room with its bright fire, its carefully-shaded lights and pretty bright furniture. Nevertheless, the young man went in and looked under the big Chesterfield, behind the heavy velvet curtains and the heavier pieces of furniture.

"Nothing here—so much is certain. Now for the small library," he said. "Lock this door, Jenkins. Nobody is in there now, and nobody shall go in there until I have finished looking round."

The small library was at the end of the short passage out of which the morning-room opened. A door opposite to that of the latter room gave easy access to the still-room and the housekeeper's apartments.

Sir Arthur touched the handle doubtfully.

"Could she have made a mistake, gone through here and got bewildered among the passages at the back?" he debated.

"I could stake my oath she never came through there, Sir Arthur," Mrs. Parkyns took the answer upon herself. "I was there in my room with the door open for above an hour just about that time."

"Still, if you had your back to the door and she passed quickly," Sir Arthur argued. "However"—as she sniffed displeasedly—"that can wait; every passage in the house will have to be looked through presently if we don't find her."

He went into the library; its severely plain furniture and book-lined walls afforded little scope for concealment of any kind. Sir Arthur glanced under the table, and then moved towards the door at the other end of the room, stumbling over some small object on the floor.

"Hallo! What is this?" he exclaimed as he picked it up. "To whom does this belong?"

It was an ordinary tobacco-pouch with a spray of flowers worked across. Jenkins shook his head.

"I couldn't say, Sir Arthur. Perhaps one of the gentlemen's."

"At any rate, I suppose Nurse Marston doesn't smoke tobacco, so it has nothing to do with her," and he threw it on the table.

The second door into the room led into the conservatory. It was standing ajar now, and Sir Arthur turned to it. "I say, mother, per-haps, thinking you were keeping her waiting a long time, she went through here to the drawing-room."

Lady Laura stiffened perceptibly.

"She would hardly do that, Arthur, when I was engaged with my guests.

"Or she has gone for a walk. By Jove, I dare say that is the expla-nation of it all!" Arthur went on, improving his opportunity.

Jenkins stepped forward.

"If you will allow me, Sir Arthur-— No, I felt sure I was not mis-taken; the door into the garden is bolted inside and locked. Her ladyship bade me always see that it was fastened at six o'clock, to prevent tramps getting in, and I don't believe there has been a day that I have been a quarter of an hour late. She couldn't have gone out this way, Sir! Arthur, without leaving the door open behind her."

This argument was unanswerable, and with a cursory glance round the drawing-room Sir Arthur led his mother back to the hall.

"Do you see the time, mother?" he said glancing at the big clock at the foot of the stairs. "A quarter to two. Time you were in bed, or we shall be having you laid up. Jenkins and I will have another look round and then I shall turn in myself. One of the maids will sit up in the nurse's place, I dare say."

"I will myself, Sir Arthur," volunteered Mrs. Parkyns. "It will be just the same to me, my lady. I shouldn't get a wink of sleep if I went to bed, I know that."

"I do not believe that I shall, either," said Lady Laura, hesitating as her son bent to kiss her. "Arthur, where can she be? You don't think anything has happened to her?"

"Happened to her, not it!" her son said reassuringly. "Don't you get nervous, mother. She has gone out for a walk or something. Back to her mother's in a huff, I dare say. Jenkins' bolts and bars won't convince me."

Lady Laura looked somewhat comforted.

"Don't you think it would be better to send to her mother, Arthur?"

"It might frighten the poor old thing into a fit," her son said lightly, though over her head his eyes met the butler's meaningly. "I will walk down the first thing in the morning, if you like. Good night, and don't alarm yourself, mother."

An hour later there was a light tap at Sir Arthur's door. He opened it instantly.

"Any news?"

"No, Sir Arthur. Her mother has not seen her since she came up, and is sure she had no intention of leaving."

"Um! The mystery thickens! What do you make of it yourself, Jenkins? Is it possible that there is a young man in the question?"

The butler glanced away from his master's face into the lighted room beyond.

"I never heard of one, Sir Arthur. The Marstons have always been folks to keep themselves to themselves. I have been wondering"—he flicked a speck carefully from his immaculate waistcoat—"whether it would not be as well for me just to go over and speak to Mr. Davenant first thing in the morning."

"Why Mr. Davenant?"

"Well, sir, he—they have always been great friends, Sir Arthur—was talking to her in the avenue this afternoon for some time. It is possible that she gave him some hint of her intentions, sir."

There was a pause. Then Sir Arthur said as he turned to close the door:

"I do not think that is at all likely, Jenkins. Had Mr. Davenant known anything of the kind he would have informed us."

The butler bowed.

"Naturally he would, Sir Arthur."

"Good night."

"Good night, Sir Arthur."

Chapter Six

"SUPERINTEDENT Stokes would be glad if you could spare him a few minutes, Sir Arthur."

Sir Arthur tossed aside his palette impatiently.

"Show him into the small library and say that I will be with him directly, James."

"Yes, Sir Arthur."

The young man rumpled up his fair hair with a sigh of despair as he stood up and surveyed his morning's work. His great canvas was pretty well covered—the accessories, the towers of Camelot, Arthur and Guinevere, and the knights and ladies of their court were all completed, even the costume of the "lily-maid" as she lay in her golden barge. But Elaine's face remained a blank—Arthur's most strenuous efforts had failed to transfer to canvas the lovely features that, once seen, had made so strong an impression upon his imagination, and anything else would, he felt sure, only fall short of his ideal.

With an impatient shrug he told himself that he was a failure from an artistic point of view, and the next moment dwelt with a ray of hope on the possibilities of obtaining future sittings.

Before he left the room he glanced carelessly at the sketches lying on a stool beside him; all of them had the same fair, clear-cut features, the same large deep-blue eyes, but none of them, as it seemed to him, did anything like justice to the flawless perfection of the face that for one minute had lain on his breast. He glanced irresolutely at the fireplace, half inclined to burn them all, and then, changing his mind, threw them upon a small table already littered with half-dried tubes of paint and with brushes and tins of turpentine.

There was a step outside and Dr. Grieve's voice hailed him through the open door.

"Good morning, Sir Arthur. I am glad to tell you that the patient is doing better this morning—decidedly better."

Sir Arthur's face lighted up. For the week that had elapsed since he was called in, Dr. Grieve had insisted upon keeping his patient in bed. The young man began to hope that the improvement he spoke of might be the beginning of better things and to dream of the sittings for the Elaine for which he was longing.

"I am very glad to hear it," he said heartily. "The memory, doctor, how is that?"

The doctor's suave countenance became momentarily overclouded and he shook his head.

"No better, Sir Arthur, I grieve to say; I can see no improvement there at all. There is nothing for that but to trust to time. You have heard nothing as to her friends yet, I presume?"

"Nothing at all," Sir Arthur replied gloomily. "I really hardly know what to do about it, doctor. One naturally hesitates about calling the police to our aid, but so far the guarded advertisements that we have caused to be inserted have met with no response, and we have relied upon her memory's returning before long. I presume you think it is sure to do so eventually?"

The doctor spread out his hands.

"My dear Sir Arthur, this is just one of those cases in which it is impossible to predict the future with any degree of certainty. You see, we are working in the dark, as it were. If we had any idea of the nature of the predisposing cause, so to speak, the matter would be so much simpler. If some overwhelming shock, for instance, had set up the cerebral excitement which is undoubtedly present, then possibly another shock might bring about a reaction. In any other event one can but hope that with returning bodily health the memory may strengthen."

Sir Arthur did not reply immediately; his face, as he turned to accompany the doctor down the corridor, was grave and pre-occupied.

The doctor went on:

"This continued absence of Nurse Marston worries her, no doubt. Lady Laura tells me that she is continually inquiring whether the nurse has returned. I can't make that affair out myself at all, Sir Arthur. It is as great a mystery as that other one—how on earth this poor young lady, in the state she was, came into your park. I can't see daylight in either matter at all."

"Nor I," Sir Arthur acknowledged as he paused at the foot of the stairs. "My mother may have told you that we have sent for Super-intendent Stokes this morning. I hear great things of his ability and possibly he may be able to suggest something in the matter of Nurse Marston."

"No, Lady Laura didn't mention it," the doctor replied, drawing on his gloves. "But I think you are right, Sir Arthur. I quite think you are right. If only for her mother's sake, one would wish to elu-cidate the mystery that hangs over her departure and discover her present whereabouts."

"Naturally," Sir Arthur assented. "Will you come and help to interview Stokes, if your time is not too valuable this morning? He is in the small library now."

Dr. Grieve's eyes sparkled. An arrant old gossip, he asked nothing better than to make a third at the interview. Nevertheless, for professional reasons he thought it best to dissemble a little. Drawing out his old-fashioned repeater, he sounded it.

"Ah! I have no appointment this morning until noon; that gives me an hour to place at your disposal, Sir Arthur, I am sure that any advice or assistance I can give is at your service."

Sir Arthur led the way to the small library, Superintendent Stokes was standing near the window. He was a big, burly man, who had been only recently appointed to the Lockford constabulary, but he came with a great reputation from his preceding post, and was reported to owe his rapid rise from the ranks entirely to his cleverness in solving difficult cases, though, looking at his self-satisfied countenance, Sir Arthur was inclined to fancy that his abilities must have been considerably over-rated.

A keener observer, however, might have noted that the small, deeply-set eyes had a trick of glancing at most things, that the full-lipped mouth was not without a certain measure of shrewdness.

He saluted as Sir Arthur entered.

"Good morning, Sir Arthur."

"Good morning, Stokes," the young man returned genially. "I suppose you have been over the house? I told Jenkins to show you round. Sit down."

"Thank you, Sir Arthur, thank you," the superintendent replied as he took the chair the baronet indicated. "Yes, I have just looked about me a bit."

"What do you make of things?"

Superintendent Stokes glanced idly through the window.

"It is early to form a definite opinion, Sir Arthur. The only point I am clear about is that some one who was in your house that night, either guest or servant, knows where Nurse Marston is to be found, or how she left the house."

"You think so?" Arthur's tone betrayed some surprise. "The servants have all denied it most positively. As for guests, they are out of the question, certainly."

"Certainly, Sir Arthur."

To Dr. Grieve, looking from one to the other of the speakers, the superintendent's tone hardly suggested complete acquiescence with this view. He waited, eagerly on the alert for any suspicion of scandal.

Superintendent Stokes stroked his clean-shaven chin and looked at the fireplace.

"As for the servants denying it, Sir Arthur—well, if they had their reasons no doubt they could keep their own counsel. There is one other possibility, however. Could she have slipped out when your guests were leaving? Mr. Jenkins is very positive she did not."

Arthur shook his head.

"I think that is improbable in the extreme. James would be at the door, and Jenkins and Charles, as well as myself, a good deal of the time in the hall. No, I think that idea must be dismissed at once."

"Then there is nothing to fall back upon but the other theory—a confidant—that I can see. Mr. Jenkins tells me he fastened all the doors and French windows himself that night at six o'clock. It is an early hour for closing, Sir Arthur."

"It is," the young man assented, "and an inconvenient one. It is a fad of Lady Laura's. You may have heard that some suspicious look-ing characters got in the house through one of the side entrances about six months ago, and the affair naturally alarmed my mother; this early closing"—with a laugh—"has been the result."

"Ah, yes, I think I heard of that affair!" Superintendent Stokes said thoughtfully. "I have made a few inquiries on my own account since you spoke to me, Sir Arthur, but so far I have not discovered anything calculated to elucidate matters. Take it altogether, it is one of the queerest cases I have ever been engaged upon. That disappearance of the tobacco pouch, now, what do you make of that? It might have given us a clue."

"Oh, I scarcely think so! It might have been there for days."

"Or it might not," the superintendent remarked sapiently. "At any rate, I should have liked to have had a look at it. Worked with flowers, your butler tells me."

"Oh, yes. Just an ordinary-looking pouch, I have seen hundreds like it," Sir Arthur replied carelessly. He was inclined to think Superintendent Stokes something of a Jack in office. "I threw it down on the table, and the next morning it could not be found. Still, its loss can scarcely be regarded as of any importance."

The superintendent made no further comment. He apparently waited for further information, and his eyes glanced indifferently round the room.

Dr. Grieve leaned forward.

"I must protest against that tobacco-pouch being regarded as having any bearing on the case whatever," he remarked fussily. "Nurse Marston and her mother have been known to me for years—respectable, well-conducted women, both of them. The idea that is apparently gaining ground in some quarters that a clandestine love affair is at the bottom of the girl's disappearance is, I am persuaded, entirely without foundation."

The superintendent slowly brought his eyes back from the survey of the room and fixed them on the doctor's face.

"I hope you may be right, sir, I am sure. You see, I have not been long at Lockford, and the opinions of a gentleman like yourself, who has known the folks all their lives, must be invaluable to a stranger such as I am. The young woman came here on your recommendation, I understand, sir?"

"Certainly! I knew her to be a thoroughly capable and conscientious nurse, and when her name was mentioned to me by Mr. Garth Davenant I had no hesitation in agreeing with him that she was an eminently suitable person to undertake the case."

The superintendent stroked his chin once more thoughtfully for a moment.

"Ah, Mr. Garth Davenant spoke of her!" he repeated. "I don't know that gentleman very well, but I happened to be in Exeter some little time ago, and I think I saw him walking with this very young woman."

"In Exeter? Scarcely, I should imagine," the doctor remarked.

"I hardly think I was mistaken," Superintendent Stokes went on deferentially. "Still, if you—"

"Old Mrs. Marston was years in the employ of Lady Davenant; she nursed both of the sons, and I know that Lady Davenant has the highest opinion both of Mrs. Marston and her daughter," Sir Arthur interposed haughtily. He was inclined to resent the present trend of the conversation. "I know that Sir John Davenant and Garth respect her very highly, and her daughter also."

"Naturally they would," the superintendent acquiesced blandly. "Still, I think I should just like to ask Mr. Garth Davenant whether Nurse Marston said anything then that might cast a light on her subsequent disappearance."

"Had she done so Mr. Davenant would certainly have informed us." Sir Arthur's tone was distinctly one of displeasure now. "He knows the trouble and anxiety her absence is causing us."

"She might have let drop a word or two that he overlooked at the time, and yet if he came to think of them now they might bear another meaning," the superintendent suggested.

Arthur rose and pressed the bell.

"At any rate the matter can soon be placed beyond doubt. Mr. Davenant is, I believe, in the house at the present moment. Jenkins"—as the butler made his appearance—"ask Mr. Garth to come here for a few moments."

There was an awkward pause as the old man departed on his errand. Sir Arthur sat drumming his fingers on the table, his brows contracted, his expression one of bored irritation. Dr. Grieve took off his spectacles, polished them deliberately with his handkerchief, and then replaced them, and sat watching the door, evidently on the qui vive for any fresh sensation. The placid, plump countenance of the police officer alone remained unmoved; his eyes were fixed absently on the pictures, and as he rose and bowed when Garth entered there was absolutely no change in his expression.

Davenant looked distinctly surprised as he turned to his future brother-in-law.

"I thought you were quite alone, Arthur. Jenkins said you wished to see me, but I have not much time to spare this morning; Mavis is waiting for me. I am going to drive her to Friar's Key—"

"We shall not delay you long," Arthur said quickly. "We—that is to say, Superintendent Stokes, who is investigating the circumstance surrounding Nurse Marston's disappearance, wanted to ask you a few questions."

Garth Davenant's face cleared, and he turned briskly to the police officer.

"I am sure that any information that I possess is heartily at your service. My only difficulty is that I am afraid I know nothing likely to be of any value. I did not even see Nurse Marston that night."

"No," the superintendent agreed. "So I have heard before, sir; but you were talking to her in the avenue in the afternoon. May I ask if she alluded in any way to anything that might call her away—whether she hinted at any trouble?"

"Nothing of the kind. Oh, I am sure she had no intention of leaving then. I cannot understand her departure at all," the young man answered readily.

"Or when you met with her in Exeter the Saturday before?" the superintendent went on blandly, his face looking merely mildly interested, though his sharp, ferrety eyes took in every change of expression in Garth Davenant's features, and not one note of the different intonation in the young man's voice escaped his keen ears.

There was a distinct pause before the answer.

"Certainly not!"

Sir Arthur turned to Garth and said:

"That would be the day after you came down—the day you had promised to ride with Mavis?"

"Yes, I had to go to Exeter on business instead."

"But what was Nurse Marston doing in Exeter?" Dr. Grieve speculated. "Did she give you any idea, Mr. Garth?"

Garth hesitated.

"Whatever her business in Exeter might be, I can answer for it that it had no connexion with her subsequent disappearance."

"Then I take it that you have some definite knowledge of that business?" the superintendent interposed smartly, while Dr. Grieve was still considering the last answer.

"To a certain extent, yes," Garth acknowledged, with reservation.

The superintendent leaned forward.

"Can't you enlighten us further, Mr. Davenant? As a barrister you must understand that in a case of this kind it is necessary that the police should be in possession of every detail, however apparently insignificant, that may have any bearing on the case."

"This can have none."

The response was quick and decisive, yet the superintendent looked by no means satisfied.

"Are we to understand that you deliberately refuse to give us any further information, Mr. Davenant?"

"I have none that could possibly assist you in any way," Garth said slowly.

Sir Arthur turned and stared at him in amazement.

"Well, but really, you know, Davenant, you must speak out. Why, the whole thing is making my mother quite ill, to say nothing of Mavis and Dorothy. You really must do what you can to help us."

Garth's dark face looked set and stern.

"I have already said that a knowledge of Nurse Marston's errand in Exeter could in no sense help you. Besides"—he paused and hesitated—"it is not an affair of my own. I can say no more."

"That is your last word?"

"It is."

"Well, upon my word, Davenant—"

"One moment, if you please, Sir Arthur," the superintendent said. "There is another question which I must ask permission to put in different forms to every one who was in this house on the 6th of June. Perhaps Mr. Davenant would kindly answer it now?"

With an air of relief Garth turned to him.

"Certainly—I am at your service."

There was a light step outside, and after a preliminary tap at the door it was thrown open and Mavis appeared.

"This is really too bad of you, Arthur. You are keeping Garth a most unconscionable time—you and Dr. Grieve," with a smile at the old man. "We shall be late at Friar's Key, and you know how particular Lady Maynard is."

"I shall be ready in a moment," Garth answered for himself, with a smile at her, though his face looked worried and anxious. "What was it you wanted to ask me, superintendent?"

"Perhaps another time, sir," Stokes suggested smoothly.

"Oh, it will be better to get it done with now! You can wait a moment, Mavis," Sir Arthur said with fraternal unconcern. "Now then, Stokes!"

"It is only that, just as a matter of form, I should like to ask Mr. Davenant whether he has in his possession a gutta-percha tobacco-pouch ornamented with a spray of flowers in silk?"

"Why, certainly he has!" Mavis interrupted with a gay laugh. "I worked it for him myself—roses and lilies, wasn't it, Garth? Awfully old-fashioned they are too; but it is so difficult to know what you can work for a man. Have you got it with you, Garth?"

He looked embarrassed, and the other three men gazed across at him in silent expectation.

"Not to-day, Mavis."

"When I gave it to you you said you would always carry it about with you. Where is it? You do not— Oh, Garth," in a tone of deep reproach, "I believe you have lost it."

Davenant's smile was a trifle forced.

"It—I have mislaid it for the time being, Mavis. I shall find it again in a day or two, I have no doubt."

"In the meantime"—the superintendent's mellifluous accents interposed—"I believe Miss Hargreave saw the one that was found in this room on the night of the 6th of June. Perhaps she could tell us whether it was the one she worked?"

"I am sure I couldn't," Mavis said indifferently. "I hardly glanced at it. It looked dirty, I remember. I should have noticed it more particularly had I guessed the care you took of my presents, Garth."

"The spray across, as I remember, was pink and white," Sir Arthur said slowly. "Garth, I—"

"I will never forgive you if you left it lying about to be picked up by anybody," Mavis finished. "I am sorry I can't wait to hear you describe it more accurately, Arthur, but I am afraid Lady Maynard would think it a poor compliment to her luncheon-party if she could see us standing here discussing that wretched pouch when we ought to be on our way. Come, Garth, we really must make a start," and with a laughing nod she took him away.

Chapter Seven

"Oh, if one could only realize one's ideals in this world!"

"Does it not satisfy you now?" Hilda asked softly.

She was lying back on the great roomy sofa in Lady Laura's morning-room. Her clinging white wrapper, as Arthur had assured her, was the very garment for the lily-maid, and the warm rug across her feet took, for the nonce, the place of the coverlet of cloth of gold.

She had acceded with a little blush and smile to her host's eager request for a sitting, and since then Sir Arthur, having transferred his sketch-book and himself from the studio to the morning-room, had spent most of his time in making attempts, which invariably ended in failure, to portray her in the character of Elaine.

Dorothy was sitting a little behind her. She leant forward.

"Why, Arthur, that is beautiful! If it does not content you, you must indeed be hard to please."

"How can I be satisfied when I look at the original?" Arthur inquired gloomily. "That glowing colour—I wonder whether I dare ask you to let your hair down, Miss Hilda? I want it to fall on both sides like that—do you see?"

The girl's delicate colour deepened a little, her long lashes drooped beneath his gaze, but she raised no objection.

"I will let it down with pleasure," she declared at once, "but I am afraid it will come far short of the required length, Sir Arthur."

She drew out the pins as she spoke, and both Dorothy and Arthur made exclamations as the hair fell around in a glittering golden mass.

"It is beautiful," Dorothy said with honest enthusiasm, "and it curls so prettily round your head, Hilda."

"It is a lot of trouble to keep in order," Hilda complained with a pout, a little flickering smile playing round her mouth as Arthur, with a gesture of despair, went back to his paint-box.

"Oh, to catch that wonderful sheen!" he cried as he turned over the tubes despairingly. "But it is hope-less!" rumpling up his hair. "How can one dream of obtaining it with paint and canvas?"

"I am sorry I am such a difficult subject," Hilda said demurely, "but I have never been painted before, and I must plead that as an excuse."

Dorothy lifted her brown eyes and glanced at her cousin; the significance of the remark was apparently lost on him. With evident love in his eyes he was gazing at his beautiful model.

Dorothy saw that if advantage was to be taken of this apparent return of memory on their mysterious visitor's part she must be the one to avail herself of it; her cousin's absorption in his work and his model was so great that he had not even noticed it.

She put a stitch or two in her work before she spoke, then she said in a carefully matter-of-fact tone:

"Have you ever been photographed, Hilda? A good photograph is often a great help."

The blue eyes looked at her for a second vaguely.

"I don't think I have a very good one," the girl began slowly, then her face clouded over, and she put up her hands to her head. "I think I have a photograph somewhere—in fancy dress—I seem to see it—but I can't remember. Oh, why did you ask me? It is so dreadful not to know." She burst into a passion of tears.

Dorothy drew back in dismay.

"I did not mean—Indeed, I am so sorry," she faltered.

Sir Arthur flung down his palette, his eyes full of a passionate pity.

"Do not think of it, do not try to remember. It will come back some day—all the doctors are agreed upon that. In the meantime you know how delighted we are to have you with us; if we could only teach you to look upon the Manor as your home."

"You are all so kind to me," the girl said as she sobbed, "far too kind, and I am very stupid and ungrateful. But it seems to bring it home to me somehow what an absolute waif I am when I am asked a simple question like that and cannot answer it."

Sir Arthur's face darkened as he glanced impatiently at his cousin.

"Dorothy should not have asked it," he said shortly. "I thought you had been warned, Dorothy—that you had been told all excitement was to be avoided."

Two hot red spots burned in Dorothy's cheeks; it was the first time her cousin had ever spoken to her in that tone and the tears were very near the surface.

"Indeed, Arthur, I am very sorry," she said penitently. "But Hilda spoke of not having been painted before, and I thought if I answered her in the same strain it was possible that she might recollect."

Arthur frowned irritably.

"Thought!" he repeated testily. "I wish you would use a little more discretion, Dorothy. Don't you see how bad all this is for her?"

The girl made no reply, her lips were trembling, her eyes were full of unshed tears.

Sir Arthur glanced from her to Hilda. The latter was apparently making a brave attempt to conquer her sobs.

"I shall be all right directly, thank you!" she murmured. "You must not be vexed with Miss Dorothy, it was all my own stupidity; she did not mean to hurt me."

"I am sure she did not," Arthur assented more calmly; his momentary annoyance with his cousin was passing, and he gave her a kindly glance. "I am very sorry it has happened. I cannot have my Elaine upset."

This was too much for Dorothy's equanimity. That Arthur should blame her—as she felt unjustly—was bad enough, but that Hilda should make excuses for her to him was the last straw. Forgetting that Lady Laura and Mavis were both out, and that she had promised to sit in the improvised studio until their return, she caught up her work and hurried out of the room.

Upstairs, throwing herself down by her bed, she burst into an agony of sobs. Those shy, sweet hopes, which she had hitherto hardly dared to put into words, even to herself, but which a month ago had seemed so near fruition, were now withering away. Ever since Hilda's coming to the Manor she had fancied that there was a distinct change in Arthur's manner; she had done her best to persuade herself that she was mistaken, that he was the same as ever, but this morning she told herself that it would be folly to deceive herself any longer.

Evidently Arthur had found out that his feeling for her was merely cousinly affection, and this beautiful stranger was absorbing his whole thoughts in a fashion which, she knew well, she had never been able to do.

There, on her knees, wrestling with her first agony of humiliation that she should have given her love unsought, Dorothy told herself that she could have borne it if she could have believed that the object of Arthur's devotion was worthy of it—that the love itself would make for his happiness; but despite her best efforts, though she knew that Lady Laura and Mavis had succumbed to her charm,

Dorothy had never been able to bring herself to like Hilda, and the utmost she could do was to resolve that no word or look of hers should reveal her feelings to others.

In the meantime, in the morning-room, Arthur was making dangerous strides in his intimacy with Hilda.

She, finding herself left alone with him, had made obvious efforts to control her agitation, and smiled resolutely through her tears into his concerned face.

"Do go on with your picture, Sir Arthur, or I shall feel that I have wasted your morning, and you will say that I am a shocking model."

"You are so absolutely an ideal Elaine that the impossibility of doing the subject justice is almost driving me crazy," Arthur declared, tossing his fair hair back from his forehead as he gazed despairingly at his morning's work. Nevertheless, he went to work with feverish energy and painted away with a sort of fierce absorption for a short time.

Presently he looked up.

"That is better, I think. I am not tiring you, I hope, Miss Hilda!"

The girl twisted up her hair with a laugh as she nestled into her cushions.

"I am the most luxuriously-served of models, and one could hardly get tired of lying on this couch, but I must confess it is a relief to turn over sometimes."

"I was a brute not to remember before," Arthur said contritely, "but the fact is, when I am looking at you, I can think of nothing but Elaine."

He was mixing his paints on his palette as he spoke.

Hilda looked at him in silence for a few minutes. At last she spoke in a subdued tone:

"Sir Arthur, may I ask you something?"

Sir Arthur looked up, palette knife in hand, in some surprise.

"Anything I can tell you—"

Hilda glanced round her fearfully a moment before she spoke.

"Where is Nurse Marston, Sir Arthur?"

The young man started; he hesitated a moment before replying, for he knew that the mystery attaching to Nurse Marston's curious departure from the Manor had been hitherto kept from her patient, but it seemed to him, looking at the girl's agitated face, that some hint of the circumstances must have reached her, and he deliberated as to whether it might not now be more expedient to speak out.

Hilda's eyes were fixed upon his wavering face, as if they would wring the secret from him.

"Where is Nurse Marston?" she reiterated. "Where did she go when she left the Manor? "

"I do not know," Sir Arthur said slowly at last. "I wish I did," he added.

Hilda pushed back the heavy mass of hair from her white forehead.

"What do you mean?" she asked, bewildered. "Do you know why she left?"

"What has made you ask me?" he inquired.

The girl's face was noticeably paler, her blue eyes looked strained and terrified.

"When I was lying only partially conscious, I caught words and phrases which, disconnected as they were, made me fancy later on when I was better, and could put things together, that there was something strange—some story about her. Then yesterday Minnie was helping me to dress—Mavis is so kind, she always sends her— and I asked how it was that Nurse Marston went away so suddenly. She turned absolutely ashen white as soon as I mentioned the name and began to tremble all over. Then when I persisted she burst into tears and I could extract nothing from her."

"Minnie's behaviour has been to me one of the queerest things about the whole affair," Sir Arthur acknowledged. "I cannot for the life of me see how it concerns her. Yet she goes about looking like a ghost and seems to be terrified at the mention of Nurse Marston's name."

"You have not answered my question—what has become of Nurse Marston?" Hilda reminded him. "You must tell me all, please, Sir Arthur."

"All is not much," the young man responded. "When Nurse Marston left your room on the night of the 6th of last month it was ostensibly to go to an interview with my mother in the small library."

"Well?" Hilda said breathlessly, a queer look coming over her face.

Sir Arthur rose.

"You are faint," he said concernedly. "You must have some wine or something. I will ring—"

Hilda put out her hands and stopped him.

"No, no," she whispered fearfully. "It is not that; don't you see that it is the dread of what I am going to hear? Tell me the worst, please, Sir Arthur, at once. Nothing could be more terrible than some of the fancies I have had. Did she die?"

"Die? No," the young man said reassuringly. "Nurse Marston is alive and well, I firmly believe, Miss Hilda. The only thing is that she did not keep an appointment she had made with my mother that night, and we none of us can make out where she did go. In fact I suppose for some reasons of her own she disappeared."

"She disappeared!" Hilda breathed slowly, her very lips looking stiff and white. "Do you mean that she was not in the house—that you could not find her?"

"We could not find her in the house or out of it," Sir Arthur assented. "From that day, try as we will, we have not been able to discover any tidings of her whereabouts. It is one of the strangest affairs I have ever heard of."

A tinge of colour was stealing back to Hilda's pale face.

"She must have had some reason for going, Sir Arthur."

"As I said just now," he acquiesced, "but the difficulty is to find out where she did go. She disappeared, and there is the minor puzzle of how she went. Jenkins declares that the doors and windows were all locked and fastened and that it was impossible she should have gone out at them."

Hilda's returning colour paled again.

"You do not mean that she is still in the house, alive or—dead?" she said as she shivered. "Oh, Sir Arthur—"

"No, no," Arthur said reassuringly. "That has been ascertained beyond all doubt. The police have searched every nook and cranny—even your room when you were out of it," he said. "No. She got out of the house somehow. Either Jenkins overlooked some door or window or some one in the house knows why she went and secured the door after her. One curious feature of the affair is that she apparently took nothing with her but the clothes she stood up in. Nothing that she was known to have with her was missing, and two of the servants spoke to her as she went down and testify that she was not carrying anything. Still, she might have had any amount of things outside."

"It is absolutely unaccountable—I never heard anything like it!" Hilda said breathlessly. "Then she really disappeared when she left my room that night?"

"Yes—up till now," Sir Arthur said unwillingly. He was beginning to fear the result of the girl's excessive agitation. "I think we may hear from her any day. To me it seems evident that she went away of her own free will. I feel sure no harm has happened to her."

Hilda made no reply, but lay gazing apparently at the fire, her large blue eyes looking bigger than ever by contrast with the unnatural pallor of her face.

Arthur turned to his Elaine again; there was much that could be done without actually posing Hilda, and he went on with it, casting a glance at the girl's averted profile every now and then. Presently he saw that great tears were rolling slowly down her face and that she was trembling from head to foot. He threw down his brushes impetuously and crossed over to her.

"Will you not tell me what is troubling you? It may be that in some way I could help you."

Hilda shook her head as she pulled out her handkerchief.

"You are very kind—you are all of you kindness itself to me; but it seems that no one can help me—no one can clear up the mystery overhanging my life. You can have no idea what it feels like to be a mere waif—without a home, without friends or a name even. Ah, when shall I remember?" She covered her face with her hands.

Arthur ventured to touch them softly; the sight of the girl's distress almost unmanned him.

"Do not," he besought her eagerly, "please do not! How can you say you have no friends when you are with us—that you are alone in the world when you know that it is the greatest joy to have you here?"

"Ah, no! I was ungrateful!" Hilda said with a pathetic little attempt at a smile as she dried her eyes. "I ought to have remembered what you have all done for me. You must forgive me; but this disappearance of the nurse is so strange that it seems all a part of the misfortune that pursues me. Do you believe in fate, Sir Arthur?"

"I can't say I do," Sir Arthur said in some embarrassment. He had all the ordinary young Englishman's distaste for metaphysics, and, greatly as he sympathized with Hilda, he would have infinitely preferred to keep the conversation on less abstract lines.

"I do most thoroughly. I believe in a fate—a power that may neither be evaded nor defied," Hilda went on to his complete discomfort; "and I feel sure that this—this woman's disappearance is all part of the mystery that overhangs me."

"Come, come, Miss Hilda, now you are getting quite out of my depth!" Arthur expostulated, taking a low chair and drawing it up near the couch. "How could the two things be connected in any way? Besides, I don't suppose there is much mystery about either of them really. Nurse Marston may turn up sooner or later, and when you are a little stronger you will remember who you are and this time next year we shall be laughing to think how puzzled we were."

Hilda's eyes were full of trouble, the colour had not come back to her cheeks, her lips drooped pathetically.

"I have tried—oh, how I have tried!—to remember where I came from, and it is all no use."

"Isn't that just what the doctors said you were not to do?"

"I can't help it. How can I?" Hilda broke out passionately. "Sometimes I fancy I am on the verge of recalling everything, and then it all goes away again. When I think of that night—the time I came here—try as I will it only seems like a sort of maze—a bad dream. I imagine that some one was unkind to me—I fancy I can remember angry words, and then it was dark and wet everywhere, and I was cold, so cold. Then through the mist and the damp I saw your face, and you were good to me—very, very good to me. Ah, I can never forget your kindness, even if I do not remember my own name!"

Arthur's own eyes were misty now, and there was a suspicious trembling in his voice.

"Ah, if only I could make you understand how thankful we are to have you here—how desolate this house will be to some of us when you go!"

He leaned forward and dared to lay his hands on hers, and was not repulsed.

"When I go!" Hilda repeated forlornly, her hand resting in his as if unconsciously. "Ah, I must—I am sure I ought to go; and perhaps I know enough to teach, if that has not all gone too! But who would take me, Sir Arthur? I should have no references—I could give no account of myself."

"Stop!" Arthur cried hoarsely. "Do not say another word of that sort. You know we—my mother and I—would never consent to anything of the kind. We look upon you as our special charge, sent to us from Heaven. Hilda, promise me that you will not speak of that again—that you will stay with us until you find your own home!"

"But when will that be?" Hilda's eyes were downcast; her long lashes lay like dark shadows on her fair skin.

"Never mind! Promise!" said Arthur imperiously.

The girl gave him one shy upward glance.

"I—promise," she murmured obediently, "since you are so kind as to wish to keep me."

Meanwhile upstairs in her room Dorothy was making desperate attempts to remove the traces of her agitation; she smoothed her hair and bathed her face, but as she looked at the forlorn reflection in the glass her tears threatened to break out again.

"If only she is good enough for him," she murmured as she rubbed her pale cheeks in a vain attempt to bring back her colour, "if only she will make him happy, I do not mind; it does not matter about me."

Chapter Eight

"YOU ARE fond of music, Miss Hilda?" Garth Davenant had been standing by the piano turning the leaves of her music while Mavis tried over a new song. He crossed now to Hilda, who, with Sir Arthur in close attendance, was listening with an absorbed face.

"I love it," she said, with an abstracted air. "I cannot help thinking—I seem to have heard that song before."

"Well, it is not exactly new," Mavis said with a light laugh. "I dare say you will hear it a good many times yet, for I don't learn anything very easily."

"Do you play or sing yourself, Miss Hilda?" Garth asked, watching the girl's changing face.

"I—I don't know." She hesitated and looked round appealingly. "I—I can't remember."

"Try!" he said, going over to her and silencing Arthur s objection with a glance. "Come, I am sure by your face that you do!"

The girl rose and stood for a moment, her hands pressed to her head, then she crossed the room slowly. As she sat down to the piano her expression altered.

"Oh!" she exclaimed delightedly. "I—I think—I believe—I remember!"

Davenant placed a symphony of Beethoven's on the stand and took his place beside her, watching her face critically.

For a moment the white fingers strayed over the keys in a vague uncertain fashion; then they altered, settled on the right notes, and the opening chords rang out. It was evident from the beginning to all in the room that they were listening to a real musician, one, too, whose touch and technique showed that she must have received a careful training.

"Capital! Thank you very much!" Davenant said as she finished and rose from her seat with flushed cheeks.

"That was quite right, was it not?" she asked with childish delight. "It is a step in the right direction, I believe. Fancy, until to-day I have not known that I could do anything! The rest—ah, surely the rest will come soon, will it not, Mr. Davenant?"

Sir Arthur had joined the group at the piano.

"Are you so tired of us then?" Davenant heard him whisper under cover of rearranging the music; he caught too the upward look with which she rewarded the speech, and his face darkened.

But Hilda had appealed to him.

"Oh, yes. I feel quite sure that your memory will be as good as ever in a very short time," he said as he looked across the room. "Mavis, do you remember you promised to be kind to me this morning? I want you to walk as for as the village with me. Will you?"

Mavis hesitated a moment, but a glance at his anxious face decided her. She caught up the coat and hat she had thrown down a few minutes before and put them on.

"Don't say that I keep you waiting. You will not mind if I take the dogs—they are waiting for me in the hall."

Outside the air was fresh, in spite of the heat; rain had fallen heavily during the preceding night, and the storm had served to clear the air; the dogs gambolled round joyfully.

Mavis lifted up her face appreciatively and drew a deep breath.

"How charming everything smells! We will go by the Home Coppice and across the footpath that brings us out near the Wishing Well. It is the nearest way, and it will be delightfully cool this morning. What do you think of Hilda, Garth?"

"She is very beautiful."

Mavis laughed as, screened from the house by the trees, she tucked her arm under his.

"Certainly, anyone can see that, stupid boy! I mean, how do you like her? Is she not perfectly delightful?"

Garth hesitated; he looked away from the gay, piquante face of the girl at his side into the green, leafy depths of the Home Coppice.

Mavis gave his arm a little shake.

"If you let your mind stray to your briefs when you are with me, sir, I shall turn back. Why do you not answer my question?"

"Well, I paused," Garth said reluctantly, "because I am afraid my answer, if I speak truthfully, will not please you, Mavis, and—"

"What do you mean?" Mavis asked, looking at him in astonishment. "Surely you do not mean that you do not like Hilda?—Oh, Garth, and she is so sweet and lovable!"

Garth pulled his moustache perplexedly.

"I don't trust her," he said slowly at last. "To my mind there is something about her that does not ring true, but I think she is a capital actress, Mavis."

Mavis drew her hand from his arm.

"What do you mean?" she said coldly. "Garth, it is not like you to be so suspicious, and when you know how fond I am of Hilda—"

"Ah, don't you see that is just what makes me so anxious, because you are brought into daily contact with her?" Garth interrupted. "Mavis, you know I never liked the idea of this girl staying on at the Manor in the way she's doing for an indefinite length of time, and now that I have seen her—"

"Well, now that you have seen her—" Mavis repeated in displeased accents.

"I dislike that idea more than ever," Garth finished. "I think I could give a pretty good guess at her object in coming to you, Mavis. I wondered to-day whether you were all blind but myself. If Lady

Laura were to take the course I should advise, and send her to the seaside with a nurse or an elderly woman to look after her, I would guarantee that the young lady would soon recover her memory."

Mavis came to a sudden stop in the middle of the pathway.

"Which is as much as to say you think that she has not lost it at all—that she is pretending and deceiving us all!" she cried indignantly. "Oh, Garth, I did not think you would be so uncharitable!"

Garth looked down at her flushed face tenderly.

"I can't help having my own opinion, Mavis. Her pleasure in finding she could play and that pretty little speech about it were all done for effect, I am certain."

Mavis's mouth looked mutinous and she drew away from the hand he outstretched to her.

"Do you imagine that you know better than the doctors?"

"I may be a better judge of human nature than the doctor who has seen her," Garth said quietly. "I have had a pretty wide experience of the scurvy side of things at the courts, you know, but I merely give you my opinion for what it is worth, Mavis. You may all be right and I may be entirely wrong, only I know that I hate the thought of you living with this woman seeing her every day and— Oh, can't I make you understand how I hate it for you?"

Meeting the appeal in his eyes, Mavis softened.

"Silly boy!" she said with a laugh. "What harm could she do me, I should like to know, even if it were as you fancy, which I am quite sure it is not?"

"I don't know," said Garth thoughtfully. "Yet I have the strangest feeling—presentiment—call it what you will—that harm will come of it. Naturally Lady Laura—none of you—can have failed to note Arthur's growing infatuation."

"Ah, no. Poor boy, you are looking at everything through jaundiced eyes," Mavis said, patting his arm, her short-lived wrath evaporating as she saw the real anxiety in his face. "Arthur thinks her very beautiful—he is painting her for his Elaine—but it is Dorothy he cares for."

Garth made no response, but his dark face looked unconvinced. He drew Mavis's arm through his.

"Don't let us talk of it any more, Mavis. I have something much nearer my heart to say to you this morning; my father was talking to me last night. He is very anxious to see me settled, Mavis."

"Oh!" The swift, hot colour surged over the girl's face; her hand fluttered restlessly and tried to draw itself away.

Garth held it in a close, warm clasp.

"He was speaking of ways and means, Mavis. To all intents and purposes he is putting me into poor Walter's place and making the eldest son of me—that is, as far as the unentailed property is concerned. The title, naturally, must be Walter's, and the secured estate and the income of the latter, after my father's death, if we should be in ignorance of his whereabouts, will have to accumulate for him, or for his children if he should have any. My father suggests that he should make over to us the house at Overdeen—the Priory, it is called; and then—for you would not have me give up my profession, would you, Mavis?—I thought I might look out for a little house in Kensington, and you will come to me. You will not keep me waiting long, will you, sweetheart?"

The girl's hot face was downcast; beneath the brim of her hat Garth could only catch a glimpse of the pretty, tremulous mouth. But the warm, soft fingers clung to his now. He stooped and pressed his lips to them.

"Oh, Mavis, my darling, my own sweetheart! How can I thank you?"

Mavis tore herself away.

"Oh, Garth, some one is coming—I heard the leaves rustling!" her cheeks still aflame. "And, see, what in the world has Pompey got there?"

She darted away. Garth, his eyes fixed fondly on her, followed more slowly.

"It is a chain," she said. "And what is this—a little book?" taking it from the dog's mouth. "Be quiet, Pompey! No, sir, you shall not have it," as he sprang upon her. "I wonder who has lost this—it is evidently a notebook from a chatelaine." She unfastened the clasp with some difficulty and looked inside. "Garth"—the colour ebbing from her cheeks—"look at this!"

"What is it, Mavis? What is the matter?"

Mavis held it out and pointed to the name written on the first page, her hands trembling visibly.

Garth looked over her shoulder. The little book had evidently lain in the damp for some time; the leaves were stained and discoloured, the cover tarnished, but the inscription written in ink on the fly-leaf was still perfectly legible—"Mary Anne Marston, from Lady Davenant."

"Mary Anne Marston!" Garth repeated in amazement. "Why, then, this is—it must be—part of the chatelaine my mother gave Nurse Marston when she first left home! We all made her some little present, and I know this was my mother's, for I remember well how particular she was that everything should be put on the chain that she thought could be useful to a nurse—scissors and a knife and such like. This is the notebook, certainly. But how in the world did it come here? What is frightening you, Mavis?"

For Mavis was ghastly pale and shivering apparently with fright.

"Don't you see that she must have dropped it after she left our house that night?" she said in a low, awestruck tone. "Don't you remember that the note she wrote to my mother to say she wanted to see her was written on a page torn from this very book? Look!" she turned rapidly to the end and held it out to him. "There—that is the place she tore it from! Oh, Garth, don't you see?"

"I see!" Garth took it from her and looked at it carefully as he turned it about. "Well, at all events this proves that she came through the Home Coppice on her way from the Manor, and so it is valuable to us as the first clue that we have been able to find since she left her patient's room. But then we knew she must have gone somewhere, so I am not sure that it tells us much. Still, I think as we go through the village we had better call at the police station and show them this and explain exactly how we found it."

Mavis clasped his arm tightly and looked round her with wide open, terrified eyes.

"Surely you do not imagine that I shall go on after seeing this, Garth? Nothing would induce me to go any farther through this dreadful wood."

"My dear child, this is really—" Garth was beginning when the steps that Mavis had heard before sounded nearer on a parallel path to them, and then as the two walks merged into one Tom Greyson came into sight. He was looking particularly gloomy and disconsolate as he strode along with his dog at his heels, but as he touched his hat he glanced in some surprise at the girl's agitated face.

She put out her hand and stopped him.

"Don't go on, Tom; you must stay and help us now. I am so frightened"—a little sob catching her throat.

"Frightened, Miss Hargreave?" Greyson repeated in a puzzled tone.

Garth passed his arm round her trembling form.

"Come, come, Mavis; you must not give way like this; there is nothing really to alarm you! It is only that we, or rather the dogs, have found something that belonged to Nurse Marston, and it has upset Miss Hargreave. It is a notebook, and must have been dropped after she left the Manor."

A gleam of interest lighted up Greyson's moody face.

"She did come this way then, sir? I have always said she must ha' done; but she would come right out close to her mother's cottage. It puzzles me why she did not go in and speak to the old woman, just to set her mind at rest, as it were. She is getting worn to a shadow is Mrs. Marston with all the worry of it."

"I cannot understand it at all," Garth said thoughtfully.

"She came into this wood," Mavis said, shuddering from head to foot with a vague intangible horror. "It may have been to see her mother, or anything, I don't know what, but perhaps she never came out. Oh, don't you see what I mean, Garth? She may have been taken ill here and lain down among the trees and died, or she may have met a tramp and been murdered, and—and—be lying here still!"

She uttered the last words in a low, terrified tone beneath her breath.

The eyes of the two men met in one long significant glance as she paused; then Garth said with a resolutely cheerful air:

"My dear Mavis, we have not the least reason for supposing that Nurse Marston is dead. She is probably alive and well and will give us her own reasons for this mysterious absence when she returns. Come, you are tired and over-wrought; I will take you back to the Manor. Greyson, I think it might be as well to let the police know of this discovery, if you are going that way."

"I will tell them, sir," the man said as he touched his hat.

"First you must look to see that she is not lying here," Mavis said with an effort, putting up her hands and clutching nervously at her throat as she spoke. "The—the dogs were moving about among the moss and leaves over there. Behind, farther in the wood, there is a hollow. I shall not go away—I could not—until I know. Garth, you must look—you must!"

"No, no, sir! You stay with Miss Hargreave, sir," Tom Greyson interposed quickly. "I'll go and look. Don't you frighten yourself, miss. Why, we are all over this coppice of nights now that the pheasants are nesting! If there had been anything of that sort here we should ha' been bound to find it before now. Under that oak you said the dogs were, didn't you, miss?"

He sprang off. Garth drew Mavis to a fallen tree-trunk near and made her sit down.

"Why, Mavis, I didn't think you were so nervous!"

"I think somehow a horror of the whole affair came over me— not quite at the first, but very soon after—with regard to Nurse Marston's disappearance," she said slowly. "It was all so strange when you think of it—that cry Dorothy heard; and Jenkins was so certain she could not have got out of the house."

"Ah, well! It is perfectly obvious now that the old man was wrong there," Garth said, with as much cheerfulness as he could assume, for in truth her nervousness was beginning to infect him. "As for the shriek Dorothy heard—well, I have never been able to connect that with Nurse Marston. If she had been taken ill in the house, or any evil had happened to her there, she must have been found before now. Probably Dorothy fancied it, or perhaps one of the maidservants had a fit of hysterics. Well, Greyson, what is the result of your search?"

"She isn't there, sir," the man said. "I made sure she wasn't. We know our woods a bit too well for that to happen, as I told Miss Hargreave."

But it struck Garth, that, in spite of his apparent confidence, the man's ruddy face was some degrees paler than it had been a few minutes before.

"Well, now you are satisfied, I hope," he said, turning to Mavis, whose colour was beginning to return. "Come, it is no use our staying here any longer. Greyson, you might look round the wood farther in just to satisfy Miss Hargreave—or stay, what are you going to do now?"

"Going to have my dinner, sir. I live right by the side of the coppice, but that don't matter if there is anything you would like me to do first."

"No, no! Have your dinner, and then come up to the Manor. I shall be there and we can ask Sir Arthur what he thinks is best to be done now."

"Very good, sir!" Greyson touched his hat again as they turned away.

As Davenant held the gate into the park open for Mavis she looked up at him wistfully.

"Garth, I want to ask you to do something for me."

"What is it, Mavis? You know anything I can do—"

"Garth, will you tell me what you were doing with Nurse Marston in Exeter the day before she came to us?"

Davenant did not look pleased.

"Talking to her," he answered shortly.

"You were walking up the street. Superintendent Stokes said he saw you."

"And I declined to give him any further explanation." Davenant's tone was curt.

"Yes, to tell him," Mavis went on softly. "But I did not think you would have secrets from me, Garth."

He stopped and took both her hands in his and looked down at her gravely, compelling her to meet his gaze.

"Nor will I of my own, Mavis. This belongs to some one else, but it has absolutely no connexion with Nurse Marston's disappearance. That I can vouch for. For the rest, aren't you going to trust me?"

The tenderness of the tone disarmed the girl's rising resentment, and her naturally sweet temper reasserted itself.

"I will trust you, Garth, even though all the rest of the world should doubt you," she said softly.

Davenant's glance and the close clasp of his hand were eloquent of his gratitude.

Inside the hall the rest of the party, assembled apparently to see the progress of Arthur's painting, were surprised to see their speedy return, and their explanation was listened to with much astonished comment, in the midst of which Garth had time to note the ghastly pallor of Hilda's face.

Before the story, with the surprise it evoked, was finished, one of the footmen came into the hall.

"Greyson would be glad if you would speak to him for a few moments, Sir Arthur."

Arthur looked across at Davenant, and the two men went together to the plainly-furnished room known as the magistrates' room—a relic of Sir Noel's days on the bench—in which Sir Arthur generally transacted his business and gave interviews to his tenants and employees.

"Well, Greyson, you haven't taken long over your dinner," Garth began as they entered.

"I did not think any more of that, sir. As soon as you and Miss Hargreave were out of sight I made across the paddock the near way and came up here. For though I wouldn't say anything before Miss Hargreave, seeing how frightened she was, when I was looking about, though it is true I didn't see anything of Nurse Marston, I found this."

Both men looked at him in surprise as he drew something out of his pocket, and held it to them.

It was apparently a small piece of some whitish material. Garth bent forward.

"What is it, Greyson? I don't see—"

"It is a cuff, sir—one of those wide ones that nurses wear," Greyson replied. "See, here is the name on it—'M. Marston'—plain enough."

Chapter Nine

LADY DAVENANT pulled the check-string of her carriage.

"I will get out here. Come back in half an hour, Robert."

"Yes, my lady." The footman touched his hat when he had helped her out, sprang to his seat, and the carriage bowled swiftly away.

Lady Davenant turned to Mrs. Marston's cottage; it looked bright and homelike in the sunlight, with its gay little flower-beds bordering the flagged path on either side, and the climbing plants covering the porch and hanging down in festoons of greenery.

Through the open doorway one had a glimpse of the kitchen, with its red-brick floor scrubbed as spotless as hands could make it, and the round deal table standing in the middle of the room. It looked a pleasant, peaceful scene, and Mrs. Marston in her snowy cap with the white kerchief folded round her shoulders and her knitting in her hand, looked in keeping with all the rest. But as she heard the click of the gate and looked up, and the onlooker caught a glimpse of the unutterable woe in her dim old eyes, of the quivering dread visible in the tense lines of her mouth, the meaning of everything was changed, and something was revealed of the tragedy that underlay that apparently peaceful life.

Lady Davenant came swiftly up the garden-path.

"How are you this afternoon, Mrs. Marston?"

Mrs. Marston's lips quivered as she got up and made her old-fashioned curtsy.

"Much about the same, thank you, my lady! I don't look to feel any better until I know what has become of my girl."

Lady Davenant's eyes filled with tears as she took the wrinkled hand in hers.

"Ah, this suspense is so bad for you! You have heard no news yet?"

"No, my lady, nor ever shall till I hear how she died," Mrs. Marston answered slowly. "They come to me," she added, a touch of passion in her trembling tones—"Sir Arthur, Mr. Garth, Superintendent Stokes, and all of them. 'You have patience,' they say, 'and she will come back to you safe and sound. No doubt she has her own reasons for staying away.' My lady, I know my girl wouldn't have left me to fret and worry myself into my grave without knowing what had become of her, not if she was alive. She was always one to think so much of her old mother, was Mary, although she had got on in the world. Mr. Garth will have told you what they found in the Home Coppice, him and Miss Mavis, my lady?"

"Yes, he told me, and I don't know what to make of it all," Lady Davenant acknowledged frankly, with a troubled look in her mild eyes. "Mr. Garth does not either; and I hear the police are quite at a loss. What could she have been doing there in the dark late at night?"

Mrs. Marston wiped her eyes.

"She must ha' been 'ticed down there somehow, to the Home Coppice, my lady, by some villain, though it is not for me to say how, and then murdered—my own poor Mary! That cuff was blood-stained, you know, my lady."

"Yes, I know!" Lady Davenant said hurriedly. "But that does not prove that anything dreadful happened to her, Mrs. Marston. She might have cut her hand. And"—lowering her voice—"you know they have searched the wood thoroughly, and there was nothing there."

"I know they found nothing, my lady," Mrs. Marston said significantly, "but—but"—beginning to tremble—"I don't say she is there. I don't know where she is, my poor child; and sometimes I think I never shall know."

Lady Davenant's own eyes were wet as she gently put the old woman back in her chair and took one of the wide seats in the little porch beside her.

"I am sorry for you," she said brokenly, pressing the old woman's hand between both of hers. "You are in my thoughts continually. It is such a dreadful trouble for you."

"Ah, my lady, it is indeed! I ought to remember as I am not the only one, I know. We all have our troubles and your ladyship has had her share of them too, but—"

"Ah, I have indeed," Lady Davenant said with a sigh, "and I can sympathize so fully with you in all this! It is so terrible not to know where one's loved ones are. And my poor boy—"

"Ay! I have often said it has been a sore trial for your ladyship, and Mr. Garth too. Never was brothers fonder of one another than him and poor Mr. Walter. He has been untold good to me, has Mr. Garth, my lady. It is seldom the day passes as he does not turn in to have a word with me. Superintendent Stokes, he comes in the other day. 'I wonder what Mr. Garth Davenant was a-talking about to your daughter in Exeter,' he says. 'Which if you did know,' I made bold to answer him, my lady, 'I'll back you would be none the forwarder.' Mr. Garth don't know anything about where my girl is—I could take my oath on that."

"I am sure he does not. The whole affair has been a great trouble to him, but I do wish he had never suggested to Dr. Grieve—though one doesn't know how any harm could have happened to her through that," Lady Davenant said in a puzzled tone.

There was a pause. Mrs. Marston looked absently down the path and into the village street beyond; some figures were turning the corner; she rose and put her spectacles on.

"No, it isn't anybody but Farmer Weston and his son as went for a soldier," she said as she sat down again. "That is the worst of it, my lady, it is the uncertainty. Night or day I can't rest; everybody as comes up the street, I think it is perhaps some one come to bring me some news of my Mary. Every noise I hear I think maybe they have found out something. Then when I do get a wink of sleep, my lady, I have dreams."

"Dreams!" echoed Lady Davenant, looking at her in surprise, "I don't understand—"

"Ay, dreams!" Mrs. Marston repeated. "I don't know as I was ever one to put much faith in that kind of thing before, my lady, but I mind when I was a child how my mother used to set great store by them—messages from the other world, she used to call them, and she was a practical woman, my lady, and a Scotchwoman too. But she used to tell of some queer things as she had learnt from dreams. Of late I have begun to think she must have been right, for these past weeks Mary has come to me every night—sometimes in the morning. I can't remember all about it clearly, only I know she always tells me as it won't last much longer, this separation."

"There, you see, then surely you ought to feel more hopeful!" Lady Davenant remarked in a relieved tone.

"Ay! But it isn't that sort of ending she means. Mary never comes to me as a living breathing woman—it is always as a disembodied spirit—one who has done with the troubles of this world and sees as it has all been for the best. Sometimes she tells me she isn't far off. I don't rightly know whether she means that her body is near here or that her spirit is hovering around," the old woman finished speculatively.

Lady Davenant's face grew obviously paler and she shivered.

"Oh, I don't think you should take any notice of that sort of thing!" she said, trying to speak naturally. "You are thinking of her all the time, and you are likely to dream of her."

Mrs. Marston shook her head.

"Not such dreams as them, my lady," she said obstinately. "It is my Mary as can't make herself happy, knowing what I'm going through here, as is doing her best to prepare me for what is coming. I am prepared to hear as she is dead, my lady—nay, I could be thankful to know she was laid in her quiet grave. The other night I dreamt I asked her how she come not to let any of us know what was happening to her. 'I did my best, mother,' she made answer, 'but they was too cunning for me altogether.' It was her shriek as Miss Dorothy heard, my lady, as I take it. That's what she meant by doing her best, poor thing!"

The tears were running down Lady Davenant's cheeks now.

"Oh, you poor mother—poor thing, I am sorry for you!" she said. "I do hope things will turn out better than you think; but I wish we could do something for you in the meantime. You have some one with you in the house, my son told me."

"Yes, my lady, my son Tom's wife, she come first, but she couldn't bide so long from her children, so now her sister's come—a tidy, well-respecting woman enough. She has never known Mary, though, and seems to make up her mind as she will come back all right in a day or two. Still, I have nothing against her, and it is better than being in the house alone, for often in the night I fancy I hear my girl calling me and stepping about at her work, and it is so lonesome when you have nobody to speak to."

"I should think so," Lady Davenant said with a shudder as she rose. "I am glad you have some one with you though we should have taken care you were not alone. Mr. Garth asked about that the very first thing. But I must not keep the horses standing—Sir John is always so particular about that. Good-bye, and I do hope you will have better news soon! Be sure you send up to us if there is anything you want!"

"Thank you kindly for coming in, my lady. It does me a bit of good to talk to some one as has known what trouble is herself, like your ladyship."

"Indeed I have, sore trouble too, Mrs. Marston." Lady Davenant pulled down her veil to hide the traces of her tears.

"Mr. Garth was telling me that as soon as Sir Arthur's coming of age was over, him and Miss Mavis was going to get married and live at Overdeen. When your ladyship has them, and later on it may be, their children, coming over to see you, it will brighten you up and Sir John."

"Ah, well, I hope so!" Lady Davenant concluded, as, nodding her good-bye to the old woman, she walked down the path.

Left alone, Mrs. Marston picked up her knitting and made a pretence of putting in a few stitches, but she could not settle herself to work, and soon she gave it up and sat with her hands idle before her, her eyes glancing restlessly from side to side or peering anxiously down the village street.

Presently, however, she started violently and sprang up from her chair. It seemed to her that a figure coming down the long dusty road leading from the station had a curiously familiar air. She hurried down the path as fast as her trembling limbs would carry her, only stopping to call out loudly:

"Ruth! Ruth!"

A comely, pleasant-looking woman of middle age came out of the cottage, drying her wet hands on her apron.

"La, Mrs. Marston, what is the matter? I declare you quite frighted me! What call have you to put yourself in this state? Didn't Dr. Grieve say as you was not to excite yourself?"

The old woman paid scant heed to her words; she drew her to the gate and laid her shaking hand on her arm.

"Who—what is it as you see a-comin' down the road, Ruth Carson?" she demanded. "Is it my old eyes is deceivin' me or—"

Ruth shaded her eyes with her hand.

"The sun is right agen me, but it is some one as is dressed like a nurse—I can see that much," she said slowly.

"What is she like? Can't you see nothing more?" Mrs. Marston interrupted eagerly. "My head is all of a swim," clutching at the gate.

Ruth glanced at her anxiously ere she looked up the street again.

"I can see as she is short and inclined to be stout, and I think she is dark," Ruth said after a pause, during which Mrs. Marston's eyes were strained on her face with pitiful intentness.

She gave a cry as the woman ended.

"If it should be her! If it should be my Mary! Go at once and see, woman, go and see—tell her as her old mother is a-waiting for her! Tell—her—"

In the intensity of her excitement the old woman was falling back against the gatepost, a waxy paleness was overspreading her drawn features, her eyes were closed. Ruth caught her round the waist and looked up for help.

The nurse whom they had been watching was coming straight down the street, walking briskly along with quick, decided steps. Ruth Carson, her helpless burden still supported in her arms, watched her drawing nearer in a species of half-terrified fascination.

Was this indeed the Mary whose disappearance had caused more talk than anything that had ever happened at Lockford, and of whose safe return even her nearest and dearest were beginning to despair? Ruth was inclined to think that the description she had heard of the missing woman tallied in some particulars with the new-comer's appearance as she came within speaking distance.

The nurse halted outside the cottage-gate and looked at the two women in evident surprise.

"Is there anything the matter?" she demanded.

"Mrs. Marston is just overcome with the shock," Ruth Carson explained. "She will soon be better if it turns out as—you are Mary, aren't you? It was seeing you so sudden-like."

Chapter Ten

THE STRANGER stared at Ruth Carson in her turn.

"Why, what on earth do you mean? Certainly I am not Mary Marston! This is her home, isn't it? That is her mother? Why should she faint if she did think I was Mary?"

Ruth Carson answered the question by asking another.

"If you are not Mary, who are you?"

"A friend of hers—Charlotte Gidden by name," was the brisk reply. "Pray, do you Lockford folk think that there is only one nurse in the world and that her name is Mary Marston? We were at Guy's together, Mary and I; and as I am spending my holidays at Plymouth I thought I would come over and look her up. But let me see what I can do here."

She helped Ruth to assist the half-unconscious Mrs. Marston up the path and deposited her in the arm-chair. Then she took command of the situation and despatched Ruth for simple remedies; after these had been applied for a few minutes Mrs. Marston opened her eyes.

"Mary!" she said feebly. "Mary!"

The nurse drew a little out of sight, and Ruth answered: "No, it was not Mary, Mrs. Marston, but it was a friend of hers."

"A friend of Mary's," the weak voice replied. "Who is it? I should like to see her. Has she brought any news?"

"She will do now," Nurse Gidden said as she stepped forward. "Yes, I am Mary's friend, Charlotte Gidden; I am sure you have heard her speak of me, haven't you, Mrs. Marston? Now I think the best thing for you would be a cup of tea; I can hear the kettle singing away on the fire, and I wonder if you would be good enough to give me a cup with you? It is a hot walk from the station."

"Ay, for sure!" Mrs. Marston said feebly. "You are kindly welcome to everything I have, for Mary's sake. Many's the time I have heard her speak of you. You know as she's lost, maybe?"

Charlotte Gidden looked bewildered.

"Lost! Mary lost! I don't know what you are talking about, Mrs. Marston."

"It is lost she is though, poor girl!" Mrs. Marston went on. "The trouble of it is like to kill me. Nursing that poor young lady up at the Manor she was, and just walked out of the room and never been heard of since."

"Never been heard of since!" Nurse Gidden turned to Ruth Carson, who, nothing loath, supplied the details in the intervals of laying the cloth and pouring out the tea.

Charlotte Gidden, eating a slice of the thin bread and butter that Ruth had cut and sipping her tea, thought that she had never listened to a more extraordinary story.

"Why on earth should she go away like that?" she debated. "I had a letter from her after she went to the Manor, and I am sure she was not thinking of leaving then, though she seemed put about over the young lady. She had seen her somewhere before, she said, and she thought it was her duty to tell Lady Laura Hargreave so at once, though she doubted how it would be taken, as she hadn't much proof of what she said, and they were all so taken up with the young lady."

Mrs. Marston and Ruth were both gazing at her in amazement. The former was the first to speak:

"You don't mean you heard from her after she went to the Manor?"

"Yes—the very night she got there," Charlotte affirmed, helping herself to another slice of bread and butter. "She had just seen her patient when she wrote. What did they say when they found she had recognized her, Mrs. Marston? Were they surprised?"

"Don't you see, they never did know!" Ruth Carson burst out. "Mary had left the young lady with Miss Mavis while she told her ladyship, and she never saw my lady or nobody else. That letter of yours must have been wrote while she was waiting, and it was the last as she ever did write, poor thing—leastways, as we have been able to hear of."

"But—but it couldn't have been that night she went away," said Nurse Gidden. "She had no such notion in her head, I am sure, when she wrote to me."

"She had no notion of going away the day before she went up to the Manor, I am sure," Mrs. Marston said tearfully. "We were sitting having our bit of dinner together as cheerful as possible and Mary, she was saying how glad she was to be at home with me for a bit, when Mr. Garth come in and asked her if she would go up and nurse the young lady that had lost her memory. I don't think she would have gone, only being as it was Mr. Garth she couldn't well refuse."

"Why not?" Nurse Gidden asked sharply. "She said in my letter she only came because Mr. Garth Davenant asked her. Who is he?"

"Oh, Mary was so fond of all the Davenants," said Mrs. Marston, "that I believe she would have gone anywhere for them! I nursed Mr. Garth and Mr. Walter both—Mr. Walter he was delicate, and I was as fond of him as if he had been my own child, and I had Mr. Garth till he was going on for two and I got married. My lady and all of them have been untold good to Mary—it was through her ladyship as she first took up with nursing. I wish she never had now," the poor woman added, with a catch in her voice. "Maybe she would be here with me safe and sound but for that."

Nurse Gidden's bewilderment appeared to increase as she thought the matter over.

"What on earth could have induced her to go off like that! It seems to me"—thoughtfully—"that some one must have had a pretty strong influence over her to induce her first to go away and then to keep her silent all this time. I suppose this—"

"They took the best way of keeping her quiet," Mrs. Marston interrupted with a groan. "They made sure of that. Do you think anything would have kept my girl from letting me know where she was if she was alive? Her that thought so much of her old mother! If I only knew where they have put her!"

In spite of her strong practical common sense, Charlotte Gidden shuddered, and her rosy, matter-of-fact countenance turned many degrees paler. To her, realizing to the full Mary Marston's kindly, straightforward nature, as well as her love for her mother, it did seem almost an impossibility that she, knowing the anxiety she must be causing, should keep silence as to her whereabouts for six weeks. Yet she could not bring herself to believe that serious harm could have befallen her friend.

"Perhaps her letters have been stopped?" she cogitated. "Everybody liked Mary who knew her; no one would want to hurt her, I am sure. But somebody must know where she is and have a motive for keeping quiet. The young lady she was nursing—I fancy Mary thought she would not like her speaking out—I suppose she couldn't have anything to do with it?"

"No, no! She was in bed and unconscious, poor thing! She knowed nothing about it. A sweet, pretty young lady she is too!"

Ruth Carson took the answer upon herself.

"Beside, Miss Hargreave was sitting with her; she took the nurse's place when she went away, and stayed there till they came and told her she was lost. Superintendent Stokes, he called here the other day and asked if Mary had ever a sweetheart."

"Sweetheart! Rubbish!" Nurse Gidden drew in her lips scornfully. "We nurses have something else to do than run about after them. No! Somebody that Mary thought a lot of must have met her on her way down to Lady Laura's room and persuaded her to go somewhere else. Now we know that she wouldn't have gone to the Manor but Mr. Garth Davenant asked her, and she couldn't refuse him. How if he asked her to go somewhere else that night?"

Ruth laughed.

"Superintendent Stokes, he has always been suspicious that Mr. Garth Davenant knows more about it than he will say, but I have seen a deal of Mr. Garth since I've been here. There's hardly ever a day passes that he doesn't pop in to ask how Mrs. Marston is, and a nice, civil-spoken young gentleman he is. I don't think he had any hand in it, though it was funny as his tobacco-pouch should be in the room, as the superintendent says."

Nurse Gidden pricked up her ears.

"Tobacco-pouch! You didn't tell me about that!"

"Well, there isn't much to tell," Ruth went on, unconsciously colouring her narrative. "Mr. Garth's tobacco-pouch as Miss Mavis worked for him was found in the small library that night. He might have left it there days before; he said himself he did not know where it was, but he felt sure he hadn't had it there. He didn't believe it was his."

"Well, if Miss Mavis worked it for him they could see it was his."

"Well, they could," went on Ruth more slowly, feeling the difficulty of her story. "But when they come to look for it in the morning it was gone—somebody had took it away."

Charlotte Gidden's eyes grew more wide open than ever.

"Well, there has been some nice underhand work going on somewhere!" she exclaimed, drawing a long breath. "Nice dunderheads the police down here must be not to have found something out before now! I believe I should have done a lot better myself. I wonder, Mrs. Marston"—her expression grew more thoughtful, a little frown came between her brows—"I have got a week longer at Plymouth, and then my holidays begin—if you haven't heard of Mary before then, which I expect you will—but I wonder, if I came to Lockford, if you could give me a shakedown. I fancy if I were here on the spot I must find out where she is."

A gleam of interest lighted up Mrs. Marston's worn face.

"You can have Mary's room, and kindly welcome. It is kind of you to think of troubling about my poor girl. I am sure if you can find out anything—" wiping away a tear.

"Then that is settled," said Charlotte briskly. "I'm much obliged to you, Mrs. Marston. I'll come and see what I can do. First of all, I should devote some particular attention to Mr. Garth Davenant."

Mrs. Marston roused herself a little and sat up.

"You needn't," she said, excitement gathering in her quavering old tones. "Mr. Garth Davenant wouldn't have harmed my girl, I know that. The Davenants were always her best friends."

"Well, well!" Charlotte said soothingly as she took her leave. "I don't suppose he has harmed her. I can't bring myself to think that anybody would; but I shall come and look round, Mrs. Marston."

Ruth attended the visitor to the gate.

"She is breaking up fast," she said with a backward jerk of her head. "If so be as Mary is well, if she don't come home soon, she won't find her mother here."

Charlotte did not dissent from this view.

"It is the anxiety, and I shouldn't think she has ever been one of the strongest. Who are these people in the pony carriage?"

Ruth looked up.

"Why, it is Sir Arthur himself and the young lady—the one as Mary went to nurse! Ain't she a picture?"

The keen eyes of Nurse Gidden glanced critically at Hilda's fair, flushed face as she smiled up into Sir Arthur's face.

"Um! Pretty well for that! I wonder whether her hair is that colour naturally? It looks to me as if she had doctored it up a bit. And who pays for her clothes? I suppose she didn't bring her luggage into the park with her? That grey thing she has got on must have cost a mint of money!"

"I suppose her ladyship must be giving them to her," hazarded Ruth Carson; "I have heard they think a lot of her."

"One of them does, it is evident," remarked Charlotte significantly. "What'll my lady say to that? A girl dropped from nowhere wouldn't be everybody's fancy as a daughter-in-law!"

Ruth Carson raised her hands.

"Oh, Nurse Gidden, what will you say next? Sir Arthur Hargreave wouldn't so much as think of the likes of her. Besides, I have heard it whispered that he is in love with his cousin, Miss Dorothy Hargreave."

"Oh, have you?" remarked Charlotte in a satirical tone. "Certainly, then, he would not dream of looking at anybody else, more than Mr. Garth Davenant would think of sending Mary off on some of his dirty work and stopping her letters home." She picked up her skirts and stepped out into the road. "Ah, you are an innocent lot here at Lockford, all of you! Good afternoon, Ruth Carson."

Meanwhile, unconscious of the comment they were exciting, Sir Arthur drove his fair model carefully towards the Manor; as they entered the park he checked the ponies and let them walk up the Avenue.

"I was startled a few minutes ago," he avowed, "when I saw that nurse in the street. She was standing by the Marstons' cottage, and for a moment I thought it might be Mary."

Hilda's pretty colour faded, the smile died out of her eyes.

"Was that the Marstons' cottage? I did not know," with a shiver. "And are you positive that it was not Nurse Marston? You could not have seen much of her, and I am sure I should not recognize her myself in different circumstances."

Sir Arthur smiled.

"I dare say you would not, but I have known Mary Marston by sight for years, and though this woman was about the same build I am quite sure it was not Mary. I wish it had been!"

"So do I!" Hilda said. "I lie awake at night and wonder where she is."

"Then you must not do anything of the kind," said Sir Arthur lightly. "Mary Marston will come back again in her own time, no doubt; people are not made away with nowadays at Hargreave Manor."

"Not at the Manor perhaps, but—" Hilda shuddered.

"Nor anywhere else," Sir Arthur said, affecting a certainty he was far from feeling. "But I am not going to let you talk about it any more. I want you to come and look at my orchids, will you?"

He threw the reins to the groom as he sprang out. For a moment he fancied she hesitated and a shade of unwillingness passed over her face; then he told himself that he must have been mistaken as she turned to him with a bright smile.

"I shall be delighted, though I don't know much about orchids!"

Her cheeks were flushed and her eyes looked very bright and restless as Arthur helped her out and led the way across the terrace to the orchid-houses.

"They are not much to boast of," he said, with becoming humility. "But we have been fortunate enough to secure one or two good specimens, and I have a first-rate man to look after them. Ah, here he is! Well, Gregory, how are you getting on to-day? I have brought this lady to see what you are doing."

"Well, Sir Arthur, I am glad to say we have something to show you to-day," the man said respectfully as he stood aside to let them pass. "That last one that Mr. Brookes brought is in bloom."

"What!" Arthur's tone was enthusiastic, and he hurried forward. "And a beauty it is, Gregory, pure white, with just that touch of gold in the centre. See, Miss Hilda, this is a root that has never blossomed in this country before! My friend Brookes brought it from the interior of South America, and up till now we have been doubtful whether we had got the atmosphere right. But it seems to have answered; your coming has brought me luck, and you must promise me to wear this first flower to-night. You must let me cut it for you."

Gregory's face darkened; quite evidently he grudged this sacrifice.

"Mr. Gribdale has been looking to see it, sir, and maybe he will be over to-morrow."

"He must wait for the next," Sir Arthur said recklessly as he opened his knife.

Hilda laid her hand on his arm.

"Please do not, Sir Arthur. It looks so lovely where it is, and I can come and see it every day. It will only last one night if it is cut."

Sir Arthur looked obstinate. He glanced again at the delicately poised blossom, looking just like some tropical butterfly springing from the gnarled brown root.

"It will be just the thing to wear with your white gown, Miss Hilda," and he cut it off deliberately and presented it to her.

Gregory's dark face frowned; evidently he would have openly resented this spoliation if he had dared. Hilda flushed painfully.

"It does seem a shame, Sir Arthur," she said.

"It is honoured by your wearing it," he remarked with a glance that made her eyes droop. "Now I must get something for Mavis and Dorothy."

He moved forward. Hilda turned to Gregory.

"It is a lovely flower, and I am sure it must have given you a great deal of trouble to grow," she said with a pretty, courteous smile. "I wish you could tell me—"

Sir Arthur, busy among his cattleyas, did not catch the rest of the sentence. His thoughts were occupied with Hilda. How lovely she had looked in her confusion just now, her long light cloak throwing up her brilliant colouring as she bent over the white flower! When he turned round Gregory was standing close to the girl, drawing forward a scarlet orchid of Japan.

"You must!"

Sir Arthur looked up quickly. Gregory's back was to him, but he could see that Hilda's eyes were fixed on the man's face, her red lips were parted. Surely it could not have been to her that Gregory was speaking in that low, brusque tone.

As the young man hesitated her face broke into smiles.

"I am afraid it would be impossible," she said, "I do not think I should ever have patience. Gregory is giving me some instructions in orchid-growing, Sir Arthur. I am afraid he does not find me an apt pupil."

"I shall be very pleased to tell you anything that you want to know," Sir Arthur remarked. "What were you explaining, Gregory?"

"I was just telling the young lady that the Rhenanthera—"

With a little cry Hilda interrupted him:

"Oh, Sir Arthur, please do not make him go over it again—my poor brain gets quite bewildered with all those long names! For the future I shall be quite content to admire the flowers and leave the practical part to you clever people."

"That will do," Sir Arthur said curtly to Gregory. "Mind the temperature does not get lowered at night. It has been cold in the evenings all last week."

Outside he turned to Hilda.

"I could not hear very plainly, but was not that fellow speaking to you in an unwarrantably insolent tone?"

Hilda opened her eyes to their fullest extent.

"Oh, dear, no! Poor man, I think he was just a little disappointed about this," laying her lips lightly to the blossom she was carrying. "I could not be surprised at that. After having watched it gradually coming into flower he must have felt sad when he saw it carried away. But what a nice, well-informed man he seems to be, Sir Arthur. I quite took a fancy to him."

"He is very well in his place," said Arthur, only half convinced. "But if I caught him—if I caught the best man about the place speaking disrespectfully to you, he should go at once."

Chapter Eleven

"It is perfect, it seems to me." Mavis glanced critically from her brother's painting to Hilda's flushed face. "You have caught just the pale cream tint of the complexion and that lovely hair. Oh, Hilda! I do envy you! Are you not proud of it? But you look pale this morning. What is the matter, dear?"

"I—it is only—" Hilda began, then her full underlip quivered, her eyes filled, and to the consternation of both brother and sister she burst into an agony of tears.

Mavis put her arms round her.

"What is the matter, Hilda? Has anybody vexed you? Tell me what is wrong with you."

Sir Arthur left his painting and came over to his sister, "I have over-tired her, that is what it must be; in my selfishness I have been thinking only of my picture. Haven't you got smelling-salts or something to give her, Mavis? Shall I get her some wine?"

Mavis, still bending over the weeping girl, shook her head decidedly. "I don't think it is that. I think something is vexing her. Can't you tell me what it is, dear?" stroking the girl's ruffled golden hair.

"Perhaps it would be better if you left us a while, Arthur; I dare say she will tell me all about it when we are alone."

Hilda sat and put out her hands.

"No, no, it is only that I am stupid; I know I ought not to bother you with my troubles. Please go on with your painting, Sir Arthur. I will try to be more sensible in the future."

Mavis bent over her and kissed the hot cheeks.

"Can't you tell us about it, dear? I often think when one has talked over a trouble, it seems less."

"This is only—but I know you will say I ought to put it out of my mind, and I can't do that. Besides, I am sure I am trouble enough to you all."

"How can you—" Sir Arthur began impetuously.

Mavis hushed him with a look.

"I thought you knew that I love you, Hilda," she said reproachfully. "You should not talk of trouble, dear. We look upon you as one of ourselves. Mother said yesterday that this must be your home until your own was found."

"Ah, when will that be?" Hilda said. Her eyes, still wet, looked straight before her, her hands lay motionless in her lap, her lips were still quivering. "What sort of a home will it be when it is found?" she added bitterly. "Sir Arthur, Mavis, have you heard that a friend of Nurse Marston's was in the village last week and she said she had had a letter from her, written the night she—she disappeared?"

Mavis looked amazed.

"How in the world did you hear that? Mother told all the servants they were not to mention it to you. One of them must have disobeyed her. Who was it, Hilda? If Minnie—"

Hilda caught the girl's hand and laid it against her cheek.

"I can't tell you how I heard it, Mavis—I promised not to, dear. It really does not matter—a thing like that was sure to come to my ears sooner or later. But I am answered—it is true, then?"

"It is true she had a letter—" Mavis began, looking at her brother perplexedly.

"To be correct, it is true that she said she had had a letter from Nurse Marston, written that night," Arthur interposed, "but the letter itself she said she did not keep, so that we only have her word for it."

"Still," Mavis said, "Superintendent Stokes told Garth that he had made inquiries and Nurse Marston did have a letter posted, Arthur, and this Nurse Gidden bears a very high character too, he said. I don't think there is any reason to doubt her."

"Oh, dear, no! I didn't mean to throw any aspersion on her character or general credibility," Sir Arthur observed as he went back to the easel. "From all I hear she seems to be a most exemplary woman; but what I mean to say is that when a person cannot produce a letter, has lost or destroyed it, one cannot exactly take that person's account of what was written in the said letter as if it were gospel truth, especially in a case like this, when her first impression would doubtless be coloured by what she had heard later on."

A faint smile curved Hilda's lips, though her eyes looked wistful and troubled.

"I think, Sir Arthur, that tells me what I wanted to know. This Nurse Gidden says that Nurse Marston recognized me, does she not, and implies that it was something discreditable that she knew about me?"

"Oh, no, no!" Mavis said quickly. "All Nurse Giddens said was that Nurse Marston said that no one knew who you were, and that she had seen you in circumstances which she thought ought to be told to my mother at once. That really tells us nothing, because we have no idea what the circumstances may have been. A nurse sees all sorts of people, and naturally she would know what trouble your loss might be causing to your people, so that it was her duty to go to mother at once."

"I see," Hilda said, leaning her head on her hand and drawing herself a little away from Mavis. "And I see too that everybody will say that it was in discreditable circumstances that she saw me—that there is something against me. The worst of it is that it may be true, Mavis. I don't know what I may have been. Have you ever realized it? I may have done anything. You would all be much wiser not to have anything to do with me."

Mavis laughed.

"Should we? I think I can guarantee that you will not turn out to be anything very dreadful. What do you say, Arthur?"

"I could stake my life on it," replied the young man with unusual fervour.

"Well, at any rate you have obtained one backer, Hilda," said Mavis.

The girl hardly seemed to heed her words; she was wrinkling up her brows, her mouth was twitching nervously.

"If I could only remember one little thing, anything, however slight, that happened to me before that night. But, do what I can, try my very hardest, as I may, it is no use. I cannot even remember my own name, my own surname, and though I suppose I must have been called Hilda it does not seem a bit familiar to me."

"Now don't get morbid," Mavis reproved brightly. "Surely you can't see to paint by this light, Arthur," as her brother took up his palette again.

He fidgeted about restlessly.

"Oh, the light is good for half an hour yet! Here is Davenant coming up the drive, Mavis."

"Oh!" His sister's cheeks flushed rosily, a new light shone in her brown eyes. "I didn't think he would be back so soon; he went up to town yesterday. He—he promised to do some commissions for me."

Arthur laughed.

"No excuse is needed, Mavis. We quite understand that you wish to have a few words quietly with your young man before introducing him to the family circle," he said with brotherly candour. "Run along, we will make all due allowances for you."

"How absurd you are, Arthur! It is only that I asked him—"

"Don't trouble to particularize," Arthur said, with a flourish of his paint-brush, "or you may miss your opportunity—

Garth's voice became audible in the hall.

"I will be back in a minute," his sister said with a vengeful glance in his direction as she gave Hilda a hasty kiss. "You are better, now, aren't you, Hilda? I will tell Dorothy to come to you. She is playing to mother in the drawing-room."

There was a silence when she had left the room—one of those silences which seem to be pregnant with electric meaning. Sir Arthur was mixing a colour; mechanically he squeezed the tube until almost the whole contents lay on the palette; then with a guilty feeling he glanced at Hilda.

She was half leaning, half lying on the wide couch on which she had posed for Elaine, but evidently her thoughts were far away from the picture.

She looked up at the same moment. As her eyes met his gaze, she started violently, her colour deepened, and she put up her hand to her hair with a gesture at once confused and conscious. Sir Arthur threw down his palette and crossed to her.

"Hilda, I—you must know what I want to say," he cried in a low voice of intense feeling, "that I love you —that I have loved you ever since I first saw you. Dear, tell me, is there any hope for me?"

"No, no!" Hilda cried pushing him from her as he would have knelt beside her. "No, no! I cannot! Don't you see that I cannot—" covering her face with her hands.

Sir Arthur's forehead flushed a dull crimson; his eyes dwelt eagerly on the loveliness of the girl's half-averted face.

"I see my own unworthiness plainly enough, Hilda," he answered simply. "Is that what you mean, dear?"

Hilda turned her face farther towards the cushions.

"No, no, you know it is not that," she said in a muffled voice.

Something in her accent seemed to raise Sir Arthur's hopes. He dropped on one knee and ventured to take the hand that was hanging limply by her side.

"What then, Hilda? Will you not let me try to teach you to care for me?"

The girl sat up and threw the cushions behind her.

"Don't you see that that is not the question—that it is beside it altogether—that such things are not for me"—her delicate hands pulling the lace on her bodice to pieces—"a nameless nobody?"

Sir Arthur did not move away.

"Ah, how can you? But let me give you a name, Hilda—my name—be my wife, dear?" he urged.

The girl gave a little moan, her white teeth bit her under-lip.

"You do not know what you are saying, you do not in the least realize how things would be. What would the world say if Sir Arthur Hargreave married a waif—a piece of flotsam and jetsam that fate had cast up at his doors? What would—"

Sir Arthur captured one of the fluttering, trembling hands once more.

"All that is beside the question, as you said just now, Hilda; the real crux of the matter lies between you and me. Tell me the truth, dear, is it that you do not—cannot care for me?"

Hilda caught her breath quickly.

"Ah, no. How could it be that, when you have been so kind, so more than kind to me? When yours was the first face I saw smiling at me out of that dreadful darkness and chaos—"

Sir Arthur laid his lips softly to the hand he held in his.

"Then that is all that matters, Hilda—the rest is nothing to us."

The girl snatched her hand away.

"Ah, no, no! I must not forget. There are others to whom this would mean misery—Lady Laura, and Sir Arthur, your cousin—"

As the last word left her lips two little straight lines came between Hargreave's level brows.

"My cousin!" he repeated, and a slight nuance in his tone might have told a keen listener that the reference had grated upon him. "My cousin Dorothy is almost my sister, Hilda; she will soon be prepared to give a sister's love to you, I hope."

In spite of the confident words, however, there was an element of doubt apparent in his manner. The mutual antagonism between the two girls could hardly have failed to make itself felt, especially by him; and he was uncomfortably conscious that, though no binding words had been spoken between them, Dorothy could hardly hold him blameless.

"As for my mother," he went on, "she will—she does—love you. But what does all that matter now?" his eyes softening and growing more eager as they rested on her bent golden head. "I cannot think of that now. For these few golden minutes there is no one in the world but just ourselves, Hilda. Ah"—his arms stealing round her, his lips seeking hers—"tell me you care for me just a little, darling!"

With a passionate gesture of self-surrender Hilda yielded herself to his embrace, and as he took his first kisses from her red lips she murmured brokenly as she turned her face a little away:

"How could I help it when you have been so good—so good to me? How could I help it?"

"Thank Heaven you could not help it, my darling!" Sir Arthur said reverently as he drew her head again to its resting-place on his shoulder. "Hilda, Hilda, I can scarcely believe that such happiness can be real!"

"Perhaps it is not," the girl whispered unsteadily. "Because do you not see that first"—with a shy hesitating glance—"we must find out who I am?"

"No, I don't see," said Sir Arthur steadily. "I shall tell my mother to-night that I have been lucky enough to win your love. Hilda, Hilda, I can hardly believe—"

The opening of the door made them start apart with flushed guilty faces as Dorothy came in, glancing at them in an uncertain, doubtful fashion.

"Aunt Laura says she is sure that you cannot see to paint so late as this, Arthur, and the coffee is in the drawing-room."

Meanwhile outside Mavis found herself waylaid by her maid.

"Oh, if you please, miss, I have just heard that my mother is feeling very poorly to-day. Could you spare me just to run down and see how she is?"

"Why, certainly, Minnie," the girl said kindly, "and I hope you will find her better. Isn't it rather late for you, though. But perhaps Gregory is going to walk down with you?"

"No, miss, he can't to-night, he is busy in his houses; but Mrs. Parkyns, she said Alice might come with me."

"That is all right then," Mavis nodded. "Don't hurry yourself, Minnie, if you're not afraid of being out in the dusk. I daresay the walk will do you good. You have not been looking very well lately."

"I am quite well, thank you, miss! Maybe the heat makes me a bit pale—it does some folks."

"Well, if you feel all right, that is the main thing," Mavis said. "Ask Mrs. Parkyns if she has anything she can give you to take to your mother, Minnie."

"Thank you, miss."

Mavis turned to meet Garth in the hall; Minnie ran quickly downstairs to tell the still-room maid that she had gained the requisite permission and in a very few minutes the two girls sallied forth. Minnie carefully carrying a covered basket containing certain delicacies provided by Mrs. Parkyns.

"We will go down the drive," she said as they turned out of the big paved yard into the shrubbery. "I don't care for going through the Home Coppice now, it is getting dark."

"I don't care for it, not in the day-time," Alice avowed openly, "not since they found those things of Nurse Marston's in it. I—I think I should faint if I should see anything like that."

Minnie's face looked a curiously ashen colour in the twilight.

"There's nothing more to be found in the Home Coppice," she said. "Superintendent Stokes told Jim Gregory that they had searched every inch of it. It is poachers and such-like I think of when I am in the wood."

"Or keepers," Alice suggested with a giggle, glancing at Minnie's unresponsive face. "I hear that Tom Greyson goes about with a long face enough to turn milk sour. If Nurse Marston went out of the house by the conservatory door"—with a sudden change of subject—"I wonder if she went across the lawn and by the pinetum to the park on her way to the Home Coppice, or whether—"

"Who says that she went through the conservatory door?" Minnie demanded.

"Nobody that I know of. You needn't be so sharp, Minnie Spencer," the other said in an injured tone. "I only said if she did—being as it was the nearest way out from the small library, and she must have got out somehow, spite of Mr. Jenkins telling us all the doors were shut. It stands to sense she wasn't spirited away. Well, as I was saying just now, when you took me up, I wonder whether she made her way by the pinetum and the park, or came through this shrubbery—it would be a bit farther this way, but I reckon she'd choose it on account of being seen as she crossed the lawn. I have thought sometimes as she came no farther."

Minnie shivered.

"How can you talk so, Alice Brown? Do you think—"

"I mean as I shouldn't wonder if she had promised to run off for a few minutes just to speak to some murderin' villain," said Alice, dropping her voice to a whisper and looking round fearfully. "There—there is no knowing where she may be now! I wouldn't come through after dark by myself for a hundred pounds. Who knows if he didn't make away with her here? Those things found in the Home Coppice the other day show that she was made away with plain enough, I say."

"Ugh!" Minnie caught her companion's arm. "If I had known you were going to talk like this I wouldn't have come a step—Mercy sakes alive! What was that?"

Right across the path the two girls were traversing—the widest of those intersecting the shrubbery and the one used by tradesmen and others coming to the back-door of the Manor—another ran at some little distance before them at right angles. As the two girls looked up it seemed to them that a figure dressed in a nurse's costume and looking away from them walked slowly past and down the path. Simultaneously they caught hold of one another. Alice Brown gave a terrified sob.

"It is her—-it is Nurse Marston!" she whispered.

As they stood clinging together, staring at the spot with fascinated eyes as if unable to stir, the same figure came slowly into sight once more, and, halting, stood as if looking at them. With a sound like nothing but a howl of terror Minnie threw herself on the ground. Alice, shivering with fright, saw the figure raise its hand as if beckoning to them and make a few steps forward. With an awful shriek of horror she dragged Minnie up.

"It—it is coming to us, Minnie!"

Stumbling, running, sobbing, how they got back to the house they never could afterwards tell, but the fear of what might be behind them quickened their footsteps as nothing in the world could have done.

Then, seeing through the open door a vision of the great kitchen beyond, with the servants passing and re-passing in all the pleasant bustle inseparable from a big country house, leaning against the outer doorpost, Alice opened her lips and tried to call out, to make herself heard, but the words refused to come; twice she caught her breath with a curious gasping sound, then a loud hoarse cry rang through the hall—a cry that roused the cook and the frightened maids in the kitchen, that reached Mrs. Parkyns, sitting in her solitary dignity in the housekeeper's room, and brought her on the scene.

"What on earth is the meaning of this, Minnie Spencer?" she demanded sternly. "And Alice Brown—have you taken eave of your senses, both of you?"

At this moment two fresh auditors appeared on the scene—Jim Gregory, who had brought down some flowers for Lady Laura's room, appeared from the back regions, and Tom Greyson ran round the corner from the stableyard.

He hurried up to the two girls, while Gregory stood staring at them in amazement.

"Why, Minnie, what is the matter? Are you ill?" he cried, catching her in his arms as she was apparently about to fall to the ground.

"I should like to know what is the matter with both of them!" remarked Mrs. Parkyns in an exasperated tone. "Starting us out of our wits by shouting in such a fashion as that, and then struck dumb as far as I can see; and there—I declare if you haven't smashed those nice fresh eggs I gave you to take to your mother, Minnie Spencer! Of all the aggravating girls—"

"Oh, Mrs. Parkyns, don't!" sobbed Alice Brown, finding her voice at last. "I'm sure I'm all of a shiver—but we have just seen something—seen her—in the shrubbery!"

Minnie gave a little groan and clutched wildly at Greyson's arm. Gregory stepped forward quickly, scowling at his rival.

"Minnie, let me—"

"Now Heaven give me patience, Alice Brown!" cried Mrs. Parkyns irritably. "I am sure I have need of it to-night. Who have you seen in the shrubbery, girl?"

"Nurse Marston—leastways it was her ghost!" said Alice. "We both saw it, Mrs. Parkyns, me and Minnie, and I don't suppose either of us will forget it till our dying day."

"Well, of all the couple of simpletons!" said the housekeeper wrathfully, though her florid face had turned some degrees paler. "Who told you that Nurse Marston was dead, pray? Ghosts indeed! Fiddlesticks!"

"Oh, Mrs. Parkyns, doesn't everybody feel sure she was made away with that night? Doesn't her spirit come back to her mother in her dreams? I tell you we saw her to-night as plain as could be, in her bonnet and cuffs and all," said Alice, rallying somewhat now that the familiar faces were round her. "I—I thought she wanted to speak to us; she raised her hand and pointed. Perhaps," shuddering, "she wanted to show us where she was buried."

"Well, of all things, Alice Brown!" said Mrs. Parkyns with uplifted hands. "What are you going to say next, I wonder? A pack of rubbish! Buried, indeed!"

Minnie Spencer was still clinging to Greyson's arm, seeming to derive some comfort from the contact. Gregory had halted a few paces in apparent discomfiture; even in that dim light it was obvious that his tanned complexion had altered to one of a curious leaden pallor.

"Nurse Marston's ghost in the shrubbery!" he repeated, staring at them. "Minnie, it can't be true!"

"True!" echoed Greyson, as Minnie at last raised herself and drew away from him. "I have heard you jeer at us country folk for superstition, Jim Gregory, but I tell you if Mary Marston is in the shrubbery it is herself and no ghost. I am going to see into it, I can tell you that. Don't you frighten yourself, Minnie, I'll soon find your ghost and settle it for you. Anybody like to come with me?"

Two stable-men who had lately been added to the group volunteered, and so did Gregory, after a moment's hesitation, which did not pass unremarked by Greyson.

They were gone some little time—it seemed hours to the waiting women as they stood there wondering what the next news might be; but at last they heard the footsteps returning.

"Well, Mr. Greyson, what news?" Mrs. Parkyns called out as they came round the corner.

"None at all, ma'am. We have been all over the shrubbery and we haven't seen so much as a sign of anybody or anything," said Greyson in a reassuring tone.

"I never thought you would," Mrs. Parkyns responded, with a relieved air. "You dreamt it all, you two girls, that is about it—a pair of geese! Well, I'm much obliged to you for your trouble, Mr. Greyson. As to you, Minnie Spencer, I suppose now you have put yourself into this state you won't dare to go down to the village, and that nice pudding I gave you for your mother will be wasted, to say nothing of those eggs you have spoilt! Well, well!"

Minnie was standing by Gregory, who had drawn her hand through his arm. Greyson reached over and took the basket from her.

"I'll take your pudding for you, Minnie," he said gruffly. "I have got to go down to Lockford, and I will bring you word how your mother is before I go my rounds."

Chapter Twelve

"It is only what I expected!" Garth Davenant's face was very grave as he stood before the mantelpiece and looked at Mavis's anxious face. "What does your mother say about it, Mavis?"

"Oh, mother is in dreadful trouble! You know how she always hoped it would be Dorothy; in fact, I think she had persuaded herself that it was quite a settled thing, and that was how it was she never minded Hilda's being here. But why do you say you expected it, Garth?"

Davenant shrugged his shoulders.

"It is not an unusual thing when a young man as impressionable as Arthur is thrown into the daily and hourly companionship of a beautiful woman older than himself."

"Garth!" Mavis interrupted him with a little cry. "Hilda herself does not know her age, and we can only guess, but we feel quite sure that she is not more than nineteen. She says herself that 'twenty' sounds unfamiliar."

"Oh, yes. I should fancy it is a good while since that particular number was used in connexion with her age," remarked Davenant dryly.

Mavis looked at him with amazed eyes.

"What do you mean, Garth? I am sure she does not look more—"

"Are you?" Garth said cynically. "Well, I must confess that I have not the unquestioning faith of the inhabitants of Hargreave Manor, and I have studied your fair friend's face on one or two occasions in the open sunlight, away from the couches and subdued lights she usually affects, and I think she is considerably older than you imagine."

"Oh, don't!" exclaimed Mavis miserably. "You make me feel so unhappy, Garth—as if I ought not to believe in anyone!"

Her lover put out his arm and drew her to him.

"I am a suspicious, world-hardened wretch, Mavis, am I not? I don't want any trouble to come to you that I can help, and I am afraid—"

"Afraid that trouble will come if Arthur married her?" Mavis finished, her head resting against his shoulder.

"I feel sure of it if he should be mad enough to contemplate such a step before something is known about her," said Davenant in alarm. "But I hardly thought matters had got so far as that even from your account."

Mavis raised her head.

"Hilda seemed to want to wait until things were cleared up, but Arthur seems quite determined that the engagement shall be announced at once—and he is his own master. I am afraid that mother's remonstrances only made him more positive. What she implied about Dorothy only annoyed him so much he said he had made up his mind that there should be no more misconception. Don't you think you may be mistaken about Hilda, Garth? I know it sounds a mad sort of thing for Arthur to do—to marry a woman we know nothing about; but I must say that to a certain extent I cannot help sympathizing with him. Hilda is so very pretty and charming that I feel positive if I were a man I should want to marry her myself."

"I should certainly interfere to prevent you," said Garth, laughing and catching her hand. "Seriously, darling, cannot you see how queer the whole business is? Here is this girl, dropped apparently from the clouds on your doorstep, and nobody makes the smallest inquiry after her. One would naturally have supposed that if a girl of our class, as she appears to be, were missing, there would be such a hue and cry after her that the whole country would be roused, yet, though a description has been published and advertisements inserted, you get no reply from her friends at all!"

"Yes, yes. I know it sounds strange," Mavis admitted at once. "But I am sure there is some satisfactory explanation of it all. Hilda and I were talking about it yesterday, and we came to the conclusion that there must have been some wrongdoing somewhere. Perhaps she may be heiress to some property which some one else wants to secure, and they may have treated her in some way that reduced her to the state she was in. Very likely they think she is dead!"

Garth's lips curled curiously.

"I fancy I could pick a few holes in that theory, Mavis. However, shall we say no more about it? Time may prove that you are right and I am wrong. In the meantime before the wedding we will set all our wits to work. We must save Arthur from this folly if possible."

"Oh, dear!" Mavis said with a sigh as she turned away her head.

"What is the matter with you, Mavis?" Garth's voice was very tender, his clasp grew closer.

Mavis moved restlessly.

"Everything is so altered, Garth," she complained miserably. "And it is such a little time ago since we were so happy; but now the very air of the Manor seems full of mystery and suspicion. One does not know whom to trust."

Garth's hand smoothed her brown hair gently.

"One thing is not altered, I hope, Mavis—our love for one another."

Mavis's fingers lingered on his arm caressingly.

"Oh, no! That is the same always; but, Garth, sometimes it seems hardly right for me to be happy in your love when I am afraid that Dorothy—"

Davenant's dark face clouded.

"Hush, child! Poor little Dorothy! We must have patience and it will all come right some time."

Mavis did not reply, but rested quiescent in his arms, feeling a certain comfort from the close contact with his strength, from the firmness of his clasp as he bent over her.

There was a step in the conservatory and Mavis freed herself.

"Oh, there you are!" Lady Laura said as she caught sight of them through the glass door. "I was looking for you, Mavis. You must see this person for me," glancing at the card she held in her hand. "I'm really so upset this morning that I cannot talk to anyone. What do you say to this folly—this madness of Arthur's, Garth?"

"It is what I have been fearing for some time. I was afraid—"

"I never thought of such a thing," Lady Laura said plaintively. "How could I imagine a man would want to marry a girl, however beautiful, who could not remember even her own name? I concluded that that put it entirely out of the question. I should have thought it quite as improbable as that Arthur, visiting a lunatic asylum, should fall in love with one of its inmates and want to marry her. I can see now that I have been imprudent in allowing them to see so much of one another, but I assure you that was how I looked at it."

Garth laughed in spite of his real vexation.

"There is something to be said for that point of view, Lady Laura, but I question whether the marriage can take place until the girl recovers her memory. We don't even know that she is free."

Lady Laura clasped her hands.

"Certainly we do not! Garth, that had not occurred to me. You must have a long talk with my poor boy. He will not listen to anything I can say. It seems useless to speak, and yet to see him throwing away his happiness in this way is heart-breaking."

Mavis took the card from her hand.

"Nurse Gidden," she read, and then underneath in pencil, "From Mrs. Marston."

"Oh, mother, what does she want?" she asked.

"I do not know—something to do with Nurse Marston I suppose," Lady Laura said tearfully. "But I really cannot stand any more worry this morning, Mavis; I am not fit for it."

"Poor little mumsy!" Mavis kissed her heartily. "I will hear what she has to say. May I tell Jenkins to show her in here, then Garth can help me perhaps?"

"Oh, see her where you like," Lady Laura acquiesced fretfully. "I am going out for a drive. I think it may help to steady my nerves."

"The best thing you can do, mother dear," Mavis agreed as she rang the bell and Lady Laura hurried out through the conservatory.

Garth Davenant glanced up curiously as Gidden was ushered in. He saw a plain-featured, resolute-looking woman of middle height and apparently of middle age, with a firmly-set humorous mouth and bright dark eyes. Looking at her he came to the conclusion that he would rather have Nurse Gidden as a friend than an enemy.

"You wished to speak to my mother?" said Mavis, advancing. "I am so sorry she is not able to see you this morning, but if there is anything that I can tell you—you are a friend of Nurse Marston's are you not?"

"Her greatest friend, I believe," Charlotte returned in her brisk, matter-of-fact tones. "We were probationers together, though Mary was some years the younger, and we have kept in communication with one another ever since. Ah, I see you did not think I was a nurse"—as Mavis glanced at her serviceable green dress and plain hat—"but I don't wear uniform as a rule in my holidays! To tell the truth it is a relief to get out of it and dress like other people sometimes. I have a month off, Miss Hargreave, and I came to Lockford yesterday. I mean to find out what has become of Mary Marston, and I want you to help me."

"I only wish I could," Mavis said earnestly. "But nothing we do seems any good. You know my brother has had a detective down?"

"I have heard so." There was a pause. Charlotte was apparently studying the pattern of the carpet. Garth, from the point of vantage he had taken up in a distant window-seat, watched her, and decided that she was at a loss how to begin. "I am sure of one thing—that Mary Marston had no idea of going away of her own free will that night; her letter to me proved it."

Mavis drew a long breath.

"Ah, I heard you had a letter, but she must have left the house of her own free will, I think! I should like to see the letter."

Charlotte raised her hands.

"I wish you could!" she said. "I never thought it was of any particular importance, and I should have my work cut out for me, with my luggage, going about as I do, if I hoarded up letters. I always burn them after they are read."

"Oh, what a pity it is!" Mavis said as she drew up a chair. "Sit down, Nurse Gidden; you must be tired if you walked up."

"Yes, it is a goodish way by the road—thank you!" Charlotte said as she accepted the courtesy. "Not but what I remember pretty well what was in the letter," she resumed after a pause. "She said that nobody knew who the young lady was that she was nursing, but that she herself had seen her in different circumstances, and she felt it was her duty to tell Lady Laura at once, as she thought Lady Laura ought to know who she had in the house. I can't remember that she said anything more definite"—wrinkling up her brows—"but I know the impression left on my mind was that she thought Lady Laura would soon get rid of the young lady when she did know. The other thing I can recall is that she had only come to the Manor temporarily, that she said she didn't like leaving her mother just then, and if it had been anybody but Mr. Garth Davenant who asked her to she didn't think she should have gone."

"Oh, yes," Mavis said quickly. "I can understand that! Her mother nursed Mr. Garth Davenant and his brother, and they have always been very kind to the Marstons."

"So I have heard. That part of the letter does not puzzle me, Miss Hargreave," remarked Charlotte composedly. "It shows though that Mr. Garth Davenant had a pretty strong influence over her—that is what I notice; but my opinion, looking at the case all round, is that that young lady she was nursing knew she was recognized, and, having her own motives for stopping at the Manor, contrived to get Miss Marston out of the way somehow, so that she should not tell Lady Laura who she was. That is where I fancy you can help me, Miss Hargreave."

Mavis shook her head.

"You are quite on the wrong tack, Nurse Gidden—I can vouch for that. Hilda was lying in a semi-conscious state all the time the nurse was in the room. I don't think she had any idea that Nurse Marston had recognized her, and that she had nothing to do with her subsequent disappearance I am absolutely certain, because I went into her room when the nurse came out to see my mother, and remained there until her absence caused uneasiness and they came to make inquiries. It is out of the question that Hilda could have had anything to do with it."

"Not herself, certainly; she could have got some one to do it for her perhaps," suggested the other.

"Impossible! Nobody had been in the room all day but ourselves and my maid. After the nurse came she sat by the bed all the time. Hilda had no opportunity of plotting anything of the kind, even if she were inclined, which I do not believe for one moment. Nurse Marston's disappearance and the rumours connecting her with it have been a real trouble to her."

"Um!" Nurse Gidden, evidently a lady of free and easy manners, unfastened her coat and leaned back in her chair. "Well, what you say does seem to put this young lady out of count," she observed;

"but I don't know what to make of it. Can't you help me at all, Miss Hargreave?"

"I wish I could," Mavis said, with a heartfelt sigh. "I was just saying when you came in that the atmosphere of the Manor is dreadful just now. Suspicion seems to be in the very air."

"It is bad for you—anyone can see that," Charlotte agreed sympathetically. "Well, as it is no use thinking any more of the lady, I must trust to the gentleman and look after Mr. Garth Davenant a little more closely than I fancy he has been looked after yet."

Mavis started, her eyes flashed.

"I do not—"

Garth interrupted her.

"One moment," he said, coming forward. "I think before you go on, Nurse Gidden, I ought to tell you that I am Garth Davenant."

Charlotte did not seem in the faintest degree discomposed; her clear grey eyes met his frankly with just a touch of amusement in their glance.

"I guessed as much from the first," she said equably, "and I am glad to tell you to your face, Mr. Davenant, how things look to me. I say to myself, times and again, that only some very strong motive could have taken Mary out of this house that night. How she could reconcile it to her duty to her patient to go at all I cannot imagine, but some one must have had a pretty strong influence over her—the motive must have been urgent to induce her to do so. Now from her letter, as well as from her mother, I know that she would do a good deal for Mr. Garth Davenant, and I am told that only the week before she came here she was engaged on some private business with Mr. Garth Davenant in Exeter. It seems to me that it is possible that that same business might require more attention later on, and that Mary might have been persuaded to go away to look after it, and kept away. That is the only other theory that I have been able to evolve."

Garth had taken up his favourite position with his elbow against the mantelpiece, one hand shading his eyes, the other playing absently with his watch-chain. Was it Mavis's fancy, she wondered, or did his face pale as Nurse Gidden spoke?

There was a long pause. At last Davenant raised his head and straightened himself.

"Would it be any use my giving my word of honour that I have not heard one word of Nurse Marston since she left this house, that my business—the subject of which I was talking to her in Exeter—is entirely at an end, and had absolutely no connection with her disappearance—could have had none?" he added vehemently.

Charlotte looked at him doubtfully.

"Well, I am glad to hear you say so, though I can't say that I mean to place implicit reliance on what anyone else tells me," she remarked frankly. "I intend to thrash matters out for myself. But—well, I don't mind saying that I am glad I have seen you and spoken to you, Mr. Davenant." She rose. "I wanted to ask Miss Hargreave if her ladyship would allow me to see Mary's room, the one she was to have slept in."

"Oh, certainly! I am sure she would not have the slightest objection," Mavis said with a distinct touch of hauteur in her tone. She moved towards the bell, then, with her hand on it, paused. "I think I had better go with you myself. The servants seem afraid of opening the doors of those two rooms. In fact I hear that my maid will not go past them alone. I dare say you have heard that they say her ghost is seen? It has troubled us all very much lately."

"Yes, I have heard that," remarked Charlotte. "A pack of moonshine! As I say, if they have seen Mary at all they have seen her alive, not dead. But I expect they have fancied it. Her mother has dreams and thinks a lot of them, but, bless you, Miss Hargreave, I don't put any faith in such things! However, I mean to find Mary!"

"I hope you will," Mavis said as she led the way up the front stairs, the visitor's keen eyes glancing round her as they went along and taking mental notes of all she saw. "But I am quite certain when the truth is known it will be found that neither Mr. Garth nor Hilda has anything to do with it."

"Well, all persons have a right to their own opinions," Miss Gidden said calmly. "When we do know I dare say it will not much matter what any of us have thought."

Mavis made no further comment as they walked down the corridor. She opened the door of the larger room first.

"This is where the patient was—she was there some time after Nurse Marston went, but we had her moved out as soon as we possibly could."

"Nothing could be found here, then, I expect," was the comment of Miss Gidden as she looked round.

"This," Mavis said as they came out and she unlocked the next door, "is Nurse Marston's own room. All her things are still just as she left them. Her cloak and bonnet are just where every one who has been here believes she put them herself."

Charlotte went up and laid her hand on them.

"Poor thing! Poor Mary! I wonder where she is now?" she said. Then a shudder shook her from head to foot and her face turned white.

Mavis sprang forward.

"Oh, what is it?"

The older woman's eyes slowly filled with tears, and as the girl touched her she looked strangely pale and shaken.

"I—I do not know, but I feel afraid," she confessed, looking round in a furtive, terrified fashion. "I am not in the least a nervous person usually, Miss Hargreave. I came here believing that all would come right in time, and that we should have Mary back, but when I touched her clothes the oddest feeling came over me—a sort of dread of something unutterably evil, and with it a sure foreboding that I shall never see Mary again. Some terrible fate has overtaken her. I—I feel as though for one moment I had stood in an atmosphere of awful wickedness," with an irrepressible shudder.

Mavis looked bewildered and half frightened as she drew the other away gently.

"You are overwrought, over-excited, that must be it. I have been in the room ever so many times and touched her things often, and I never had the feelings you describe. But"—closing the door behind them—"I am sure you ought not to stay longer to-day. You can come again another time, you know. You will be only too welcome to any help we can give you. We should be delighted to have the mystery cleared up."

Some of the colour was coming back to Charlotte's face.

"I am ashamed of myself for having such fancies," she said energetically, "and for giving way to them and talking about them to you. It was as clear a case of nerves as I ever saw. I can't understand it, but I suppose the fact of the matter is that I have been overworked lately."

"That was it, I expect," Mavis agreed, glancing at her companion a little curiously as she came down the stairs. With her usually florid colour returning and her brisk, decided walk she scarcely looked a likely subject for a nervous attack, Mavis thought.

"Can you tell me which door she went out by?" Charlotte resumed abruptly.

Mavis shook her head.

"That is one of the points we have never been able to make out; but you shall hear. Jenkins!" she called out to the old butler, who was crossing the hall. "Nurse Gidden wants to ask you a question."

Charlotte stepped forward.

"I should like to know how Nurse Marston went out of the house—I mean, by what door."

The old man raised his hands.

"I wish I could tell you. All I know is that at sunset by her ladyship's orders, ever since last autumn, I have locked all the doors except the front one, and kept the keys myself, and fastened the windows. They were all closed that night as usual."

Charlotte looked amazed.

"But how did she go—"

Jenkins shook his head.

"I don't know how. It's one of the things I have never been able to fathom. Seeing that the young woman did not put on her outdoor things it didn't look as if she meant to go away, and I have sometimes been tempted to think—saving your presence, Miss Mavis—as she never did go out of the house."

"What do you mean? "Charlotte stared at him.

Jenkins passed his hand over his white hair.

"Sometimes when I'm by myself, I think as she is still in the Manor. There's queer holes and hiding-places in these old buildings, and who knows but she may have tumbled into something that we none of us know of? There, I mustn't talk to you young ladies like this—and Mr. Garth is coming out."

"Will you come in and rest a while?" Mavis said, turning towards the morning-room.

Charlotte drew back.

"I think I will be getting into the fresh air to think things over, if you please, Miss Hargreave," she said. "This is as about as queer a tangle as I ever heard of."

When Mavis had said good-bye, as Nurse Gidden was crossing the hall Garth Davenant stepped forward.

"I wish you success," he said pleasantly. "Rest assured that anything that I could do to elucidate matters should be done at once."

The woman did not take the proffered hand. Her sharp eyes met his coolly.

"Thank you, Mr. Garth Davenant, but as matters stand now I would rather not! It may be that some day I may know the truth and be ready to apologize to you, but it is best to be straightforward, I think, always, and I don't feel to-day as if I could bring myself to it. That is a fact!"

Chapter Thirteen

"You must be patient, Arthur, really. It is for your sake that I must refuse to give way."

"My sake!" Arthur laughed shortly as he leaned his head on the arm of her low chair. "Dear, I want all the world to know how happy, how blessed I am!"

His eyes were fixed adoringly upon the girl's brilliant face.

"You would find that the world by no means shared your opinion of your state," Hilda said with a coquettish laugh as her hand wandered softly over his close-cropped light hair.

They were sitting in the inner drawing-room; Hilda, who was being made to feel that she was no longer high in Lady Laura's favour, had retired there after dinner, and thither, when the men came up, Arthur had followed her.

It had been somewhat of the nature of a family dinner-party to-night—the Davenants, Dorothy with her friends, the Leighs, the clergyman and his wife, and old Dr. Grieve comprised the list; for, as Lady Laura fretfully observed, it was impossible to ask many people to the house while there was this uncertainty about Hilda's position—"so awkward to introduce a girl without a name."

That the difficulty would have to be met and faced, supposing the matter were not cleared up before, at the coming of age festivities Lady Laura fully recognized, but she was willing to delay matters as long as possible. All her hopes of persuading Arthur to give Hilda up had proved futile, and the poor lady was at her wits' end. None the happier was she when her husband's brother, who was Sir Arthur's guardian, hastily summoned on the scene to remonstrate with him, bluntly told her that the whole affair was entirely her own fault in keeping the girl at the house, and she could only bemoan her own short-sightedness and Arthur's folly.

To get rid of her unwelcome visitor was an impossibility now; the girl had nowhere else to go, and Sir Arthur would be in a very short time master of his own house, and would not hear of his fiancée's departure. So poor Lady Laura had to make the best of it, and confine her lamentations over the state of affairs for the most part to her daughter's ears.

To-night as she talked to her guests her attention was evidently wandering, and her eyes turned constantly to the curtained doorway, through which she could catch just a glimpse of Hilda's white frock.

That the situation was sufficiently obvious she was well aware, and she felt uncomfortably conscious that her guests could scarcely fail to see how matters stood. Meanwhile Dorothy, whom she had looked upon as her future daughter-in-law, was apparently perfectly contented with things as they were. An acuter observer than Lady Laura might have noticed that though the girl's soft gaiety was in no way dimmed, while her laughter was as frequent and as infectious as of yore, there was an extinguished look about her eyes, a pathetic drooping of her lips when in repose that told their own story.

Meanwhile in the smaller drawing-room the lovers were enjoying an uninterrupted period of bliss.

Sir Arthur caught the white hand straying over his head.

"How long is this state of things to go on, Hilda?"

"Well, I think it ought to stop now," the girl said as she laughed, wilfully misunderstanding him. "I am sure Lady Laura will think we are lost."

Sir Arthur raised himself on the low stool upon which he had taken up his position at Hilda's feet.

"You know I did not mean that. I mean how long will it be before you allow me to tell everybody—before you will become—my wife?"

The last two words had all the softness of a caress, yet Hilda shrank back as from an unexpected blow.

"Oh, I don't know—I can't think about it—not for a long time yet."

Arthur's eyes were fixed upon her face devouringly.

"Shall I tell you what I should like, dearest? To hold the coming of age and the marriage festivities together."

"Oh, no, no!" Hilda cried. "Impossible—in a month! It is entirely out of the question, Arthur—I couldn't."

Arthur put his arms round her waist and drew her nearer.

"Why not, Hilda? We can find out anything you want to know just as well afterwards. And what does it matter about your name? You shall share mine, and whatever other names you might find you possessed to me you would always be just Hilda."

For a moment the girl seemed to yield herself to him, she bent a little towards him, he felt her warm breath upon his cheek, a strand of her soft hair touched his forehead, the intoxication of her nearness thrilled through all his senses. Then with a quick, jerky movement she freed herself from his arms, pushed him from her and rose.

"No, no, Arthur! Haven't I told you that there is to be nothing—nothing—for the present? I will not be persuaded. Perhaps after your birthday—"

"After my birthday," Arthur repeated. "After my birthday, Hilda—"

The girl flashed one brilliant, unfathomable glance at him as she parted the curtains.

"Ah, then we shall see!" she replied enigmatically.

And with that Arthur had to be satisfied.

As he entered the room, Mrs. Mainwaring, the rector's wife, looked up.

"We have been talking of the Blue Diamond, Sir Arthur, the 'Luck of the Hargreaves.' Do you know that neither my husband nor I have ever seen it? And we hear so much about it. Miss Hargreave has just told me that she thinks if I ask you very nicely"—with a would-be fascinating smile—"that you might perhaps let us have just one peep at it."

Sir Arthur frowned. Mrs. Mainwaring was no particular favourite, and he did not feel altogether inclined to grant her request, but before he could refuse Hilda interposed:

"Neither have I. The Blue Diamond! That sounds very attractive. You must certainly let us see it, please, Sir Arthur!"

"Oh, certainly, if you wish to," Sir Arthur agreed at once. "We do not often show it, but in the circumstances—if you will excuse me a moment, I will go and get it myself."

"Oh, really, Sir Arthur, I never thought of giving you so much trouble!" Mrs. Mainwaring began, but she was too late, Sir Arthur had left the room. Hilda took a seat beside her.

"I am so glad you thought of asking to see it, Mrs. Mainwaring. I love looking at jewels."

"Well, naturally, as a resident in the neighbourhood," said the good lady with some emphasis, "I am anxious to see it, but I dare say you will be interested"—patronizingly—"for the Hargreaves have been so good to you, and you have been here for so long that you must feel almost as if you belonged to the place. It is so awkward for you, as I say to Mr. Mainwaring, not knowing where you do come from. I am sure I do not know what I should do in such circumstances. Your memory is too bad to permit you to teach or anything of that kind, is it not?" searching the girl's face with a rapid inquisitive glance.

Hilda did not shrink from her scrutiny, but raised her eyes and smiled at Mrs. Mainwaring.

"I am afraid it is at present, but I think it is getting better, and I hope soon to be able to do something for myself. Then I was thinking of asking you to advise me, Mrs. Mainwaring. Perhaps I may come to the Rectory and talk to you some day."

If Mrs. Mainwaring loved anything on earth better than her meek husband and the little Mainwarings who filled the Rectory, it was managing other people's business. Hilda could not have taken a better way of placating her.

"I should be delighted, I am sure!" she said, instantly mollified. "You must come up and spend a long afternoon with me one day soon, and we will discuss the whole matter. I quite understand your feeling!"

"I felt sure you would," Hilda responded with a grateful glance, "and I shall look forward so much to my visit."

Mrs. Mainwaring's face shone with mingled pleasure and self-importance.

"Now, when shall it be? I am afraid that next week—oh, here is Sir Arthur!"

Sir Arthur looked round for Hilda, then, as she came forward a step behind Mrs. Mainwaring, he turned towards her.

"This is the 'Luck of the Hargreaves'," with a laugh as he opened the case.

Mrs. Mainwaring uttered a cry of amazement.

"Oh, my dear Sir Arthur, I never imagined anything quite so magnificent!"

Hilda did not speak, but her eyes were fixed on the gleaming stones with a curiously rapt expression, and one long, fluttering breath escaped her. The rest of the party gathered round, eager to have another look at the famous diamonds.

Mrs. Mainwaring kept well in the front.

"It is the big one in the centre that is really called the 'Luck,' isn't it, Sir Arthur? I wonder how the name originated."

"I fancy the reason is lost in the mists of antiquity," Sir Arthur said lightly, "but I believe the loss of the Blue Diamond would presage some fearful misfortune to all the Hargreaves. That is why we take such care of it. It is only worn on rare occasions by the wife of the head of the house, or by the bride of the heir on her wedding-day."

His eyes sought Hilda's, but the girl did not respond to his glance, and apparently her whole attention was absorbed by the diamonds.

The Hargreaves proudly claimed that their necklace was absolutely unique; certainly it was remarkable even when contrasted with the Crown jewels of modern reigning houses. It consisted of seven rows of diamonds, each row being clasped to the next one in front in the centre by a larger stone of great brilliance, and as a pendant to the lower one there gleamed resplendent, seeming almost like a living, burning flame as Arthur turned it about in the light, the great Blue Diamond — the "Luck" itself.

"You must feel quite nervous when you are wearing them, Lady Laura," Mrs. Mainwaring said at last, Lady Laura laughed.

"I—I have never done so. Had my husband succeeded his brother I should have worn them, but as it is they are put by for Arthur's wife."

"I see!"

A sudden silence fell on the group. Mrs. Mainwaring, with questionable taste, looked across at Dorothy, who was just now smiling bravely at her cousin. Garth Davenant glanced significantly at Mavis. To his mind there was something curiously suggestive in the way in which Hilda was absorbed in the contemplation of the diamonds to the exclusion apparently of everything else. She and Dorothy were standing almost in a line, and it seemed to Davenant that even contrasted with Hilda's loveliness the younger girl held her own.

There had always been something spiritual in Dorothy's beauty, and to-night a certain air of fragility about the small, flower-like head and the immature curves of her slim young body struck Davenant afresh with a sense of delicacy, enhanced as it was by a touch of languor in her whole pose, in her large clear eyes and softly curving lips.

Hilda's brilliant colouring was wont to overshadow and dwarf all other less striking beauty, but now as her eyes were fixed on the Blue Diamond her face was for the nonce off its guard, and Davenant noted not only a coarseness about the modelling of her features, but certain little lines about the mouth and eyes which convinced him that his estimate of her age was not unjust.

Just as the pause was becoming oppressive Dr. Grieve bustled forward—the old man could always be relied upon to fill up an awkward interval.

"I see you have not adopted the modern plan of sending your valuables to the bank, Sir Arthur? You still stick to your own safe and strong room."

"Oh, yes. I fancy they are more secure in my care than they would be in the bank," Arthur smiled. "I assure you it would be a very difficult matter for thieves to break through and steal the 'Luck,' Dr. Grieve. Have you ever seen our strong-room? It was made before the days of jerry-building."

"No, I haven't, but—" the doctor was beginning.

Hilda interrupted him.

"Do show it to us, Sir Arthur! It doesn't seem to me that you could do enough to keep the treasure safe."

Lady Laura looked manifestly displeased. Sir Arthur hesitated, but a look at Hilda's eager face decided him.

"I will show it to any of you with pleasure. I shall have to put away the necklace myself, for we do not trust it to the servants, not even to one so trusted as Jenkins. So if you like to come with me, Dr. Grieve, I shall be delighted to exhibit our precautions to you."

"Oh, do let us all see them, Sir Arthur!" Mrs. Mainwaring pleaded. "It would be so interesting—quite a novel experience. You will go with us, will you not, Miss Dorothy?"

The girl drew back.

"I think not—thanks!" she said.

Mrs. Mainwaring glanced round in indecision, but already Hilda and Dr. Grieve were at the door, and Garth Davenant was following. She moved forward.

"You do not mind, Lady Laura?"

"Certainly not!" said Lady Laura with a little air of coldness. "I hope you will find it as delightful as you imagine."

Mr. Mainwaring glanced meaningly at his wife; quite evidently he saw that the proposed expedition did not meet with Lady Laura's favour; but with Mrs. Mainwaring, for once, curiosity overcame her fear of incurring Lady Laura's displeasure, and she hurried after the others.

Sir Arthur held open the green baize door which gave access to the back of the house, and led the way down a wide passage, stopping before a heavy oak door, which he unlocked. The door opened outwardly, and they saw inside a second one of metal.

"This is the outer strong-room," Sir Arthur said as he fitted the key," where all the plate and valuables in daily use are kept. To it there are two keys—one I have and one Jenkins has. Now this is a different matter," moving towards a smaller inner door at the opposite end. "This key is never out of my possession, and even should any unauthorized person get hold of it you see there is an electric alarm-bell which rings at the top of the house—one of my Uncle Noel's latest improvements." He switched it off as he spoke and drew out a small key. "Now, Mrs. Mainwaring, you are in the heart of the mystery."

They all glanced curiously round the small oblong room into which there was no opening save by the narrow doorway, and which was lined on three sides by iron cupboards.

"Rather stuffy, isn't it?" Arthur said as he went across. "But you would risk it, remember. Now this"—pointing to the wall, which was apparently blank—"is the real home of the necklace." He touched a spring and the wall opened backwards, revealing a strong iron safe.

"And this," he went on, "is the crux of the whole matter."

He made a rapid movement with his hand and the door of the safe opened. He laid the diamonds carefully on a shelf and closed the door with a click. "Now," he went on, "it would puzzle you to open that door, doctor, even if I lent you the key. You have heard of the letter-locks, I dare say. This is one of the most complicated."

"Is it now—is it indeed?" The doctor stepped forward quickly. "Really, this is most interesting. A letter-lock! I have, as you say, heard of such things, but I have never seen one. How does it work, Sir Arthur?"

The young man smiled.

"Ah, that is my secret, Dr. Grieve. As I tell you, even if I gave you the key, you could not unlock the door."

"Ah, no. You must have the secret of the combination of the letters, must you not?" It was Hilda's voice, but sounding so curiously strained and harsh that every one instinctively turned towards her. Her hand was pressed to her forehead, her eyes were wide-open, the pupils looking dark and dilated. "I think I have seen one like it before somewhere," she said slowly, with a little fluttering gasp between each word. "A minute ago I thought I knew the word, but now I seem to forget again. Was it 'Keep'?"

"This is not," Arthur said. "But I do not know—"

Dr. Grieve glanced from him to Hilda meaningly. All his little mannerisms seemed to fall away for a moment.

"Now I wonder what it is?" he went on benevolently after a momentary hesitation. "Something short, you think, Miss Hilda?— 'Safe'? How would that be? Very appropriate, I should say," with a little laugh at his own joke.

Moving forward almost like a person in a dream, Hilda put him aside and fumbled helplessly with the letters, as the others gathered round. "'Luck,' 'Manor,' 'Keep'. No, no—they are not right! I cannot remember!" a distressed pucker coming between her brows, her lips trembling childishly. "Oh, I wish I could! I wish I could!"

Dr. Grieve laid his hand on her arm.

"Don't try any more to-day, my dear young lady. Rest assured you will recall everything before long. I consider that you have made wonderful progress lately, I do indeed; and very soon I feel sure everything will come back to you. Well, Sir Arthur, you have shown us what care you take of the precious Blue Diamond, and I think I may say, speaking for all of us, that we are intensely obliged to you; but now I fancy we had better be making our way back to the drawing-room. I want to have a little talk with this young lady here," patting Hilda's hand in a fatherly fashion.

He led the girl away without further ado, and the rest of the party followed, almost more interested in the promise of a solution of the mystery that had puzzled them all so long than in the precautions taken for the safeguarding of the Hargreave treasure.

They watched eagerly as Dr. Grieve took Hilda across the drawing-room to a distant settee and seated himself beside her.

Mrs. Mainwaring turned to Lady Laura; Garth crossed to Mavis, who was talking to the rector; Sir Arthur found himself close to Dorothy.

"When are you coming back to the Manor, Dorothy?" he began, anxious to appear on the same friendly footing, but obviously ill at ease. "We miss you very much, little cousin. I don't think you can be spared to the Leighs much longer."

The girl raised her eyes to his, smiling bravely.

"I shall come for the birthday celebrations. Mavis has told me your news, Arthur. You must let me congratulate you and wish you both every happiness, though it is not public property yet.—I—I was not altogether taken by surprise—I had been expecting it."

"You are very kind, Dorothy." To the girl who loved him Arthur's embarrassment was painful. "You know it is by Hilda's wish that it is not made known at once?"

"Yes. Mavis said that Hilda wanted to wait till all was cleared up. One can understand that as well as your impatience, for she is very beautiful, Arthur. I hope she will let me be her friend too," with a tiny catch in her voice.

"We shall always think of you with Mavis," he said. "I have always looked upon you as a dear little sister, Dorothy, and Hilda—"

Dr. Grieve interrupted them.

"The exigencies of a doctor must be my excuse for an early farewell, Sir Arthur; but before I go I must tell you that I have every hope that in a short time Miss Hilda will be quite restored. If she accidentally makes any allusion to the past do not appear to be surprised; lead her on to speak of it gently, and you will probably get the clue for which we are waiting. It is only a question of time. I consider the progress most satisfactory."

Chapter Fourteen

"If you please, Sir Arthur, could you come into the houses for a minute? I am not quite satisfied with that new root from Chile. There's a dryness—"

"All right, Gregory, I will be back directly; I must just see the ladies to the house, and then—"

Mavis stood still.

"How absurd, Arthur! As if Hilda and I could not take care of ourselves for that little bit of a way! You can go at once, can't he, Hilda? We shall be perfectly safe."

"Certainly! Please go," Hilda agreed promptly. "Indeed, I would rather you did. We should feel obliged to hurry if we knew we were keeping you from your orchids, whereas Mavis and I can dawdle as much as we like, and I think it is lovely to be out in the gloaming."

"So do I," agreed Mavis, putting her arm through the other girl's. "Go on, Arthur, we will look after ourselves."

"Well, if you really do not mind," Arthur conceded reluctantly. "I dare say I shall catch you up before you get to the house."

He hurried away. The two girls walked leisurely towards the house, laughing as they talked over the approaching festivities, for Arthur's coming of age was only three weeks distant now; and though their engagement was a secret to the world at large the young man insisted that Hilda should be consulted with regard to all the arrangements. Lady Laura's dislike to the whole affair had in no way abated, but, realizing her helplessness, she had ceased to offer any opposition, trusting that time might show Sir Arthur the folly of the proceeding.

It seemed to Mavis sometimes, looking on, that his love for their beautiful visitor increased rather than diminished, and she had little faith in matters turning out as her mother wished. The longed-for improvement in Hilda's memory had not taken place. Mavis very often doubted whether it ever would—the girl herself seemed so well now, so full of vitality in every way, save for that fatal blank in her recollection.

Notwithstanding her real love for Dorothy and Garth Davenant's avowed distrust of Hilda, Mavis had from the first fallen under the girl's fascination to almost as great an extent as her brother, and Hilda had responded to her evident affection with a caressing, wayward wilfulness that the other girl found very winning.

"Have you decided on your frock for the ball yet, Mavis?" Hilda asked as they turned through the shrubbery. "You really must make up your mind about the colour to-night and then let me arrange it all for you. I will write to Madame Sternforth and tell her just what I have designed for you. I know exactly how it ought to be made to suit your style and to charm Mr. Davenant," she ended with a little laugh.

Mavis paused.

"Now, Hilda, you know that I have told you I will not do anything towards getting my gown until you have promised to have one too. You remember mother said we were to have them alike in every respect."

A slight smile curled Hilda's lips—only too well did she divine who had dictated Lady Laura's offer.

"Don't you see, dear, that I owe everything I wear, everything I eat, to your mother's kindness? I must not go on carelessly piling up a debt which I may never be able to pay."

"You know we have told you not to think of it like that. Arthur would be very angry."

"Oh, Arthur is all that is good and kind," Hilda interrupted "and so is Arthur's sister"—with an affectionate squeeze of the girl's arm—"but I should not like to think—Mavis, did you notice anything? Listen! There, I am sure I heard a step! Somebody is following us!"

"It is Arthur, I expect. You know he said he should not be long; but I don't hear anything."

"No, no!" Hilda continued quickly. "It was not decided enough for Arthur. It had a stealthy, gliding sound, as if some one did not want to be heard. There, I believe it is coming again."

They stood still and listened, and Hilda turned round.

"There, you see, it was your fancy!" Mavis said, moving a step away. "Come along, Hilda—you make me feel quite creepy. What—what is it?" as the other clutched her arm.

"Look! Look!" Hilda cried hoarsely, her fingers gripping Mavis nervously. "It is she—it is Nurse Marston!"

With a sharp exclamation Mavis turned. Right behind them, some little way back on the path down which they had just come, there stood a woman. Mavis caught sight of her dark cloak and little close nurse's bonnet, as Hilda spoke, of the broad white cuffs and collar. With a little fluttering sob she caught at Hilda.

"How did she come? Oh, Hilda, let me speak to her!" She tried to move forward, but her knees felt strangely numbed and tottering.

Hilda held her back.

"Ah, no, no, Mavis, I daren't! Indeed I daren't! It is her spirit!" with a violent shudder.

In spite of her common sense, Mavis shivered from head to foot as she turned to the terrified girl beside her.

"Hush, hush, Hilda! We must speak to her, ask her what she wants, why she has come!"

"Oh, don't!" cried Hilda, half fainting. "I know!"

"You know?" For half a minute, as if stunned, Mavis stood silent, quiescent, while the other clung round her, moaning. "Let me go Hilda! I—" She stopped and stared in amazement. It seemed to her that she had not taken her eyes from that quiet figure on the path, and yet now it had disappeared. In vain she gazed round, not a vestige of it was to be seen. "Hilda," she said in a low tone, "it—she has gone."

The girls looked at one another and Mavis made a step forward.

"Let us look for her," she said.

Hilda gave a cry of horror.

"I am frightened, frightened! Oh, Mavis, Mavis, come home!"

As Mavis yielded, not reluctantly, in spite of her brave words, a masculine step sounded behind them, there was the unmistakable aroma of a cigar, and Sir Arthur joined them.

"Oh, I say, this is splendid! I was afraid Gregory had kept me so long that I should not be able to overtake you. Now we will have a stroll round the rose garden before we turn in. Why, Hilda, my dear child, what on earth is the matter?" as the girl with a sob of terror almost threw herself into his arms.

"Oh, Arthur, Arthur!" she cried, clinging to him as a drowning man clutches his rescuer. "She is there in the shrubbery—Nurse Marston! Take me away! Take me away! I shall die if I see her again!"

Her agitation was so excessive that Arthur, who had started at the mention of Nurse Marston and looked back, could not release himself, and was obliged to apply himself to the task of consoling and calming her. Presently he and Mavis between them half led, half carried her back to the house. Mavis in the meantime, in the intervals of attempting to soothe Hilda, gave him a short account of what had taken place.

As soon as they were safely in the hall Hilda burst into a passion of tears.

"Oh, Arthur, it is dreadful! She—I think she appeared to me because I was the cause of her death! If she had not been nursing me—"

"Death! Death!" Arthur repeated in as cheerful a tone as he could assume, for as a matter of fact recent occurrences at the Manor were beginning to puzzle him sorely. "Who says Nurse Marston is dead? I should imagine, on the contrary, that if you saw her in the shrubbery to-night she is alive and well."

"No, no!" wailed Hilda. "Don't you understand that it was her spirit we saw? She wants to tell us something. I think it is where she is buried. Perhaps"—with a violent shudder—"the place where she was standing was her grave!"

"Oh, hush, hush, Hilda!" Mavis said quickly. "I do not think she wanted to speak to us. Why should she have gone away so suddenly if she had? You did not see anything of her, I conclude, Arthur?" she went on, turning to her brother. "It seemed to me that if she turned back she must have met you, for I fancied we heard your footsteps almost directly she disappeared."

"Disappeared indeed!" Arthur repeated in a mocking tone. "Do say 'When she walked away,' Mavis. Do not tell me that you too believe it was a spirit?"

"No, I do not think it was," said Mavis slowly, "It looked to me too solid somehow. I have always fancied a ghost altogether more spiritualized. Besides, though I noticed nothing myself, before we saw her Hilda heard footsteps—"

"I—I don't now feel sure that I did," Hilda interposed. She was recovering her composure somewhat, and a little colour was slowly coming back to her cheeks as she sipped the wine that Arthur had ordered for her.

"You spoke of it to me, so I think there must have been the sound," said Mavis. "You certainly had the impression that there was a sound, Hilda."

"That settles the question," Sir Arthur cried, springing to his feet. "Ghosts don't make any audible sound as they walk, or so I have always been informed. If Nurse Marston, for some reason of her own, is lurking about the shrubbery frightening people we will have her out to-night. Jenkins," to the butler, who was hovering round at a discreet distance, not averse doubtless to learning what was the cause of the unusual commotion, "tell two of the stable-men to come round, and I will take James too. We will soon learn whether there is anyone in the shrubbery."

"Yes, sir," The old man moved nearer his master. "I—I don't fancy as you'll discover anything there, Sir Arthur. Two of the men—one from the stables, and Jones, the second in the hothouses, they saw her—Nurse Marston—two or three nights ago, close to the conservatory, but the moment they were after her she was gone. I don't suppose we shall get rid of the ghost, Sir Arthur, not until the poor young woman's fate is known."

"Now, Jenkins, don't you talk such rubbish!" reproved Sir Arthur, calling to James and giving the orders for the other men himself. "Poor young woman, indeed!" he went on as he turned back for a moment. "That is not precisely the epithet I should apply to Miss Mary Marston when I catch her. I suppose she is hiding somewhere near—in her mother's cottage, I dare say; though she does declare she knows nothing of her, no doubt it is all a part of the plot—and then coming prowling up here to scare people out of their senses. When I do find her I shall be in two minds about prosecuting her. I believe she is liable to it."

Old Jenkins shook his head.

"Ah, Sir Arthur, I misdoubt me if you will never get the opportunity!

"You old pessimist!" said Sir Arthur, with a laugh, fully persuaded in his own mind that the solution of the mystery that had puzzled them all for so long was at hand. "Well, don't frighten the ladies. I shall have some news for you when I come back. Mavis, you will look after Hilda, don't let her alarm herself. I shall be back very soon. Come along, James!—Are the other men outside?"

The young man hurried away and they heard his voice outside as he issued his orders to the stable-men.

Mavis turned to Hilda.

"I think we had better go into the drawing-room."

Hilda rose, still shaking, her eyes looking fearfully around.

"Mavis," she whispered, as soon as the door was shut behind them, "did you know before that she—that the servants had seen her?"

"I heard a whisper of it," Mavis answered reluctantly, "but I attached no importance to it. I thought it was merely an idle tale until to-night. Then—"

"A—h!" Hilda shuddered. "Don't speak of it, Mavis!"

"I must ask you one thing," Mavis said gravely. "Hilda, what did you mean when you said that you knew why she had come back?"

There was a silence. Mavis's eyes were fixed on the other girl's downcast face.

At last Hilda raised her head.

"Didn't you hear me just now—didn't I tell you that I knew she had come to show us where she was buried?" she said, her teeth chattering. "I—I am sure she did, Mavis."

Mavis's clear eyes looked searchingly at Hilda's.

"Was that what you meant, then? It seemed to me—"

"Certainly it was what I meant!" Hilda said pettishly. "Really, Mavis—"

The door opened and Lady Laura came in looking excited. Hilda turned to her with an unusual air of relief, and Mavis said no more; but for the first time, glancing at the fair face before her, a faint distrust of her future sister-in-law crept into the mind.

Lady Laura carried an open letter in her hand.

"Oh, my dears, such news! But Hilda, what is the matter?" The traces of the girl's emotion were still plainly to be seen on her face. "Have you heard—"

"Oh, Lady Laura, we have seen Nurse Marston in the shrubbery—Mavis and I!" Hilda burst out, disregarding Mavis's signal to her to be silent.

Lady Laura stared at her.

"My dear child, what do you mean?"

Hilda poured forth the whole story, much to Mavis's vexation; the girl was anxious that as much as possible the affair should be kept from her mother and Dorothy. It was useless attempting to stop Hilda, however, and she could only keep her closely to the facts.

To her daughter's relief Lady Laura did not seem inclined to take the matter seriously.

"You must have imagined the whole thing, both of you," she said decidedly, "and I am not altogether surprised. Very often when

I am thinking of the affair it gets on my nerves until I am sure I could fancy anything."

"Arthur thinks it is Nurse Marston herself—that she is doing it for a trick," Mavis said doubtfully.

Lady Laura laughed.

"Oh, my dear Mavis, how absurd! Do you, or does Arthur imagine that a sensible woman like Nurse Marston would wish to play a silly trick of that kind? I should advise you to put the whole thing out of your heads, all of you, and also to give up wandering about outside the house when it is getting dusk. You know how I dislike the idea of it for you, Mavis. I am sure it is positively unsafe. One does not know what suspicious characters may be about. I expect if poor Nurse Marston had been content to stay indoors she would have been safe enough. Now we will say no more about that," as Hilda, who had been growing more composed, began to tremble. "You have not asked me about my news."

"No, I think we were far too excited about our own adventure," said Mavis. "What is the news? Something pleasant this time, I hope."

Lady Laura held up her letter.

"This is from some one who thinks Hilda is her daughter!"

"What?" With a cry the girl sprang to her feet. "Oh, Lady Laura, is it true, is it true? Let me see the letter!"

Lady Laura kept it in her own hands.

"It is from a Mrs. Leparge. Do you recognize the name, my dear?"

Hilda's demonstration ceased.

"I don't think so. Is—is it mine, Lady Laura?"

"I think that very probably it is. Mrs. Leparge writes that her daughter, whose name was Hilda Frances, has disappeared from the school where she was a parlour- boarder. Mrs. Leparge has been away from the country, travelling in New Zealand, and the schoolmistress seems to have decided in her own mind that it was a case of elopement. However, on her return to this country Mrs. Leparge was not inclined to accept this theory, and put the matter into the hands of a private inquiry agent; he naturally had heard of our search for Hilda's friends, and thought that probably Mrs. Leparge would turn out to be her mother."

Hilda sank into a settee and buried her face in her hands.

"Oh, is she, is she?" she said as she sobbed.

Lady Laura laid her hand on her shoulder.

"Try to calm yourself, my dear. We shall soon know, for Mrs. Leparge writes that, too impatient to wait, she is following her letter, and will call upon us to-morrow, in the expectation of finding her daughter. I hope sincerely, for your sake, my child, that she may do so."

"Oh, I hope so! I hope so!" Hilda's voice was choked by her tears.

Lady Laura, her resentful feelings of the last few weeks momentarily forgotten in her pity, bent over her.

"There is Arthur!" Mavis exclaimed as she heard the front door open and her brother's voice in the hall.

She hurried out.

"Any news, Arthur, did you find her?"

He was looking moody and distrait as he handed his hat and coat to Jenkins.

"There is not a vestige of anybody to be seen about the place. We have been up and down, inside and out, all over the shrubbery, and we are at least pretty certain of one thing—there is nobody there now."

"Still, you were a long time before you started," Mavis said doubtfully, "and it seems to me that she would have had plenty of time to get away before you began your search."

"If she was ever there," Arthur said sceptically. He was feeling cross and tired; his unsuccessful search and the loss of his chat with Hilda, to which he had been looking forward, had made him irritable. "I expect you had been frightening Hilda and yourself by talking about Nurse Marston until you both fancied you saw her. I only hope you won't let your imagination run away with you in this fashion often, or we shall not be able to get a servant to stay in the place."

Mavis coloured a little. It was so seldom Arthur had spoken to her in that tone.

"There was no fancy about it, Arthur. I was not thinking of Nurse Marston—I had not mentioned her for days—when Hilda called out and I saw her on the path."

Her manner impressed her brother. He turned back with his hand on the drawing-room door.

"You really believe she was there?"

"I saw her as plainly as I see you now, except that she was farther away," Mavis said impressively. "She was there, Arthur—and I do not believe in ghosts."

"Ghosts! No." Arthur said impatiently, though his manner was softened. "Well, if that is so, Mavis, we must find her. What on earth her motive can be for dodging about the house like this I can't think, unless she is out of her mind."

"I think she must be," Mavis conceded, as he opened the door.

Chapter Fifteen

"AH, IF I only knew! It may be that it is my own mother coming to see me, and I, her daughter, know nothing about it!"

"Well, it will soon be settled one way or the other," remarked Mavis prosaically. "Mrs. Leparge said she would be here early in the morning, and it is nearly eleven now."

Hilda turned and caught her hands.

"Suppose she is not a nice woman, Mavis? suppose she should say that I am her daughter and take me away with her, and it should be all a lie—I should not be able to contradict her."

Mavis disengaged herself a little coldly. Since the preceding evening there had been a shade of aloofness in her manner towards Hilda, which so far did not seem to have made itself felt by the other girl.

"Surely you cannot imagine that Arthur would let her interfere with you in any way without having given him full proofs of her claim?"

"He might imagine she had," said Hilda hopelessly. "Yet they might be forged or something of that kind, might they not? I am very ignorant, Mavis, but the mere thought of this interview frightens me."

"Don't think of it then," Mavis advised. "Let us talk of something else. What do you think of the very palest shade of blush pink for the gown I am to wear at the Tenants' Ball?"

Hilda threw a quick glance at her betokening anything but amiability, but she made no comment as she dried her eyes and came to the table where Mavis was idly turning over fashion papers.

"Pink is your colour, there is no doubt, and if you had it veiled with some of Lady Laura's exquisite lace—Mavis, there is a carriage!"

Mavis sprang up.

"Come along," she cried as she swept both Hilda and the fashion-papers into the conservatory. "You know mother and Arthur want to see her first."

It was a quiet-looking, middle-aged woman, in a widow's conventional garb, who rose when Lady Laura and her son entered.

Lady Laura glanced searchingly at the somewhat worn features, at the pale, red-rimmed eyes and weak-looking mouth. Certainly if this were Hilda's mother she in no wise resembled her daughter, she decided.

"You, I am sure you understood that I could not remain away, Lady Laura," she began, dashing straight into her subject without offering any preliminary greeting whatever. "The agents I employed wanted me to wait to send photographs, to ask for them from you, but I could not. I felt that I must come straight off as soon as I heard of the poor child's whereabouts without telling them anything about it. She will remember her mother when she sees her, I said."

"Still, I am sure you will recognize that we must ask you a few questions before we allow you to see her," Lady Laura said courteously. Checking her son with a look as he was about to speak, she invited her visitor to sit down and then went on more slowly, "Will you tell me some of your reasons for thinking that Hilda is your daughter?"

"The name, the description, everything tallies," the other said excitedly. "Lady Laura, you are not going to tell me that she is not my child after all, that I have been deceiving myself with false hopes?"

"No; on the contrary," Lady Laura said with polite interest, "I think all the probabilities point to Hilda being your daughter. But will you tell me a little of the circumstance under which you lost her?"

Mrs. Leparge passed her handkerchief over her dry lips.

"I can only tell you the facts of the case as they were related to me by the schoolmistress in whose charge I left her, for you must understand that I was abroad; it has been so dreadful to me that I have known nothing—that I have had to rely upon others for everything. She—Miss Chesterton—told me that before Hilda's disappearance, though unknown to her at the time, it had been a matter of common talk that some man staying at one of the big hotels on the front—did I tell you she was at Brighton?—was always watching for Hilda and following her about when they were out for their walks; they called him 'The Unknown' and joked about him, as schoolgirls will. But when—when she went away they remembered it."

"Surely they had the man traced?" Arthur interposed, his face looking hot and wrathful. "Though I do not for one moment believe that this is—"

"They made inquiries at once," Mrs. Leparge went on. "He had been known at the hotel as Mr. James Duncan, and his only address given in the books was West Kensington. No such name appears in the directory, and the hotel authorities admit having some reason to believe it to be assumed, but they speak of him as a man apparently possessed of great wealth, and I am convinced that he decoyed my poor darling away."

"What a dreadful thing!" said Lady Laura, shuddering. "I wonder there was not more said about it in the papers."

"Oh, Miss Chesterton was like all schoolmistresses!" said Mrs. Leparge impatiently. "She thought first of the credit of the school—my poor Hilda came distinctly second. Lady Laura, when may I see her? You do not realize my anxiety or you would not delay our meeting."

"One more question," said Lady Laura, detaining her as she would have risen. "When did this happen? When did your daughter leave her school?"

"On the 29th of May. She was missing when the names were called in the evening, and has never been heard of since."

"And it was the 6th of June when we found Hilda in the park, was it not, Arthur?" said Lady Laura, turning to her son. "That would leave a week unaccounted for, but still it seems probable."

Sir Arthur's face was very gloomy; the prospect of discovering Hilda's relatives in such circumstances was by no means a pleasing one to him. Moreover, he had taken a somewhat unreasonable dislike to Mrs. Leparge, and did not feel inclined to welcome her as a possible mother-in-law. A sudden thought struck him.

"I should like to show you something first." He crossed the room and drew aside the curtain that at present concealed the Elaine. "Is that your daughter?" he asked, pointing to the central figure.

Mrs. Leparge put up her lorgnette and surveyed it critically.

"I think it is," she said in an uncertain tone. "It is her colouring exactly, and the features are a good deal alike, but this looks older and so very sad, and Hilda was always bright and lively. Besides, you must remember, Sir Arthur, that I have not seen her for two years. She was sixteen when I placed her with Miss Chesterton to complete her education, as I was summoned abroad on important business connected with my husband's estate. Poor darling, I little thought what a home-coming mine would be! If that is all—"

"The age is about the same, though Hilda has always thought she was nineteen," Lady Laura said with a glance at her son, "but I think now, Arthur—"

She beckoned Mrs. Leparge to the glass doors leading into the conservatory. Inside, on the tessellated pavement, Hilda was standing with her back to them.

Mrs. Leparge looked at her for a moment.

"Oh, her hair is just the same shade as my sister Cecile's!" She opened the door in spite of Lady Laura's warning gesture. "Hilda, my darling Hilda!" she cried.

At the first sound of her name Hilda turned quickly, and then stood still, her hand on her heart, her breath coming and going in long palpitating gasps. As Mrs. Leparge hurried towards her she looked at her with frightened eyes, the pupils dilated by emotion.

"Are—are you my mother?" she asked faintly.

Mrs. Leparge, who had hastened forward at first with an air of assured confidence, now appeared to hesitate, her steps faltered, and, as Hilda stood waiting in an attitude of intense expectation, with a low moan Mrs. Leparge dropped into one of the seats.

"Oh, no, no, no! It is not my Hilda—it is a stranger! Oh, my child, my child, where are you?"

Startled, shocked apparently, Hilda did not move forward, but stood motionless, statue-like in her white dress, save that her lips were moving inaudibly.

Sir Arthur hurried to her.

"Hilda, I—"

Lady Laura turned to Mrs. Leparge, disappointment in every line of her face, in every inflection of her voice.

"Do I understand that you have made a mistake— that this is not your daughter?"

Mrs. Leparge's slight form was still shaking with sobs.

"Ah, no, no! Yet she is so like, so like!" drying her eyes. "No wonder my agent made the mistake! You must forgive me, Lady Laura, for all the trouble I have given you."

She moved as if to turn away; but Hilda, who had been listening as if frozen into stillness, taking absolutely no notice of Arthur's attempts at consolation, now walked towards her.

"Tell me, tell me!" she cried. "Are you my mother?"

Mrs. Leparge looked at her mournfully.

"Alas, my child, you are not my Hilda! Where can she be, poor unhappy darling, I dare not think!"

Hilda caught her hands.

"Oh, look—look carefully!" she cried. "Do be quite, quite sure. I want my mother so badly, so very badly. Oh, shall I never know—will it always be like this?"

"Hilda dear," Mavis began, while Arthur endeavoured unsuccessfully to draw the girl away.

Mrs. Leparge's whole face quivered as Hilda clung to her.

"I wish you were my child," she said as she took the girl in her arms. "There! There, dear, you have lost your mother and I have lost my daughter; we ought to be able to comfort one another." She drew her to one of the garden seats and looked at the others. "She is overcome and disappointed, poor girl!" she said pitifully. "She can hardly realize that she has not found her mother; yet her disappointment can hardly be so great as mine. I think perhaps if I talk to her for a little while she will realize that. Won't you, dear? You see, my little daughter—"

Already Hilda seemed quieter and rested more calmly in Mrs. Leparge's arms. Lady Laura motioned Arthur and Mavis to the other end of the conservatory.

"She will be better in a few minutes," she whispered. 'Poor girl, it is upsetting for her!"

They stood in a little group by the door, while Mrs. Leparge still held Hilda closely and talked to her in low, caressing tones. The purport of her words did not reach them, but they saw that Hilda was gradually becoming quieter, and that though her face was pale her manner was more composed when Mrs. Leparge rose.

Mavis went softly towards them.

"Remember, it must be done and without delay," she heard the widow say impressively, as she bent forward and kissed Hilda.

The words and the tone alike struck Mavis as a little odd.

"What is that you are recommending Hilda to do, Mrs. Leparge?" she asked in some curiosity.

The widow turned; for one instant Mavis fancied that she detected a shade of discomposure in her manner.

"I beg your pardon, Miss Hargreave. I had no idea you were there. I was just telling this poor child that she must make up her mind to cease fretting and trying to find out what is evidently concealed from her for some wise purpose and be very thankful that she has found so kind a home. She will make herself ill if she goes on this way, and that will not mend matters. Now, my dear, I must say good-bye. I hope that good news will come to us both soon."

Hilda suffered, rather than responded to, her embrace; there was an odd passivity about her whole manner; her eyes looked dazed and her colour had for the nonce deserted her.

Mrs. Leparge glanced back longingly as she walked up the conservatory with Lady Laura.

"Poor girl! I really do not know what to say to you, Lady Laura, or how to apologize for the trouble I have caused you. I can see now that I did wrong in coming myself instead of leaving things to the inquiry office, but I can only plead a mother's anxiety for her only child, which I am sure you can understand and sympathize with."

"I can indeed," Lady Laura responded as she allowed her visitor to precede her through the drawing-room door. "It does seem strange that there should be two cases so much alike."

"Yes, does it not? But I am beginning to be terribly afraid that my own daughter is with that man, James Duncan, as he called himself. It makes me shiver when I think of her and what her fate might be."

Mavis sat down beside Hilda.

"What was she saying to you, Hilda? It did not sound like that sort of advice, I fancied."

Hilda looked at her with dazed, bewildered eyes.

"I—I hardly know," she said hesitatingly. "The usual sort of thing, I think—that I ought not to fret, but to be patient and wait till it is Heaven's will to restore me to my friends. She meant to be very kind, I am sure; but she does not understand—nobody understands how terrible it is to have only the black darkness behind one."

"What particular bent has your mind taken this morning, may I ask?" said Arthur, seating himself beside Hilda.

Hilda did not move when he laid his hand over hers; her eyes still looked listlessly in front of her.

"I do not think I shall ever find my mother; I do not think I shall ever recover my memory," she said hopelessly in a low monotonous tone. "Arthur, you must let me go away now. I will—"

"You will stay here," Sir Arthur interrupted. "What did Dr. Grieve tell you the other day? It is only a matter of time, and then you will be restored to your mother and your friends. Do not talk of going away, Hilda. What should I do without you?" He raised her cold hand to his lips as he spoke.

It was the first open caress on which he had ventured in his mother's presence, and that lady frowned.

"As for finding Hilda's mother," she said shortly, "I am inclined to think that she has no near relatives; it is inconceivable that if she had, some inquiry about her should not have been made before now, as Mrs. Leparge says."

"At any rate," Mavis interposed," I do not think that Hilda has had any loss in discovering that Mrs. Leparge is not related to her. I took a dislike to her at once."

"To Mrs. Leparge!" Lady Laura echoed in surprise. "Oh, Mavis, my dear, how absurd! I thought her particularly charming."

"I did not!" Mavis maintained stoutly. "I did not like her face one little bit; and she had such a curious sidelong way of looking at one. Never once did she meet a glance fully. Didn't you notice it?"

"No, I did not!" replied Lady Laura tartly. "I think you are becoming very fanciful, Mavis. You should try to cure yourself of it, child; it is a very bad habit. I was feeling too sorry for the poor woman's disappointment to criticize her. Poor thing, it is too terrible for her, after being so hopeful."

Mavis was not to be disposed of so easily, and her brown eyes looked mutinous.

"Mrs. Leparge's eyes were quite dry, though she put her handkerchief to them so much. I noticed them," she said sceptically. "And I thought the way she was talking to Hilda was rather a curious one. Still it doesn't matter; we shall not be likely to see any more of her in future."

"No; but it is very wrong to allow oneself to be prejudiced against people by absurdities like that—things that probably exist only in your own imagination," Lady Laura said severely.

Poor lady, she was feeling distinctly out of gear with the whole world this morning. Her hope had been that with Hilda's belongings some barrier to her marriage with Sir Arthur might have been discovered, and, disappointed of this, it was a relief to vent her vexation upon some one.

"Garth says that that sort of thing is an instinct given us for our protection!" Mavis retorted. "He says that he has known of cases in which it has proved—"

Sir Arthur burst into a brotherly laugh.

"Oh, Garth says!" he mimicked. "But Garth is not quite such an authority to all of us as he is to you, my dear Mavis."

Chapter Sixteen

"WELL, IT is about as queer a go as I ever heard of. I can't see daylight in it at all yet, but one thing I am clear about, that there's more in the affair than meets the eye—a great deal! Some of us will be surprised before we hear the last of it, I'm thinking!" Superintendent Stokes stroked his chin thoughtfully as he looked up at the Manor House. "I just wonder if it was her or not?"

Lost in thought, he remained stationary for a few minutes. The night was dark and cloudy; little scuds of rain beat in the superintendent's face every two or three minutes; a mild westerly wind was rising and rustling the leaves.

Suddenly there was a quick step behind him, a strong hand was laid on his shoulder.

"What are you doing here, my man?"

Superintendent Stokes wrenched himself free.

"I beg your pardon, Sir Arthur!" he said as he recognized his assailant.

"Oh, is it you, Stokes? Why are you prowling about here at this time of night? I am sure I don't know what people may be taking you for if they see you. Anyhow, you may be quite sure that they will be pretty well scared. Have you heard the latest reports—that Mary Marston haunts the shrubbery and grounds? My sister and Miss Hilda"—Arthur brought out the Christian name with some hesitation; it was distinctly awkward, he often found, to have to speak of some one without a surname—"both declare they saw her the other night. I don't believe I could get either of them in the shrubbery after midnight for a king's ransom."

The superintendent nodded, still surveying the lighted windows of the house before him.

"Ay, I have heard of the ghost, Sir Arthur! I reckon there is not many in Lockford that haven't, as far as that goes. About the young ladies, I think you are mistaken, Sir Arthur. I am pretty well sure I saw one of them not many minutes ago."

"What, here alone in the dark!" Sir Arthur exclaimed incredulously. "You are out this time, Stokes; I am sure my sister would not venture—"

Superintendent Stokes paused a moment before speaking and scraped up the dry leaves into a little heap at his feet.

"I didn't say it was Miss Hargreave," he said in a deliberate tone at last, "and I didn't say she was alone."

There was a pause. Sir Arthur's face was very stern.

"What do you mean, Stokes?"

The superintendent took off his cap and held up his face to the cool, damp air with a sigh of relief.

"I saw somebody out here a quarter of an hour ago, Sir Arthur, somebody talking to a young man; I am pretty sure that it was the strange young lady. I wondered at the time what she was doing out here."

"A quarter of an hour ago!" Arthur exclaimed wrathfully. "Why, a quarter of an hour ago I was sitting with the ladies myself before I came out for a smoke, so I know that it is a mistake!"

"A quarter of an hour, more or less, I take it to be, Sir Arthur, though I did not look at my watch," the superintendent returned stolidly. "But if she was with you it could not have been the young lady—wearing a dark dress she was, and I thought I caught the gleam of her yellow hair."

"Miss Hilda has a long clinging white thing on to-night."

"Seems as it couldn't be her, then," concluded the superintendent. "Must have been one of the maids out with her young man, I suppose. It was this business of the ghost that brought me up here, Sir Arthur. To my mind it wants looking into."

"The business of the ghost brought you up!" echoed Sir Arthur in amazement. "Why, Stokes, you can't mean that you put any faith in such rubbish?"

Superintendent Stokes permitted himself a short laugh.

"I can't say as I do—not as ghosts, Sir Arthur, but they have a value of their own in a case like this disappearance of Nurse Marston."

"I believe Nurse Marston is hiding somewhere, and coming out at night to frighten people," Sir Arthur cried wrathfully. "Let me catch her, that is all, and I will—"

Stokes so far forgot his dignity as to emit a low whistle.

"What on earth has put that in your head, Sir Arthur? Mary Marston is not in hiding at Lockford—not alive," he said significantly. "You can take my word for that."

Sir Arthur shrugged his shoulders.

"Well, I am not inclined to accept the ghost theory."

"I never believed in a ghost yet, and I don't think that I am going to start now," said the superintendent placidly.

"Bless you, man! What do you think then? If it was neither Mary Marston in the flesh nor in the spirit, what was it?"

"Was there anything at all, Sir Arthur?" The superintendent's tone was oddly eager, or so the young baronet fancied.

"Oh, as to that, I do not fancy there can be any question!" he said decidedly. "My sister is not a likely person to imagine anything of the kind, and she saw her distinctly."

"Umph! Well, it is a strange case, and I don't know what to make of it," said Stokes. "I should be glad to clear it up, if only for Mrs. Marston's sake; the old woman is fretting herself to death for her daughter."

"I have sometimes thought that she may have been persuaded into taking some long journey and lost her memory in the same sort of way as Miss Hilda has," Sir Arthur went on meditatively.

Dark though it was, Stokes gave a quick glance towards him.

"Perhaps she may, Sir Arthur," he assented placidly. "But about this ghost; I should like to watch for it a bit longer, if you have no objection. I have a fancy that, if I could see it, it might clear things up for me a bit."

"Well, watch as long as you like," Sir Arthur agreed as he walked away. "I shall be glad to hear the result if you meet with any. Good night."

"Good night, Sir Arthur!"

Left alone, Superintendent Stokes judiciously stepped behind a clump of trees.

"I don't suppose I could be seen—it is too dark," he remarked inwardly. "Still, one never knows."

He had been standing there for some little time when he caught a whiff of tobacco and heard footsteps on the path. They stopped short of his hiding-place, and as the Superintendent peered forth cautiously he heard a woman say:

"No, I wouldn't come a step farther, not if it was ever so, Jim. I daren't. I should be frightened I might see her again."

"More silly you!" The superintendent fancied the voice was not very brave. "We'll stay here then. Now, Minnie, I want you to promise me that as soon as this jollification is over you will be ready for me."

"Oh, I don't know, Jim! I can't promise!"

The superintendent, looking a little farther, fancied that the girl was crying. He had his own private disappointment too, for it seemed to him that the man before him was the one whom, but a few minutes before, he had seen talking to the girl he had taken for Hilda.

"I suppose it must have been this one all the time," he soliloquized. "Yet I made sure it was the other. Well, well! A bit of a hint won't do Sir Arthur any harm, anyway."

He paid a little attention to the pair on the path; very soon he had gathered that the man was pleading for a speedy marriage, which the girl was tearfully refusing, but all this was not particularly interesting to Stokes, with his mind full of a different subject. He had allowed his fancy to travel along an obscure path, and was knitting his brows over a difficult problem he had encountered, when a sentence spoken by the girl roused him effectually from his absorption.

"I can't do it, Jim," Minnie was saying in a voice broken by sobs. "I can't bring myself to it, not until we know what became of her—Nurse Marston."

"Haven't I told you times without number that that has got nothing to do with us where Nurse Marston went?" was the man's reply, impatiently spoken. "You have got to let that alone and make up your mind, Minnie."

"Ah, it is all very well, but I can't get it out of my head that if it hadn't been for me she might have been alive and well now."

A rough exclamation broke from the man.

"Be quiet about it, can't you? I tell you what, Minnie, many a time of late you have pretty near made me lose my patience with you."

"I can't help that," the girl wailed. "It—you don't know how I have been taking on, Jim. I have just sat down and cried and felt like a murderess."

"The more silly you, then," the man said angrily, "What call have you got to say as she is dead, if you come to that, much less as you have anything to do with it?"

"Ah, I have deceived myself long enough!" the girl murmured, with a sob. "I have tried to persuade myself as she would come back again all right after a while, and all the time something was whispering to me that she never would. Now that I have seen her I am sure. You won't shake me, Jim. She pointed at me! I have never known what it is to have one moment's peace, and I don't expect to any more. I wish I was dead, I do!"

"Ugh! Ghost!" the man said contemptuously. "Why should she point at you, pray? You go out and imagine things and then put yourself into this state about them."

"I didn't imagine that," the girl asseverated. "No, I saw her plain enough. It wasn't to say dark, and there she stood. Alice Brown saw her too—she told you she did. As to why she pointed at me—you know, Jim, you know!"

"I don't know what you are driving at," was the sullen answer." It is my belief as this is all an excuse, Minnie, and the truth of the matter is that you are hankering after that Greyson still."

"I am not—you know I am not!" Minnie cried indignantly. "It is only—"

"Well, if you are sure," the man said slowly, "I promised not to tell, but I can trust you, Minnie. Listen!"

There was a pause; the superintendent, craning forth a little further, could just make out through the darkness that the two heads were close together, that the girl was whispering to her lover. A not unreasonable disappointment overtook him; it might be that the very clue to the mystery which he was seeking lay there at his hand, and he was unable to avail himself of it. At length, while he was still impatiently chafing at his inability to hear, Minnie laughed aloud.

"So that was it?"

"That was it," the man replied. "Now, Minnie, don't you go fidgeting yourself over it again."

"Oh, no," the girl said in a satisfied tone." I shall be only too glad to put it out of my head, Jim."

"You'll think about fixing the day?" the man pleaded. "I can't wait much longer, Minnie."

"Well, I won't promise," the girl responded coquettishly, "but—"

She paused; the clock was striking.

"Ten!" she said in alarm. "Why, I don't know what Mrs. Parkyns will say!"

"I was to be at the house at ten o'clock," the man interrupted. "Sir Arthur was coming to speak to me. He may be a bit late, but I must run. You won't be afraid to go back alone, Minnie? You see, if I kept Sir Arthur waiting—"

"Oh, I shall not be a bit afraid now," the girl said cheerfully, "now I know there's no call to be! You make haste, Jim."

They separated, and the superintendent, watching them, saw the man hurry off round the corner of the house. Minnie turned back towards the kitchen entry.

Superintendent Stokes came to a sudden resolution, and stepping quickly forth from the shadows, he laid his hand on her shoulder. The girl shrieked aloud, nor did her terror seem allayed when she recognized him.

"Oh, it's the superintendent! What were you wanting with me?"

"Only just to have a little chat with you," he said blandly. "It is Miss Spencer, Miss Hargreave's maid, isn't it? Ah, I thought so! Just the person I wanted! There is a question—"

"I haven't any time to answer questions now," Minnie said, with a sulkiness underlying which there was an element of fear, as the superintendent was quick to discover. "If I am not back in a minute Mrs. Parkyns will be fine and angry."

The superintendent kept pace with her hurried steps.

"Maybe, then, I had better come in with you and tell Mrs. Parkyns how things are, and that I have a question or two to put to you," he suggested as they crossed the stable-yard and came in sight of the brightly-lighted kitchen entrance. "Perhaps that will be best; we shall be quieter than we should be out here."

Minnie stopped suddenly and faced him.

"Pretty talk there would be if you were to do anything of the kind, as you know, Mr. Stokes! Will you tell me what you want to know?"

The superintendent stood with his back to the open door, and by the light from the inside he could see the girl's face, while his own remained in shadow.

"I want to know first why you think you are as good as Mary Marston's murderess?"

The girl shrank back as if he had given her a blow.

"You—you were listening?" she gasped.

"It would be as well for you to keep a civil tongue in your head, young woman. If I am taking a walk in the shrubbery of an evening, me being employed on business as brings me there by Sir Arthur, and you and your young man choose to stand there talking out loud and taking no heed who is about—well, you must expect to have your words brought up against you, that is all I can say; and naturally, me being looking into this case of Mary Marston, when I hear a young woman say that often and often when she thinks of Nurse Marston she feels like a murderess—why, I come to her to know what she means by it."

"I never harmed Nurse Marston," said Minnie shortly, "and I don't believe anyone else did either."

He glanced at the bright, defiant eyes, at the hot red spots that were beginning to burn on her white cheeks.

"Why should you feel like a murderess, then?" he asked in the crisp, concise manner that was familiar to subordinates.

Minnie paused.

"Because I was a fool," she burst out at last. "It was me as took her message from my lady as she was to go to the small library, and it was me as showed her the way there, and if she hadn't gone there none of this might have happened."

The superintendent looked at her.

"I don't see that you have any call to blame yourself for that."

"Don't I tell you that I was a fool to think about it?" said Minnie testily. "But there, ever since that cuff was found I have had it on my mind as I was the one to take her the message. Then when we saw her the other night in the shrubbery, me and Alice Brown, she pointed at me. I thought as it was her ghost then; but now I feel sure that it was her herself."

"What has made you change your mind?"

Minnie fidgeted.

"I don't believe in ghosts."

"Sensible girl!" he commented gravely. "What has made you feel sure that there are no such things as ghosts?"

Minnie moved her head as if his steady glance embarrassed her.

"Oh, sometimes I think one thing and sometimes another!" she said evasively. "We are all alike for that, I expect."

"Just so! just so!" he assented suavely; then with an oblique glance, "It wasn't for instance, anything that Jim Gregory said to you just now that brought you round to his way of thinking?"

"Said to me!" Minnie repeated. "Why, what should Jim Gregory have to say to me about it?"

"Ah, that is for you to tell me!" parried Superintendent Stokes. "You and him had got your heads pretty close together when he was talking to you."

He fancied a shade of relief flitted over the girl's face, and she even smiled slightly as she looked down.

"Bless you, Mr. Stokes, do you think it was of Mary Marston we were talking then?" she asked coyly. "It—we have other matters to think about, Jim and me, we are going to have our banns put up a month on Sunday. If that is all you want to know I must be going in, or I shall get into trouble."

"You can't tell me any more?"

"Haven't I told you I can't?" she retorted. "You'll get no more out of me if you keep me here until midnight."

"Ah, well, I shall not do that," he said carelessly. "We will have another little talk one day before long, Miss Spencer. Good night."

He stood still a little while after she had left him.

"That girl is telling lies," he ruminated. "Why, I wonder? I can't see how she could be mixed up in it. I may have been on the wrong scent all this time, but it don't seem likely. However, I will look Miss Minnie Spencer up a bit; and while I am about it"—he pulled his lower lip out thoughtfully—"I shall devote a little of my attention to Mr. Jim Gregory also. I wish he had whispered in my ear instead of in Minnie Spencer's!"

Chapter Seventeen

"I HOPE it will be fine for Tuesday, Miss Mavis."

"So do I, Mrs. Grogram, indeed!" Mavis replied. She was standing in Lockford Street, a little basket in her hand; for the nonce she was acting as Lady Laura's deputy and distributing the tickets for her various charities. Mrs. Grogram, a lady of independent views and the parent of a numerous progeny, was leaning over her garden gate in a *négligé* costume. "I don't know what we shall do if it be wet," Mavis went on. "Certainly there will be the tents, but you will be crowded up all of you."

"Ay, and tents isn't everything if it rains!" remarked Mrs. Grogram, whose disposition was apparently pessimistic. "I mind how when I was staying with my cousin and we went to Squire Mayhew's harvest home it set on to pour, and after about half an hour it come through the marquee, as they called it, just as if it was running through a sieve."

"Well, we must hope that ours will be made of stouter stuff," said Mavis with a laugh. "You'll bring Tommy, won't you, Mrs. Grogram. My brother wants the children particularly."

"Which I call very good of him, m'm, and him having none of his own. Oh, yes, I shall bring Tommy! Mr. Garth Davenant'll be coming down, I reckon, Miss Mavis?"

Mavis's colour deepened.

"He will be at the Court to-morrow."

"Ah, I thought we should have him over, though it doesn't seem long since he went away! As I said to Grogram when he said maybe Mr. Garth would not be able to spare the time, 'Bless you, Grogram,' I says, 'he'll make time for that! Do you think he'd leave Miss Mavis alone with all the folk going in and out of the Manor, and all Sir Arthur's friends about?' Nice looking young gentlemen too, some of them, I'll be bound! No, he won't give them a chance of cutting him out!"

In spite of a touch of vexation Mavis laughed aloud.

"I don't think he is coming because he thinks I am not to be trusted, Mrs. Grogram, but because he knows that I shouldn't enjoy it a bit if he were not there."

"Ay, do you think so, indeed, miss? Well, we are all like that one time or another," Mrs. Grogram replied indulgently. "As for Mr. Garth," she added more critically, "I am not going to say but he is a fine figure of a man, but as far as looks go he isn't a patch on poor Mr. Walter. The last big 'do' as you may call it, as we had down in these parts was when he come of age, wasn't it, miss?

Mavis looked grave.

"I suppose it was," she said hesitatingly, "but that was when my uncle was alive, before we lived here, and I was only a child then."

"Were you really, miss? I am sure no one would think it to see the well-grown young lady you are now," Mrs. Grogram observed complimentarily. "Then you never see Mr. Walter, miss? But there, it wasn't long after that that it all happened. I shouldn't wonder if it don't bring it back to Mr. Garth though. The good lady as come down last week is over again for the coming of age, I suppose, miss?"

"What good lady?" asked Mavis mechanically. Her thoughts had strayed far away from Mrs. Grogram and were busy with that tragedy of old.

"The one as come here thinking she might know something about the young lady, Miss Hilda, as they call her."

Mavis frowned. Though of late, unconfessed even to herself, an element of distrust had crept into her feeling for Hilda, still loyalty to her brother demanded that Mrs. Grogram's disparaging tone, when speaking of his fiancée, should be checked.

"Oh, you mean Mrs. Leparge!" she said coldly. "No, she is not likely to be here—in fact, poor lady, she is probably too much occupied to find the time."

"Oh, no!" Mrs. Grogram said confidently. "She has got time enough, miss. She is staying down here now. An hour or so ago I had occasion to go up to Farmer Townson's, and I come across her talking to Miss Hilda over by the Home Wood."

Mavis looked surprised.

"I think you must be mistaken, Mrs. Grogram."

"Mistaken! Me, miss!" Mrs. Grogram's tone was righteously indignant. "'Tain't often as I make a mistake; more by token as I had almost to ask 'em to move to let me get over the stile. This person here, she were telling the young lady she must do something—I don't know rightly what, I'm sure, but I heard her say, 'The rest can be managed, but it remains for you to do your part.' Yes, miss, them was her very words."

"Oh!" said Mavis, feeling distinctly puzzled. "Well, I don't know, I am sure; I had no idea she was likely to be in the neighbourhood again. Perhaps her inquiries after her daughter may have brought her this way."

"Perhaps they may," Mrs. Grogram assented with a sniff as Mavis moved on. "Thank you kindly, miss! I am sure I hope the weather will hold good."

Mavis walked quickly up the lane and into the park. Very bitterly now, watching her brother's growing infatuation for Hilda, was she inclined to regret the introduction of a stranger into their home circle; more especially did she blame herself for yielding to the spell that Hilda's beauty and charm had cast over her.

She dated her first conscious feeling that Hilda was not the wife her brother should have chosen from Mrs. Leparge's visit, and she was by no means inclined to welcome the news that that lady was in the neighbourhood again. She knit her brows as she walked quickly over the short grass, crisp with the first frost of autumn, and tried to recall the events of the last three months in their true sequence, but so much seemed to have happened in them that her brain grew confused. She told herself, looking back, that she could have fancied it a phantasmagoria of bad dreams, in which the only thing that was real was her love for Garth, or, as she whispered with a tender little smile, their love for one another.

Lunch was on the table, and was indeed, being somewhat of an informal meal at the Manor, already in progress when she went into the dining-room. Hilda was looking particularly well, Mavis noticed, as she slipped into the place opposite; the pale blue gown she was wearing was one that had been run together for her by Lady Laura's maid, as Mavis knew, but its very simplicity made Hilda look younger and more girlish. She seemed bright and animated too, and was exchanging gay badinage with Arthur, from whom she glanced off to smile at Mavis.

"What do you say to this new proposal, Mavis—that you and I are to take a day in town to-morrow to choose the presents to be given at the treat next week?"

"It is out of the question for me, I am afraid," Mavis said as the man brought her a plate. "Garth comes down to-morrow. I hear you have met a friend to-day, Hilda."

"A friend!" Hilda looked bewildered. "I don't know what you mean. I think," with a wistful smile, "all the friends I know are in this room at present."

"I heard you had been having a chat with Mrs. Leparge."

"With Mrs. Leparge?" Hilda's amazement became more obvious. "Is she here?"

"Isn't she?" Mavis parried. "Have you not been talking to her?"

"I? Certainly not!"

"What bee have you got in your bonnet now, Mavis?" her brother struck in. "Hilda has not had much opportunity of talking to anybody but me; she has been out with me all the morning, and I think I have taken up most of her time."

"I suppose it was a mistake then," Mavis said, turning, her attention to her lunch. "Mrs. Grogram told me she saw you by the stile going into the Home Coppice, and that you were talking to Mrs. Leparge."

"We went through the Home Wood; I had to speak to Greyson," Sir Arthur said, "but I didn't see Mrs. Grogram."

"Oh, that was it!" Hilda exclaimed with a laugh. "While you went into Greyson's cottage and I was waiting for you, Arthur, a woman—a lady—came up and asked me a lot of questions about the neighbourhood. I was sorry I couldn't give her much information, but I didn't notice that she was like Mrs. Leparge."

"She was a stranger, then?" Mavis said.

"Evidently, because she didn't know her way about. She was asking for Townson's farm, and the directions for that were within my capability. Your Mrs. Grogram must have been a woman who pushed by us rather rudely, with a basket on her arm."

"She doesn't stand much on ceremony," Mavis said with a smile, having a lively recollection of some of the worthy woman's remarks, "but she seemed very sure about Mrs. Leparge. And you say your stranger was not like her?"

"The resemblance did not strike me at the time," said Hilda carelessly; "She was not in widow's dress, you see, which makes such a difference, but she was about Mrs. Leparge's height, and—yes—I did not think of it before, but she may have been a little like her in the face."

Mavis did not pursue the subject. Evidently Mrs. Grogram had made a mistake, she told herself, in spite of her positive words, for what possible motive could Hilda have for denying that she met Mrs. Leparge if she had done so?

Nevertheless the incident had left an unpleasant impression, and she felt by no means sorry when Arthur announced his intention of taking his fiancée for a long spin in the motor, and she was thus left free to follow her own devices.

Motoring, Arthur's latest hobby, had for the last few weeks threatened to supersede both painting and orchids; his new car was at present a source of unmixed joy, and so safely had he hitherto come through the perils inseparable from acting as his own chauffeur that even Lady Laura was becoming accustomed to seeing him depart without a single qualm.

Hilda looked particularly charming in her motor array, Arthur thought as he helped her into the car. Like himself, she disdained goggles, and the little pull-on hat which she wore, which pulled low down over her forehead, enhanced rather than concealed her brilliant complexion.

At first their progress was all that could be desired. The Manor was soon left miles behind, and Sir Arthur was loud in his praises of his new toy; then, as, regardless of regulation speed, they were swinging along over a fine stretch of level road, there was a whir, a crash, and the car came to a stop with a suddenness that sent Sir Arthur against the front of the motor.

"Something's wrong!" he said with a rueful countenance as he recovered himself.

Hilda laughed mischievously, though for one moment the colour had deserted her cheeks.

"That is certainly pretty obvious," she said.

Sir Arthur made no comment as he bent over the machine and carefully investigated various nuts and cranks.

"It will take some time, I am afraid," he said at last.

"Fortunately we are near Overdeen, and the smith there is an intelligent sort of man and, moreover, has had a good deal of practice on breakdowns. I dare say he will be able to help me. In the meantime"—he glanced perplexedly at Hilda—"there is the village inn, and Mrs. Medway is a very decent clean sort of person. If you would let me take you there while we put this thing to rights, I dare say she would get you a cup of tea."

"Delicious!" Hilda exclaimed, springing out and accepting the situation with equanimity. "But you will have to let me go alone. You can't leave the car."

"The car will not move," Arthur said grimly. "Anybody who puts that in working order before I get back will deserve the thing for his pains. Come, if you can manage it—the house is by those trees."

Mrs. Medway, the smiling buxom hostess of the Red Lion, received them with open arms. She placed a private sitting-room at their disposal, and while Sir Arthur went off to interview the smith she entertained Hilda with graphic descriptions of the different accidents that had occurred in the neighbourhood.

Finally, when Sir Arthur appeared with the tidings that the smith had declared himself fully capable of managing the repairs alone, Mrs. Medway placed a luxurious tea before the young couple and left them alone.

Sir Arthur's eyes dwelt lovingly on Hilda as she poured out the tea and handed it to him.

"I wonder what sort of a dinner that good woman thinks we should eat if we ate all the good things she has provided?" he said with a laugh. "Ah, Hilda, this is like a foretaste of the times that are coming!"

"As to quantity, do you mean?" Hilda inquired demurely.

"You know what I mean!" he went on passionately. "Of the life that we are going to share together—-of the time when we shall be alone, Hilda."

The girl bent her face over the tea-cup.

"Ah! If it comes—"

"Do not say 'if'," he cried. "Hilda, you do not know what this means to me."

The girl raised her eyes.

"Do I not? Oh, Arthur! You must not ignore the condition I made. When my memory comes back—"

Arthur caught her hand.

"Memory! Memory!" he echoed in a low deep tone. "It is not your memory I want—it is you yourself, the woman I love. When you are my wife, Hilda, I too shall have no memory, for I shall remember nothing but the fact that you are mine and that we are together."

Hilda bit her lip nervously.

"Oh, I wish I could remember—if I only knew my name—who my friends were!"

"Why do you wish for other friends?" Arthur cried, pressing his lips to the hand he still held. "Am I not enough for you? Sweetheart, you have filled my life so entirely that I want no one but you! Day after day I ask myself if it can really be true—if this wonderful thing had really happened to me—that you are indeed my own!"

Hilda drew her hand away nervously as she averted her face. Sir Arthur could see that she was very pale, but her very coldness only rendered her more attractive in his eyes.

"Darling," he pleaded, "don't turn from me! If I could only make you understand how in you everything seems completed for me! There is only one thought in my mind all day—one word fills my life, and that word is—Hilda!"

Hilda glanced round once more; her face was still pale, but a suspicion of mirth gleamed in her eyes and played round the curves of her mobile lips.

"How about the car, and the orchids, and the Elaine?" she asked mischievously. "No, no, Arthur, your heart is not like the letter-lock of your safe! It will open for more words than one."

For a moment Arthur looked distinctly aggrieved. That Hilda was not a demonstrative girl, that she was inclined apparently rather to scoff at his sentiment when they were alone, he had long since discovered, but he told himself that it was a girlish caprice, that she was only delaying the day of complete surrender, and his face brightened.

"Don't you understand how outside one's life all those things are? Hilda—"

"Is the only combination for which the key will turn," she said as she laughed, though the man saw that her slender hands were trembling and took courage. "Are you sure, Arthur? Suppose I tried orchids or motor or Elaine?"

"Elaine means Hilda to me," he smiled, entering into the spirit of her jest. "You might try that and be successful."

"Isn't it strange?" Hilda said abruptly, her mind evidently wandering from Sir Arthur's love-making. "I know I have seen one of those letter-locks before, and I cannot tell where or what the word was. I wonder whether it was the same as yours?"

"Hardly likely, I think," Sir Arthur said quickly. "Don't try to remember, Hilda. Memory is more likely to come back if you do not try to strain it."

Already the look of helpless bewilderment that he had learned to dread was coming into the girl's face; she leaned forward and put her hands over her eyes.

"Oh, I thought the cloud was lifting then! Just for a moment I seemed to have a vision of what had been — and—now—now it is all dark again!"

Sir Arthur felt desperate—consolation seemed impossible when these moods of depression overtook Hilda. He laid his hand on her shoulder.

"It will come all right some day."

The girl stirred impatiently.

"It—I seemed to see it all then; and now, with the letters, it has all faded away. But it is near—so near. Arthur"—looking at him with eyes once more filled with tears—"if I could only remember that word I feel sure that everything would come back, and something seems to tell me that it is the same as yours."

"I do not think it is very likely, dear. Ours is a very ordinary little word, and so far as I know it has never been altered."

Hilda's lips quivered pitifully.

"If I could only find out, Arthur! If you love me, help me—tell me yours."

My darling, it has always been kept a dead secret, and it could not possibly—"

Hilda's face seemed to quiver all over into sobs.

"Such a little thing, and you said you loved me; and it is so near—so near! Then all would be clear, and we could be happy as we never can be till I know."

"Hilda, dearest!" Arthur bent over her.

She pushed him away and buried her face in her hands.

"Oh, how can I make myself remember? It will kill me!"

Arthur put his arms round her and drew her, still resisting, to his heart.

"If the word will help you, sweetheart, you shall know it. And after all it is not breaking the rule, for you and I are to be one—you are to be my second self!"

"Yes, yes!" Hilda whispered, her arms stealing for one instant round his neck. "Ah, so soon, Arthur— when I know!"

"It is such a simple word," Arthur went on; "just 'm—i—n—e'—mine, you see, only we spell it backwards—'e—n—i—m.'—That is all the secret, Hilda. Now does it help you, dear?"

"I don't know. Wait a minute," the girl said slowly, her head still resting on his shoulder, her perfumed hair sweeping across his face and intoxicating his senses. "It—Oh, Arthur, I see a tall man with white hair! I remember him—he was my father, my dear father! And they called him General—General—Oh, it is going! I can't remember—"

There was a knock at the door.

"If you please, Sir Arthur, the man has brought your car round," said Mrs. Medway, discreetly averting her eyes from the young couple, whose confusion was plainly evident. "He says he hopes as you will be able to manage it home all right now."

Chapter Eighteen

"ARE THE Pontifexes coming down?"

"I think so. All our friends have been very kind; but, Garth, though we have looked forward to Arthur's coming of age all this time, now that it is at hand I don't seem to care—it is all spoilt."

Mavis's eyes were very troubled as she glanced up at her tall lover and she watched his dark face anxiously in the pause that followed.

Garth's eyes wandered from her to the other side of the room, where Hilda sat with Sir Arthur, leaning forward in a pretty attitude of attention and listening to him with her eyes fixed on his face, a diamond star, Arthur's latest gift, sparkling in her gleaming hair.

"I am very sorry, dearest," he said slowly at last, "but from the first I have seen that this—this infatuation of Arthur's could only bring trouble."

"Poor mother has to accept it because Arthur is so determined," Mavis went on, "but it is worrying her dreadfully, and she is getting quite thin. She is so disappointed because it means the downfall of her dearest hopes. Still, after all"—in a brighter tone—"one must not always look at the dark side of things. Mother doesn't really dislike Hilda, and if everything should turn out satisfactory about her I dare say she will be happy enough about the match after all."

"I hope so."

But neither Garth's countenance nor tone was expressive of confidence, and the momentary gleam of brightness in Mavis' face faded away.

"You do not think so. Garth, you have not heard— I have not told you that yesterday just for a moment Hilda had a flash of memory?

She remembered her father—a tall old man with white hair—and she said they called him General; but it all faded away before she could remember the name."

"That was unfortunate." A curious smile played for a moment round Garth's mouth. "I gave myself a holiday on Tuesday, Mavis."

The girl looked at him in surprise at the sudden change of subject.

"Did you? Where did you go? I thought you said you were so much occupied just now. Why, you said you were so busy that you could hardly spare the time to come down here!"

"So I was—so I am busy," Garth said imperturbably; "but I was determined to make time for this. I went down to Brighton."

"To Brighton?" Mavis did not look quite pleased.

"Yes. I wonder whether you will be surprised to hear that my visit was to the superintendent of police there."

"Oh, Garth! Does that mean that you have discovered anything—that you have found Hilda's—"

"I found out one thing," Garth went on, "that no daughter of Mrs. Leparge's has disappeared from a Brighton school. The whole story, as far as Brighton is concerned, is an entire fabrication."

"Garth, how could you—"

"It was not difficult. I felt very doubtful of the lady from the first moment I saw her. Her grief for her daughter did not ring true. When I found that no disappearance of the kind had been reported to the police my suspicion that the whole was a made-up story became almost a certainty; but I obtained a list of the ladies' schools in Brighton. There is no Miss Chesterton, but there are a Chester and a Chesham. I called upon both and found, as I had expected, that no Hilda Leparge had been a pupil, and that there had been no disappearance from their schools. The rest of the matter I left in the superintendent's hands. I had his report this morning. No such name is known at any of the Brighton schools, and, in short, he says that if his inquiries have made one thing more certain than another it is that no disappearance in the circumstances related by Mrs. Leparge has taken place at Brighton."

Mavis caught her breath quickly.

"Garth, what does it all mean? What object could she have had in coming here if she had not lost her daughter? I can't understand it."

"Neither can I at present," said Garth in a curiously significant tone. "But we are gathering up the threads, Mavis, and I think it will not be long before the end of this remarkably tangled skein is in our hands."

Mavis did not reply for a minute; she was looking puzzled and worried.

"I—I don't see what you mean, Garth," she said slowly. "I don't see what Mrs. Leparge's coming has to do with Hilda, unless"—thoughtfully—"Hilda has been the victim of some plot, that perhaps Mrs. Leparge has been one of the people who have ill-treated her, that they thought they could get possession of her again, and when she was here she found it hopeless as we should make so many inquiries and so gave it up. Is that what you think, Garth?"

"Not—not exactly," he said slowly. "In fact I should be puzzled to tell you what I do think, Mavis. My feeling is more one of vague suspicion than anything definite."

"Suspicion of Mrs. Leparge?"

"Oh, of her and other people."

Mavis sighed.

"Well, I hope it will all come right some day. Oh, Garth, how I should like to go to sleep and wake up and find that everything was a bad dream—everything that has happened since we dined at the Court, I mean!"

Garth looked out of the uncurtained window—the moon was so bright that, in spite of the electric light, outside things stood out almost as clearly as in the day-time; his eye was caught by a dark bank of clouds near the horizon.

"See, Mavis," he said, directing her attention to it, "those threatening clouds will spread presently and obscure all this moonlit sky, but after a while they will pass, and everything will be bright again. I think our lives are like that—when troubles come they darken and alter the face of the world for us, but some day it will be all clear again." His hand just touched hers. "Can't you believe it, Mavis?"

The girl's eyes looked up at him trustingly.

"Oh, yes. I will—I do! But it seems difficult to realize the silver lining when one only sees the cloud."

"Ah, we all feel that!" Garth said absently, his attention once more straying to his future brother-in-law, whose back was towards them, but whose attitude of admiring attention was sufficiently obvious. "Oh, by the way," he went on, "when I was in town I had a regular turn-out, made my man institute a systematic search, and I have found the pouch you worked for me, Mavis, and which the police professed to believe was the one discovered in the small library at the time of Nurse Marston's disappearance. I shall take it in and have a talk with Stokes in the morning."

"Oh, I am glad!" Mavis exclaimed. "I hate you to lose my presents, and Stokes seemed so horrid about it besides. I wonder what Arthur and Hilda will say when they know that Mrs. Leparge's daughter was not lost from Brighton." She raised her voice. "Hilda!"

"Don't say anything about it, don't tell them for the world," Davenant said in a low, emphatic tone, "or you may spoil everything."

The other two looked up in some surprise as he sauntered over to them with some excuse about the latest political *canard*, and Mavis was left alone to puzzle out the mystery of his words.

When Garth rose to take his leave she glanced once more out of the window; the dark clouds of which he had spoken had fulfilled their prophecy in so far as they had spread over the sky. Obscured by them, the moon shone slantwise across the heavens, and even as she watched a vivid flash of lightning almost blinded her for a moment, and nearly simultaneously a crash of thunder seemed to shake the very house. The girls sprang to their feet and looked at one another in consternation.

Sir Arthur turned to the window.

"It is late in the season for such lightning," he remarked. "I wonder if it has struck anything. Garth, my boy, how are you going home? The storm will be upon us directly."

Garth laughed.

"Well, I am not exactly sugar and salt. I drove Gipsy over in the high cart, and I fancy her nerves are pretty well seasoned."

Mavis laid hold of him.

"Well, mine are not," she declared positively. "No, Garth, indeed you are not going out of this house until the storm is over. Do you think I could sleep to-night if I knew that you had been out in such a storm as this promises to be? Besides, this lightning might strike you dead," as another flash lighted up the room. "Oh, no. Indeed, Garth, you must not go!"

"Why, what is this? Garth thinking of going?" Lady Laura, roused by the thunder, was sitting up and rearranging the scrap of lace, called by courtesy a cap, on her hair. "It is out of the question, my dear boy," she went on. "Here you are, and here you must stop until it is fine again. Do you hear that?" as the thunder crashed overhead, and the first few heavy drops amid the stillness that followed heralded a veritable downpour. "That settles it, I think."

Garth smiled in her harassed eyes. The two women's solicitude was very pleasant to him, and though in his heart he felt that Lady Laura was really responsible, from sheer kind-heartedness and lack of worldly wisdom, for much of her own trouble, yet his real affection for her made him long to smooth away the wrinkles from her forehead, the tired lines round her mouth.

"It does sound rather alarming, doesn't it?" he said.

"I will wait a little, if you will allow me, Lady Laura. But you are not afraid of lightning, are you?" as a vivid forked flash lit up the room and she shuddered. "There is no danger really."

"Oh, one never knows! I always feel a little nervous in these old houses; something may catch fire," and Lady Laura glanced round apprehensively.

Garth took her hands in his.

"Oh, it is passing over now. Already the thunder is more distant. Listen! And it had much better come this week than next,
you know."

Lady Laura looked at her son, who was engaged in soothing Hilda's fears.

"Yes, I should have been very sorry if it had spoilt the outdoor
amusements for the poor people," she said listlessly. "But for myself,
as you know, this affair" —nodding at the young people—"has been
such a disappointment that personally I should not care if it rained
cats and dogs the whole time."

Garth hesitated a moment; he glanced round doubtfully. He
and Lady Laura were virtually alone—Mavis, her nervousness
apparently forgotten, had retired to a distant window to watch the
progress of the storm; Arthur and Hilda were well out of earshot.
He bent towards her.

"Would it be any consolation if I told you that I feel almost certain this projected marriage will not come off, Lady Laura?"

Lady Laura sniffed in a melancholy fashion.

"Well, certainly it would, if I could believe that you were speaking
the truth about it, but unfortunately I can't," she replied honestly.
"I know Arthur better than you do, Garth, and I am sure that when
he has once made up his mind he is obstinacy itself. Besides, did
you ever see anyone so infatuated?"

"It was not of any change of mind on Arthur's part that I was
thinking," said Garth slowly. "I fancy that circumstances will inter-
vene. Perhaps you are right not to let me raise your hopes unduly,
dear Lady Laura, for after all it is only a theory of my own."

"Ah, I think I am too unhappy to be cheered up by any theories!"
Lady Laura said with a sigh." Still, it is nice to know that anybody
thinks there is a chance that it may end in smoke. It is good of you
to care, Garth."

"Mavis's mother must be mine too," he responded, and, moved
by a sudden impulse, he stooped and kissed her pale cheek. "I
believe the rain has stopped now; I must be starting, or it will be

coming on again, and I shall be on your hands for another hour." He turned to Arthur. "I think now, Hargreave—"

Mavis held up her hand.

"Who can this be in the avenue so late? How fast the horse is being driven! Do you think it is running away?"

With common consent they all moved nearer the window. Sir Arthur flung it open and leaned out. The cool night air, the fresh, sweet scent of the earth after the rain, filled the room, but outside there was not a movement, not the faintest rustle of wind; everything was still with the absolute silence that presages the coming of another storm.

Plainly now they all heard the sound of which Mavis spoke—the sound of a horse being urged up the avenue at its fullest speed.

With some instinct of impending calamity Mavis turned pale.

"What can it be?" she said.

"The fish for to-morrow's breakfast miscarried," Arthur said lightly.

"A messenger in hot haste with a brief for me," Garth suggested.

Arthur moved back and shut the window.

"Probably a message from some of the tradespeople with respect to the arrangements for next week; but I don't know why we should all stand still to listen to the not unwonted sound of a horse in the drive," ironically.

"It is unusual at this time of night," Mavis said.

"Well, we shall soon know what it is," Garth began.

Hilda laid her hand on her lover's arm.

"Arthur, suppose it should be some one come for me?" with a little sob in her throat.

"Then I shall not let them take you away," he responded playfully, with a loving glance at the girl's flushed cheeks.

Meanwhile the cart had stopped at the front door, thereby disposing of Sir Arthur's suggestions, and there was a loud, insistent peal at the bell.

No one spoke; in the silence the sound of a low-voiced altercation in the hall was plainly audible, and just as Sir Arthur, with an indistinct murmur, moved towards the door, it was opened, and Jenkins, looking curiously disturbed appeared.

"If you please, Sir Arthur," hesitating and stammering, "could you speak to Mr. Grimes, the butcher?"

"Grimes, the butcher!" Arthur exclaimed. "Well, it sounded like a butcher driving, I must say. What does he want with me, Jenkins? Something wrong with his accounts?"

The butler paused.

"No, I don't fancy it is anything of that, Sir Arthur. He—he is waiting in the hall if you could speak to him just for a minute."

Arthur glanced at him curiously a moment.

"Oh, I'll come!" he said in an altered tone. "Garth—"

Lady Laura put him aside.

"What is it, Jenkins? Something is wrong, I'm sure. Not Miss Dorothy—"

A momentary expression of relief crossed Jenkins' face.

"Oh, no, my lady, it is nothing of that kind!"

"Some private affair of Grimes's, I expect." Sir Arthur moved forward.

Lady Laura checked him.

"Then what is it, Jenkins? Speak out!"

The man glanced round as if for inspiration.

"Your ladyship heard that dreadful crash of thunder before the rain began—you saw the lightning?"

"Yes, yes, certainly I did!" Lady Laura said impatiently.

"Do you mean that it has struck something?"

"It struck the Lovers' Oak, my lady—broke a big branch off."

Lady Laura drew a deep breath of relief.

"Was that all, Jenkins?—There was no one there, was there?" she went on, her fears taking a new direction. "Nobody was hurt?"

"No, my lady; nobody was hurt," Jenkins said. "The tree was struck. That was all, my lady."

Garth, watching the man closely, saw that his eyes were glancing uneasily, appealingly, at his master, that his face had an odd look.

"All!" Sir Arthur echoed with a laugh which had something forced in its merriment. "Quite enough, too, I should think, Jenkins! Will the destruction of the Lovers' Oak mean misfortune to the lovers who have plighted their troth beneath its branches and drunk from the Wishing Well, do you think?"

"I couldn't say, I am sure, Sir Arthur." The man's stiff lips smiled in an unmirthful fashion at his master's pleasantry. "Grimes, he came straight away as soon as he heard of it to tell you, Sir Arthur."

"Ah, well, I will come and speak to him, then." At the door Arthur turned with an imperceptible sign to Garth. "We will bring you all the details in a moment, mother."

With a murmured apology to Lady Laura, Garth followed Jenkins.

Chapter Nineteen

As THE door closed behind them Sir Arthur's manner changed.

"Well, Jenkins, out with it! What do all these mysterious signals portend?"

The butler's face looked white and scared.

"If you please, Sir Arthur, I couldn't speak of it before the ladies, but it—but Mr. Grimes there will tell you about it better than I can, Sir Arthur."

Grimes, the Lockford butcher, was standing, cap in hand, near the front door. He was a big, burly man with a thick neck like one of his own oxen; ordinarily his great, clean-shaven face was of a cheerful rubicund hue, but to-night it looked grey, save that in places there were curious purple patches.

He touched his forehead.

"It—I am afraid it is a bad business, Sir Arthur! Mr. Jenkins has likely told you how the Lovers' Oak has been struck by lightning—it has broke away the biggest branch altogether—"

"Yes, yes, I have heard all this!" Sir Arthur interrupted impatiently. "But, though I am sorry enough about the old tree, I can't understand for the life of me why you should all look so tragic about it. If there is anything else to hear, man, tell us without any more beating about the bush."

Mr. Grimes looked around and scratched his head doubtfully.

"It is an awful thing, Sir Arthur," said Grimes, after a pause. "As soon as we saw that flash of lightning and heard the thunder we come out, me and my missis, and looked about us; then young Bill Grogram brought us word as it was the Lovers' Oak as was struck, and we went up to see it, me and a few more. We found the oak was split right down, Sir Arthur, and what we never knowed before at Lockford, speaking for myself, it was hollow, Sir Arthur."

"Well, there is nothing so astonishing about that," said Sir Arthur irritably, "nothing to be so tragic over, that I can see, Grimes. A tree of great size, and an old tree such as that was, often is hollow."

"Ay!" said Grimes slowly, mopping his head with his red handkerchief, and moving his feet about uneasily. "It—it wasn't its being hollow as startled us, Sir Arthur, but—but there was something inside."

"What sort of something?" asked Sir Arthur, his tone catching some of the awe in the butcher's. "What on earth do you mean, Grimes?"

"There was something inside, Sir Arthur," the man repeated slowly and ponderously. "Something—somebody, I ought to say, poor thing! Somebody as must ha' been made away with and put down there to be out of the way. They are saying down in the village—they are saying as it's that poor young woman that's been missing from the Manor since last June—Mrs. Marston's daughter, down at Lockford!"

"What?" Arthur's quick, horrified exclamation went unheeded as a hoarse, strangled shriek rang out behind him, and he turned to see Hilda with ashen face and straining eyeballs falling back apparently in violent hysterics.

With some curiosity as to Grimes's errand, and not conceiving it possible that it required anything in the nature of secrecy, Lady Laura had opened the drawing-room door just in time to hear the last speech.

"What did you say, Grimes? What is that you have found?" Lady Laura cried as Mavis caught Hilda and Arthur ran to help her.

"My lady, I can't say nothing of myself," Mr. Grimes said huskily, "save as it is some poor creature as some brute has rammed down there to be out of the way—leastways all that remains of her. There's them down there as are saying as it is Nurse Marston. I thought as it was nothing but right, seeing as she went away from the Manor, as I should drive up and tell Sir Arthur. Superintendent Stokes, he was coming up as I left, so he will tell us the rights of it all," with unintentional sarcasm. "Tom Greyson, he went off for Dr. Grieve, not as he would be any good, unless it was to speak as to who she was."

"It—it can't be true!" Lady Laura cried piteously. "Who would hurt her? Garth, tell them it is a mistake! Indeed, it is not, it cannot be Nurse Marston!"

Garth's dark face seemed to have caught Grimes's pallor as, in response to this appeal, he came forward.

"This is a terrible thing, Grimes," he began, smoothing back the hair from his brow.

"Terrible it is, you are right, sir," the man returned stolidly.

"Have you any reason for thinking that it is—that the body is that of Nurse Marston, except that she is missing?"

Grimes hesitated and turned his hat about.

"Well, naturally, Mr. Davenant, sir, it were that as made us think of her," he acknowledged frankly. "But though we couldn't recognize her face, poor thing—it were too late for that, and we didn't go for to move her, not till the police and the doctor came—it looked, as far as we could tell, as if she—it had on a nurse's dress."

"Ah!" Half convulsively Lady Laura's hand clenched itself among the foamy chiffon at her breast.

Garth drew forward a heavy oaken chair.

"This has been a great shock for you, Lady Laura, you must rest. Ah, that is right!" as she sank into it. "Now this matter must be seen to without delay. Will you take me back with you, Grimes? The Marstons have been faithful friends of ours. If this should indeed be poor Mary, though I cannot accept that yet, I should like to feel assured that everything possible is done. But perhaps you are on your way somewhere else?" as the man did not reply.

"Well, no, sir; I am going straight back," Grimes said after an appreciable pause. "And I can give you a seat if you want one."

"On second thoughts," Garth said quickly, a shade of hauteur in his tone, "I will drive myself, thanks! We will soon be back with the latest news for you, Lady Laura. Arthur, are you coming with me?" glancing with some distaste at the settle upon which Hilda had been laid and over which Sir Arthur was bending.

"In a minute," he said, looking up. "You are better, are you not, dearest?"

Hilda only moaned feebly by way of reply, but Mavis answered for her.

"Yes, indeed she is. Do go, Arthur; she will be much better alone with me. It was the shock of this horrible thing!" She shuddered violently.

"You see, I feel that I must go," Arthur said reluctantly.

"I think, Sir Arthur, perhaps if you would allow me to attend to the young ladies'—" Mrs. Parkyns' voice said behind him at this juncture.

"Come along, Hargreave!" Garth said impatiently.

But as he paused Hilda raised herself.

"Arthur, didn't I tell you when—when she appeared to us in the shrubbery that she was pointing straight at me? I am no better than a murderess!" hoarsely. "If she had not come here to nurse me she would have been safe now.'

"Eh, dear, eh, dear, Miss Hilda, and how could you help it, I should like to know, and you lying there ill on your bed?" Mrs. Parkyns asked sensibly.

Sir Arthur turned back, but the housekeeper shook her head at him.

"You only excite her, Sir Arthur, but she will be better with us, and maybe you will be able to come back soon and tell her that this is all a mistake."

"Ah, why—why should she have been sent to nurse me?" Hilda wept as Mrs. Parkyns raised her and put some pillows under her. "If it had not been for that—"

"It would have been just the same, Miss Hilda, I shouldn't wonder," Mrs. Parkyns observed. "Miss Mavis, if you could just put your arm under here I could raise her better."

"I cannot understand it!" Arthur said, as he joined Grimes, who was already outside and getting into his cart.

"No more can't we, Sir Arthur; how anyone could bring himself to harm a pleasant body like her, as had always a good word for every one, I can't think. We shall know the rights of it soon now, I hope."

"Ready, Arthur?" Garth's tone was crisp as he took the reins from the groom.

The feeling of oppression had gone from the air now, the threatening storm had apparently passed over for the time being, little puffs of wind were stirring the leaves and dashing the raindrops from the branches into Sir Arthur's face as they drove down the avenue.

"This is an awful thing, Garth!" he began. "The very idea of it has upset Hilda terribly. The poor girl is so sensitive that she fancies that because Nurse Marston was summoned to the Manor to attend to her she is in some way responsible for her fate. I have tried to argue it out of her before, but you saw how little use it was to-night."

"Yes, I saw!" Garth's tone was dry and uninterested apparently. His horse's head absorbed all his attention.

Arthur was silent for a minute.

"I cannot help thinking that we shall find it is all a mistake, and that with their imaginations fired by the story of Nurse Marston's disappearance they have taken some rubbish—there was sure to be lots of it in a hollow tree—for a body, or that it is some other poor thing."

"Do you think so?" Garth said curtly as they passed the lodge.

"Why, yes," replied Arthur. "I can't believe a ghastly thing like that could happen to an inmate of our house and that we should know nothing of it all this time. Though if it really should be Nurse Marston she must have gone out to meet some one."

Garth did not reply, and after waiting a minute or two Arthur proceeded:

"But I don't believe it is; I cannot but think when we get there that we shall find that it is some mistake."

It was impossible to drive very near the Lovers' Oak; at the entrance to the wood they had to get out and make the rest of their way on foot. They were by no means alone; the news had spread like wildfire through the village of Lockford, and, late though the hour was, most of the inhabitants were evidently making their way to the scene.

Around the Lovers' Oak quite a large crowd had already assembled, but were kept back by the police, who were now in possession, and in the middle of the cleared space of ground, Superintendent Stokes and Dr. Grieve were bending over something that lay on the ground—something over which as the doctor rose the superintendent reverently threw a mackintosh sheet. Garth and Arthur made their way through, the people respectfully parting for them.

Arthur beckoned to the superintendent.

"Who—what is it, Stokes?" he asked.

The officer's quick eyes darted from the young man's agitated face to the grave, impassive one of his companion.

"I am afraid that there can be no doubt that it is the missing woman, Sir Arthur. As clear a case of murder as I have ever had to do with, I should say."

"I don't believe it can be Nurse Marston—it must be some mistake!" said Sir Arthur, clinging to his cherished shibboleth of comfort.

The superintendent shook his head.

"I don't think there is much doubt, Sir Arthur."

At this moment Dr. Grieve, who was looking worn and shaken as he helped himself to something from a flask, caught sight of them. He hurried across.

"A terrible thing, this, Sir Arthur—terrible! I—really I don't know what to say about it. Accustomed as I am to seeing a good deal of the seamy side of life, I was not prepared for this; and it has upset me more than I can tell you."

He was moving away, but Arthur buttonholed him.

"You know what they are saying, doctor—that it is Nurse Marston? But—"

"It is Nurse Marston safe enough, Sir Arthur. I attended her for an illness three years ago and I can't be mistaken. She is in her uniform too, and wearing her chatelaine—only the notebook is missing. Yes, it is poor Mary Marston; and if I could get hold of the scoundrel who put her in that tree"—his hands working nervously—"I am an old man, but it would go hard if I couldn't—"

"How could she get there—" Arthur was beginning, and as he spoke four men with a stretcher passed them and made their way to the stricken oak.

Dr. Grieve turned to them, and Sir Arthur watched them with fascinated eyes as they carefully raised the body and laid it on the stretcher. As they moved off on their way to the village mortuary, followed by the police superintendent, Dr. Grieve looked round.

"Who would have thought there was that great hollow in the old Lovers' Oak, Sir Arthur?" he said.

The young man raised himself with a start and glanced across; the proud old tree that had been for years the delight and the trysting-place of Lockford sweethearts presented a sorry spectacle now. One great branch had been torn from the parent tree and lay maimed and broken on the ground, and the big hollow right down the great trunk was plainly visible. Standing there with its gaping, open wound it looked like an accusing witness of the crime and of the secret which the hand of Heaven had brought to light.

"I suppose that if we had ever thought about it at all we might have guessed that it would be hollow."

"Somebody knew, anyhow," the doctor said grimly. "Well, well, poor thing, her troubles are over!"

Garth Davenant moved forward to the tree and examined it, the policeman left in charge walking round with him.

"Who could it have been? How was it done? He must have been a pretty strong man to get her up there alone," Arthur remarked.

The doctor shrugged his shoulders.

"As to how it was done it is impossible to say at present; there will have to be an autopsy."

Sir Arthur's bewilderment and horror seemed to increase.

"For a woman to be done to death outside the Manor, with a houseful of people, as you may say, within earshot, seems to be incredible!"

"Yes, it does!" the doctor assented. "I'm not so sure that it was outside the house, either, mind you, Sir Arthur," he added significantly.

"What do you mean?"

"Well, so far as I can see there is nothing to indicate that she had left the house when she came by her death—nothing at this first cursory examination, you understand. She had on her house shoes and her indoor uniform. She could not have gone far out of the house in such a fashion, if indeed she went at all."

Even by the uncertain light of the lanterns, the old man could see that Sir Arthur's face was white to the lips.

"That could not be, doctor," he said passionately, answering the meaning underlying the speech. "I tell you that it was absolutely impossible that such a deed could have been done in our house."

"What about the screams Miss Dorothy heard?" the old man inquired meaningly. "I am afraid that everything points to the poor thing's being made away with inside the Manor House on the night of the 6th of June."

"I do not believe it," asserted Sir Arthur emphatically. "I can't imagine that anybody could be killed in a few minutes in the small library. Besides, you see what is implied in your theory, doctor—the murderer must have been in the house."

"An inmate for the time being, certainly," the doctor acquiesced. "But do not call it my theory, Sir Arthur. I shall be only too delighted if a different deduction can be drawn from the facts."

"I will have a different deduction drawn if I have anything to do with it," Arthur said quickly. "I shall telegraph to town first thing in the morning for the best detective to be had. Garth, I say," raising his voice, "do stop looking at that tree and come here and see what you think of this idea of Dr. Grieve's. He says he believes that this—this atrocious thing was done in the Manor—in the house itself. What do you say to that?"

"Now, now, my dear sir," the doctor remonstrated as he struggled into his overcoat, "please do not put words into my mouth. I said that I saw no indications of her having been outside the Manor that night in her dress. Neither did I."

"Which means exactly what I said," retorted Sir Arthur hotly. "What do you think, Garth?"

Davenant did not answer for a moment; his face looked haggard and strained.

"I—I hardly know what to think," he said at last, pausing between each word, while his eyes wandered restlessly back to the Lovers' Oak. "In fact, I fancy I have been far too much shocked by the whole affair to have formed any very definite ideas as yet. Are you waiting longer, doctor? There seems to be nothing to stay for."

The policemen were dispersing the loiterers, who in awestricken groups were wending their way homewards.

"Nothing!" Dr. Grieve turned with the two young men.

Garth held his cigar-case towards him.

"Please help yourself, doctor."

"No thanks. Not to-night!" Dr. Grieve's manner was brusque.

Davenant looked at him in some surprise.

"Why, doctor, I have heard you say that a smoke was the best thing for the nerves."

"Yes," the old man said gruffly as they reached the waiting conveyances, and he prepared to get into his brougham, "but I don't feel like it now, Mr. Davenant. I dare say I shall have a whiff of pipe before I turn in."

"Obstinate old man!" Arthur ejaculated as he and Garth drove off. "Now he will put into people's heads that this horrible deed was done in the Manor, which, as I tell him, is an impossibility. If that notion is to get about there is no knowing what harm may be done to Hilda, just as she is recovering too. She has such a sensitive nature, poor girl; and my mother—But how could it have been done, Garth? Do you think she stepped out of doors and some wandering tramp—"

"I don't imagine so," Garth said shortly. "But—Good heavens!"

A sudden turn in the road had brought them within sight of Mrs. Marston's cottage, and by the light of the moon, which was now shining brightly, they could see a group of villagers surrounding the old woman at the garden-gate.

As Garth pulled up the horse there was a chorus of exclamation, but one weak, quavering voice made itself heard above the rest.

"Mr. Garth! Mr. Garth, you will have heard—"

With a muttered word or two of apology, Garth threw the reins to Arthur and jumped out.

"I have heard, nurse"—going back to the name of his childish days—"and I cannot tell you how grieved I am for you."

"They have killed her—my Mary!" the poor woman wailed. "I knew that—my dreams had told me. She has been so near me all this time; and now they have carried her past the cottage—her own little home—and they've took her to the mortuary, and they say I'm not to see her—not me, her mother. I will, for all of them!" and she made a few steps forward.

Garth put his arm round her; then he turned to Arthur.

"Drive on, Hargreave, please, and send the cart back for me; I must stay a while here."

As Arthur touched the whip and the horse started he saw that, clinging to his arm as he bent his tall head to hers, the old woman was letting Garth lead her home.

Chapter Twenty

LOCKFORD Street presented an unwonted appearance; at every cottage door the inhabitants were standing in twos and threes discussing this dreadful deed that had been done in their midst. Round the Hargreave Arms quite a crowd assembled, while inside the accommodation of the long room known locally as the club-room was taxed to the uttermost by all those whose position entitled them to be present.

The inquest was to be opened that day, and public interest in the proceedings was at fever heat. The progress of the jury across to the mortuary to view the body had been watched with interest by a crowd of onlookers, and their different appearance as they emerged was freely commented upon. Now, however, a fresh rumour was going round—one that for exciting public attention had eclipsed all previous reports.

Sam Grooms, the youth with whom the rumour apparently originated, was for the time being the centre of attention, and even the advent of the closed carriages from the Manor containing Lady Laura and her daughter passed almost unnoticed.

"I don't believe it, Sam Grooms. He'd never go for to do a thing of that sort."

"Believe it or not, as you like," was the response of Mr. Samuel Grooms, a clumsy hobbledehoy just passing out of his teens. "I don't say as it's true. I had it from Jim Levett, him as is own cousin to Constable Jones."

"What was it as he said?" this from a new-comer to the group.

"Why, he would have it as there was a note found in her pocket from Mr. Garth Davenant asking her to slip out and meet him outside the Manor that night."

There was a subdued sound of horror.

"If he did ask her to meet him it don't prove as he had anything to do with what followed," remarked one voice, bolder than the rest.

Meanwhile in the club-room matters were progressing. Evidence of identity was given both by Dr. Grieve and by the dentist whom poor Mary Marston had employed, and was further corroborated by the marks on her clothes and by her dressmaker. Questioned as to the cause of death, Dr. Grieve, who had conducted the autopsy in conjunction with two well-known surgeons, gave it as his opinion that death had undoubtedly resulted from suffocation, though proof of this was difficult to obtain.

Sir Arthur was seated beside the Coroner, while Garth Davenant, who was accompanied by the family solicitor, had placed himself near the reporters' table. He was looking unwontedly pale as he listened to the evidence.

In the landlady's private sitting-room Mavis, awaiting her turn to be called as a witness, was pacing up and down in a state of intense nervous excitement, while Lady Laura lay back on the couch and tearfully inhaled smelling salts.

"I can't realize it, Mavis," she repeatedly exclaimed.

The girl's hands were tightly locked together, her brown eyes looked strained, the pupils were intensely dilated.

One report which had been communicated to her that morning by an officious housemaid Mavis had so far contrived to keep from her mother. It was that a letter from Garth Davenant, supposed to be of an incriminating character, had been found upon the dead woman, but her own nerves had been terribly upset by the rumour. Unutterably as she had dreaded having to give her evidence, she yet felt now as though, if the moment were delayed long, the tension would be too much for her, and it was with a sigh of relief that she greeted her brother when he came to fetch them.

Arthur was secretly relieved.

"That is plucky, Mavis," he said approvingly as he gave his arm to his mother. "Keep up your courage, dear, it will soon be over."

Way was made for them through the crowded room, and chairs were provided for both, but there was still a period of waiting.

Superintendent Stokes was giving his evidence with regard to the articles found on the body; the formal list had just been completed when Sir Arthur had left the room.

As the superintendent was about to leave the witness-box one of the jurymen leaned forward.

"You say that in the pocket, one pencil, one gold-plated thimble, one handkerchief marked 'M. MARSTON,' and one letter were found. Is it possible to decipher the letter?"

"Certainly. The paper is discoloured and stained, but the writing is perfectly legible."

The juror looked at the Coroner.

"Would it not be well to have the letter put in now? It might help us in the matter—we should know what questions to put."

The Coroner hesitated.

"I had thought of reserving it to a later stage of the proceedings; but if the jury wish—"

There was a pause; the jury conferred, and then the foreman spoke.

"We are agreed that it should be put in now, sir."

The Coroner gave a resigned shrug of his shoulders as he ordered the production of the letter, and his clerk, taking the sadly-discoloured note in his hand, began to read it in his loud, unsympathetic tones:

"Wednesday night.
Dear Mary,
Will you come out and speak to me? I shall not keep you more than a few moments.

Yours,

G.D."

A subdued murmur ran through the room, followed by a prolonged hush during which every one turned to look at Garth Davenant, whose expression had not altered, and whose countenance remained as impassive as ever beneath their scrutiny.

When the note had been handed to the jury for their inspection, and, after turning it about, the foreman had inquired whether anyone had been asked to identify the writing, before the Superintendent could reply, Garth Davenant rose in his place.

"I think it may save time," he said in his clear impassive tones, "if I state at once that I wrote that note to the deceased, Mary Marston."

The jury appeared profoundly impressed, and the Coroner, a man who had known the Davenants all his life, glanced keenly at the young man over the top of his spectacles.

"Do I understand, Mr. Davenant, that you admit having asked this young woman to come out and speak to you on the night of Wednesday the 6th of June last?"

"Certainly not!" Garth's voice was as firm and clear as ever. "I stated that I wrote the note produced."

"This note is dated Wednesday night," the Coroner went on more severely, "and we know that she disappeared on the night of Wednesday, the 6th of June."

"That note was written to her the week before when she was at her mother's cottage." Garth leaned forward and glanced at it. "It is most unfortunate that the day of the week should happen to be the same as that on which she disappeared, and that I should neither have dated nor directed it more definitely."

"Most unfortunate!" the Coroner echoed. "That is all for the present, Mr. Davenant. You will have an opportunity later of giving, on oath, an account of the affair. Call Miss Mavis Hargreave."

As Mavis rose for one instant Garth looked towards her, and their glances met; and then Garth sat down, quivering in every nerve in spite of his unmoved exterior. How could she bear this terrible ordeal to which her love and faith in him were about to be exposed, he marvelled, and he shaded his eyes with his hand as he heard her low, clear tones answering the Coroner's questions.

After that first swift glance she looked away from her lover, away from the crowded room, straight at the Coroner, a fatherly old man whom she had often met out at dinner. The first formal question gave her time to recover herself and to collect her thoughts, and she gave her account of that evening of the 6th of June and of Nurse Marston's anxiety to speak to her mother, clearly and lucidly.

When she had finished the Coroner studied his notes a moment.

"I think I must ask you, Miss Hargreave, when you last saw Mr. Garth Davenant that night?"

Mavis's colour rose, but she retained her self-possession.

"He said good night to me in the morning-room before I went upstairs."

"Ah!" The Coroner looked at his plan of Hargreave Manor attentively. "That would be the room here," laying his finger upon it. "The door is close to that of the small library."

"Yes, but not to the one that we went in by," Mavis said quickly. "There are two doors, one leading into the smaller drawing-room; we went in by that; the other was not opened."

"I see." But the Coroner's grave face indicated clearly to those who knew him that in his opinion Mavis was strengthening the case against her lover. "One more question, Miss Hargreave. I believe you saw the tobacco-pouch that we have been told was found in the small library. Did you recognize it as the one which you had worked for Mr. Garth Davenant?"

"I am quite sure it was not."

There was a pause, and the Coroner looked at his notes again.

"May I ask why you are so positive, Miss Hargreave? We have been told that you stated it was very like the one you gave Mr. Davenant."

"Exactly. I believe it was very like," Mavis replied with spirit. "But it was much dirtier than Mr. Davenant would have made a present from me. Besides"—holding up her head proudly and speaking very distinctly—"I am quite sure that it was not the same, because Mr. Garth Davenant told me so, and I know that I can rely upon his word."

Then for a moment Garth looked up, his eyes full of a passionate gratitude, and as Mavis smiled at him across the crowded room his heart swelled with a glad thankfulness. Mavis would not fail him whatever happened.

"Very natural, and—ahem!—a very creditable feeling, my dear young lady, I am sure," said the Coroner, "but you will understand that it is not evidence."

"Can you tell us anything of the disappearance of this pouch, Miss Hargreave?" asked the foreman.

"Nothing at all," Mavis replied decisively. "I knew nothing of it until I heard my brother mention it."

It was evident that no more was to be learned from Mavis. The Coroner intimated that he had finished and the girl stepped down.

It was Lady Laura's turn next, but her evidence was purely formal, being confined merely to describing how Nurse Marston had requested an interview, and, after having had the small library appointed for such interview, failed to put in an appearance.

Then there was a stir of expectation through the room when Garth Davenant was called.

"It is my duty to tell you, Mr. Davenant," said the Coroner, "that you are not compelled to give evidence, and also to warn you that whatever you say will be taken down and may be used in evidence against you."

The significance of his words was unmistakable. A sort of electric thrill ran through his hearers. Garth alone appeared unmoved; not one muscle of his face altered as he acknowledged the warning with a grave bow, and his tone was firm as he said: "I should prefer to give my evidence, sir."

"You remember the events of the Wednesday, the 6th of June?" the Coroner began when the witness had been duly sworn.

"I do."

"Will you relate them to us in so far as they bear upon this case."

Garth paused a moment.

"In the morning, hearing from Dr. Grieve that a nurse was required at the Manor and that there might be a difficulty in procuring one at the local hospital, I suggested Mary Marston, who, I happened to know, was at her home in the village and was unemployed."

The Coroner glanced at him quickly.

"How did you know it?"

"Because I was in the habit of calling on old Mrs. Marston, and I had seen her daughter on several occasions and heard that she was unemployed. I offered to walk down to the village and interview Mary Marston," Garth proceeded. "I did so, and though she was a little unwilling to leave her mother, who was not well, she consented to go until they could get some one else. I met her accidentally in the avenue as she was going up to the Manor in the afternoon, and that was the last time I saw her. I heard nothing more until Miss Hargreave informed me the next morning that she had disappeared."

"May I put a few questions to the witness, sir?"

The foreman of the jury was standing up, holding a piece of paper in his hand.

"Certainly!" the Coroner assented.

The foreman was a sleek and prosperous grocer, a man who had been a thorn in Sir John Davenant's side for years, partly from the fact that his shop was his own and, standing like an oasis amid the Davenant property, was a veritable Naboth's vineyard to Sir John. He was by no means inclined to let Garth off lightly.

"Do you now declare on your oath that the note produced in Court and found in the deceased's pocket was not written by you to her on the night of Wednesday, the 6th of June last?" he asked severely.

"It was not. It was written during the preceding week, on Wednesday the thirtieth of May."

Garth's tone was clear and distinctly audible throughout the room.

"Then how do you account for the fact that it was still in her pocket the following week, and also for the terms in which you addressed the deceased?" fixing a searching glance upon the young man.

Garth's countenance did not alter beneath his scrutiny.

"I can only conclude that it was slipped into her pocket and forgotten. As for the terms I employed, they were those in which I usually addressed Mary Marston."

"'Yours, G.D.' Would that be your usual signature?"

"To her it would," Garth answered without hesitation. "Mrs. Marston nursed me. I had known and liked her daughter all my life, and Mary was a favourite with us all."

As the foreman paused the Coroner interposed:

"I understand, Mr. Davenant, that you state on your oath that this note was written on the preceding Wednesday—that on Wednesday, the 6th of June, you swear you did not see Mary Marston after you met her in the avenue on her way to the house?"

"That is so, sir." Garth's tone rang out as decidedly as ever.

"Why should you ask her to come out to meet you?"

The old man's tones were sharp; he glanced keenly at Garth.

For a moment, and for the first time, there was a noticeable hesitation in Garth's manner.

"I wished to speak to her without her mother hearing what I had to say," he answered.

"Why?" The Coroner fired the word at him rather as though it had been a pistol-shot, and again Garth's pause was noticeable.

"My conversation was of a private nature. I am not at liberty to disclose it—at present." He added the last words in a lower tone.

The Coroner consulted his clerk for a moment; then he turned to the young man again, his tone markedly colder.

"I understand that you were walking with this young woman in Exeter a few days before her coming to the Manor?"

"On the Saturday before," Garth assented.

"Had you met by appointment?"

This time not only did Garth hesitate, but his colour manifestly changed.

"We had," he replied.

"For what reason?" The Coroner eyed him closely.

"It was on the business to discuss which I asked her to meet me outside her mother's cottage."

The reply was an enigmatic one, and the Coroner pondered it for a moment.

"Then you decline to enlighten us with regard to this private understanding which undoubtedly existed between Nurse Marston and yourself?"

"I have no choice but to do so at the present stage of the proceedings; I assure you"—and Garth's expressive voice was very earnest now—"that it could have had no bearing whatever on the mystery which surrounds her death."

"Um! We are hardly in a position to judge of that," said the Coroner. "You can stand down, Mr. Davenant, and I cannot help commenting upon the extremely unsatisfactory way in which you have elected to give your evidence."

Garth's mouth was set in grim lines, his eyes looked pained and tired as he moved back to his place. It seemed to him that all the eyes in the room were fixed upon him with unfriendly criticism.

Sir Arthur made his way to him.

"Mavis wants to speak to you," he said quietly. "She is in Mrs. Owens's private sitting-room."

It seemed to Garth that the young man's tone was distinctly less friendly, that his eyes rather avoided him, and he braced himself up for an ordeal. Mavis's friends must have convinced her that her faith was misplaced; he told himself bitterly that in any case it could not have lived through his evidence, and his step was heavy and his spirit flagged as he turned down the passage.

The door was open and Mavis was standing alone in the middle of the room waiting for him. As he came in sight she smiled instantly at him and held out her hands.

"Garth, my poor boy!"

The reaction was so great that as Garth held her in his arms, as she rested against his shoulder, for a moment he could not speak; his clasp became a convulsive one as he pressed his lips to her hair. Presently Mavis put up her hand and touched his cheek softly.

"I am so sorry, Garth!"

"Sorry for what, sweetheart?"

"Sorry that people are so stupid," she said, nestling up to him with a little laugh. "That they don't see you did not ask Nurse Marston to come out that night—that they don't seem to trust you!"

Garth felt her trembling as she clung to him. Very tenderly he raised her face and gazed into her eyes.

"How can I tell you how much I thank you for your brave words in the room, Mavis? Tell me—tell me that nothing has changed you, since?"

There was a moment's silence; then Mavis drew herself erect and raised her eyes bravely to his.

"I shall never change, Garth. I trust you now and for always. Tell me you will never doubt me again. It—it hurts me somehow," with a wistful, pathetic little smile.

Garth bent down and kissed her slender fingers again and again.

"It is only that I cannot realize your goodness to me," he murmured brokenly; "Oh, Mavis, Mavis, am I—is any man worthy of such love as yours?"

A sound in the passage made them start asunder; Lady Laura's skirts rustled as she came down attended by the obsequious landlady.

"We shall be ready in five minutes, Mrs. Owen," she said as she came in. "I will tell Miss Mavis—Oh, is that you, Garth?" coldly. "I wondered—"

Mavis's cheeks flamed.

"Mother, won't you tell him that you are sorry, that you believe in him?" she exclaimed unwisely.

Lady Laura looked at her with obvious displeasure.

"Certainly I believe Garth in so far as I do not suppose he had anything whatever to do with Nurse Marston's death; but—as the young man turned to her in mute gratitude—"I do think it is exceedingly tiresome of you, Garth—Yes, Mavis, I shall speak out. I think it is very annoying of you to refuse to tell exactly why you wished to see her, and thus incur all this odium and suspicion. I had not the faintest idea that you were in the habit of requesting private interviews and making clandestine appointments with young women when I gave my consent to your engagement with my daughter, or—"

Garth was about to speak, but Mavis checked him with a look as she prepared to follow Lady Laura out of the room.

"She is tired and a little cross, poor mother!" she observed softly. "All this has been a terrible shock to her."

Garth relieved her of her wraps and escorted her down to the waiting carriage. As they drove away and he turned back the echo of a loud voice speaking in the adjacent taproom caught his ear:

"Adjourned for a week to give the police time to complete their inquiries indeed! I think I could ha' helped 'em to come to a verdict sooner. It runs in the family, that is what it does; and if Mr. Garth Davenant had been a poor man—"

Chapter Twenty-One

"AND TO think that this is the day to which we have looked forward for so long!" Mavis said with a sigh as she clasped her bracelet.

"Yes, things haven't turned out as we expected, miss! But then I don't think they often do in this world. It is full of disappointments."

"That is not a very cheerful doctrine, Minnie." Mavis glanced doubtfully at her maid.

It had struck her of late that the girl was looking pale and worried, but to-day, for the first time, she fancied that something was really amiss. Minnie's lips were trembling, and there were great circles round her eyes.

"You don't look well, Minnie," she said kindly. "I wonder if you want a rest? If you would like to go home for a few days I could spare you."

Minnie shook her head.

"It isn't that, Miss Mavis. I have been a bit upset over—over things," vaguely, "and then that night we saw her—Nurse Marston—she beckoned to me. She appeared to you and Miss Hilda too, didn't she, miss?"

"Well, we did think we saw something," said Mavis reluctantly. "But now I think we must have been mistaken, Minnie."

"I didn't make any mistake, miss." Minnie shivered, her eyes growing dark with awe. "I saw her plain enough, Miss Mavis. Oh"—throwing her black silk apron over her eyes—"I shall see her till I die!"

Mavis looked at her in some perplexity.

"Your nerves are out of order, that is what it is, Minnie. If you do not seem better in a day or two I shall insist upon your taking a holiday." She glanced at her tall, slim figure in the glass. "I shall do very well. Garth always likes me in white," turning almost with a shudder from the dainty, glistening fabric that Minnie had spread out on the couch, the lovely frock of palest rose-pink chiffon that had been prepared for her to wear to-night. "You need not wait up for me, Minnie," she added as she picked up her gloves. "Make haste and get early to bed. I dare say after a good night's rest you will feel different."

Her heart was heavy in spite of her reassuring words as she went down to the drawing-room; the contrast of this evening with the one to which they had been for so long looking joyously forward could not but strike her afresh. All the festivities connected with Sir Arthur's coming of age had been abandoned or postponed, the dance would probably take place in the winter and the old people's treat would become a "Christmas Tree."

To-day, the actual day of the celebration, instead of the great gathering that had been expected, only the quietest of dinner-parties, almost a family affair, was being given—a brother of Lady Laura's, an old friend or two from a distance, the Mainwarings, and the Davenants. Mavis, in spite of some objections from Sir Arthur, had had her own way—no difference whatever was to be made in the treatment of Garth Davenant at the Manor, in spite of the suspicion that was generally cast upon him and the fact that he was popularly supposed to be under police surveillance. He was in the drawing-room now, but Mavis, who had purposely dressed early to have a little chat with him before the others were down, was disappointed to see her uncle already in possession and buttonholing Garth on the hearthrug.

"I never heard anything like it out of a novel—never!" her uncle was remarking as Mavis came into the room.

"It is too terrible, Uncle Robert," she said as Garth greeted her, "but you know we agreed that it was not to be mentioned to-night."

The Honourable Robert Gore was a short, stout, choleric-looking man, about as unlike Lady Laura as it was possible for anyone to be.

"Bless my life," he said explosively, "I am not talking about that poor murdered girl. I am speaking of Arthur's madness, for I can call it nothing else. Does he imagine that I am going to sit down quietly and let my nephew make an utter fool of himself? I used to think it was absurd of the Hargreaves to put off the heir's majority always until he was five and twenty, but upon my word I have come to the conclusion that if it had been delayed until Arthur was forty it would not have been too long. If your mother had had the gumption of a guinea-fowl the thing would never have occurred."

Mavis coloured—she was inclined to resent the blame of her mother.

"I don't think mother could have acted otherwise, Uncle Robert."

"Not have acted otherwise, not have acted otherwise!" Mr. Gore stormed, his wrath for the moment diverted to his niece. "Don't talk that nonsense to me, Mavis. She could have sent the girl to the nearest workhouse, I suppose? Do you fancy for one moment if I found some unknown young woman wandering about my place at Norman's Heath that I should ask her into my house and say, 'Will you please marry me?'"

Mavis could not forbear a smile as she caught Garth's eye.

"It was not quite so bad as that, Uncle Robert. Besides, you must see that Arthur had some excuse. Hilda is very beautiful, you must acknowledge that."

"Umph! Speaking for myself, I should never admire a lunatic!" Mr. Gore snorted. "I am surprised at you, Mavis, upholding your brother in such suicidal folly."

"I don't uphold him, indeed, Uncle Robert. I am extremely sorry about it; but what can I do?"

"Do! Do!" raged her uncle. "Why, telegraph for the best detective in London to come down here and make inquiries into her antecedents—that is what I shall do in the morning."

"Arthur has already had the police," Mavis reminded him.

"Oh, yes, I dare say Arthur has!" he mimicked, too angry to mince matters. "And I can pretty well guess what Arthur said to them. 'Here is this charming young lady whom I am going to marry—doesn't quite know how she came into our park. If you can make a few inquiries in a quiet way I shall be obliged to you'; and naturally they can make nothing out. What I shall say will be, 'Here's this fool of a nephew of mine intending to marry a girl who says she has lost her memory—she is either a lunatic or a murder-ess. Will you find out which?' That is how I shall set to work!"

"Oh, Uncle Robert, I don't think that will be quite fair!" Mavis remonstrated. "I feel sure Hilda is a lady—it is the mystery about her that I don't like; but I fancy her memory is coming back grad-ually. She suddenly remembered her father the other day and that people called him General, but she couldn't recall the name."

"I dare say she couldn't!" Mr. Gore sniffed. "I wonder you can be so simple, Mavis! She might tell me she had suddenly remembered that her father was the Shah of Persia if she pleased; I should want a little more proof than her assertion. Here Arthur comes! I have a good mind to tell him what I think of his conduct without more ado. I had no idea of the depths of his folly until your mother told me about the affair just now. She tells me your father's brother refused to come down altogether, and I am not surprised to hear it. I shall—"

"Oh, please don't say anything to-night, Uncle Robert!" Mavis entreated in alarm. "We—things are all wrong somehow, and Arthur is not very good- tempered as it is; we do want to-night to pass off without any bother."

Sir Arthur certainly did not look in the best of tempers as he strolled towards them, one of his favourite orchids in his but-tonhole, but his face brightened as Lady Laura, with Hilda and Dorothy, came into the room; Lady Laura turned to her brother, Dorothy joined Garth and Arthur drew Hilda aside.

The girl was looking her best to-night. Arthur had insisted that she should wear the gown that had been ordered for the dance from Mavis's dressmaker; it was of her favourite pale blue, and its long straight lines showed every curve of her rounded figure, while the colour threw up in high relief her brilliant complexion and the sheen of her golden hair. At her breast she wore a cluster of delicate orchids, and round her firm white throat a string of pearls, exqui-site in shape and colour—Sir Arthur's latest gift.

Arthur's gaze never left her face as they chatted in low tones. More than once the others, as if compelled by her beauty and charm, paused in their conversation to look at her; but it was obvious that the girl was nervous and ill at ease.

"You are not afraid of my uncle, surely, dearest?" asked Arthur as he bent nearer to her.

"Your uncle?" Hilda repeated vaguely; then she started. "Oh, I beg your pardon, Arthur. I was thinking —yes, I believe I am a little afraid of your uncle. He looks rather formidable."

"Oh, he only wants knowing! He will love you like everybody else directly," Arthur finished with cheerful optimism.

Despite their best efforts the dinner-party was a dreary affair: the shadow that lay over the house seemed to affect the spirits of every one, and no one was sorry when the evening came to an end.

In the hall Dorothy caught Mavis's arm.

"I—I am going to sleep with you to-night, Mavis. I can't help remembering the scream I heard. If I stayed in my own room I know I should hear it again."

Mr. Gore buttonholed his nephew.

"Come on, Arthur, you and I must have a long talk over matters."

Arthur turned towards the smoking-room with him unwillingly. Fresh from the contemplation of Hilda's beauty, he was in no mood to listen to his uncle's remonstrances patiently. Mr. Gore soon found that he was doing more harm than good, and he reluctantly concluded that he must leave the matter until he was in a position to present his argument more forcibly.

Little attention as Arthur paid to his uncle's words, they served to irritate his nerves, already overstrung by the events of the preceding week, and his dreams were haunted by forebodings of some calamity yet to come. It was with a feeling that his presentiments were about to be fulfilled that he woke up suddenly with a sense of having been called. He sat up in bed and waited.

There was a low tapping at his door, and he recognized that this was the sound that had roused him.

"Who is there?" he called out.

The answer came in a whisper.

"It is I—Mavis. Be as quiet as you can, Arthur. I think—I am sure there are burglars in the house."

"Burglars!" Arthur ejaculated as he threw himself out of bed. "Go back to your room, Mavis, like a good girl, and lock your door. I will see to this."

He hurried on his clothes and opened the door, to find Mavis still outside with Dorothy clinging to her.

"Now, where are the burglars?" he said in a reassuring tone. "I expect it is all fancy, but still—"

"It is not fancy. Dorothy could not sleep; she was nervous and worried last night, so she came into my room. As she was tossing about she thought she heard some one opening the side door which you can just see from my window, so she got out of bed, and looked out. Dark as it was she could distinguish figures outside, and they came in—somebody let them in. They—they have gone towards the strong-room, Arthur!"

"They have! Well, they will find they have a pretty hard nut to crack there," Arthur remarked philosophically, "one they will not manage in a minute or two. I shall have time to take you girls back to your room. Have you told Uncle Robert?"

"No; we came to you first." Dorothy ventured to lay her hand on his arm. "You—you will be careful, Arthur? You will take care of yourself?"

"I shall be all right, never fear, Dorothy," he said. "Lock your door; I must call the men."

So absorbed were they that none of them heard a door softly open farther down the passage, not one of them caught a glimpse of a white face peering forth.

Sir Arthur stole softly along the passages to the men's quarters, catching a glimpse of light as he passed through the swing-doors that told him that the girls' story was no mere fabrication. Very softly he roused Jenkins and the footmen and told them what was wanted. Then, arming himself with his revolver, while the men provided themselves with other weapons, the four crept down the stairs. As they reached the bottom flight they became aware for the first time of a low, filing sound. They paused in indecision. At the same moment a tall, dark figure, cloaked and thickly veiled, that had been softly stealing after them, slipped deftly behind a statue at the bend of the staircase.

One of the men looked up.

"I—I almost thought I heard something above, Sir Arthur. If they should be going upstairs—"

"No, no! It is the strong-room!" Jenkins said, with a moan, going a step or two in advance. "They have the outer door open— and all my silver! Oh, dear!"

"They will not get much farther," Arthur said beneath his breath as they tiptoed down the passage.

A moment later he found that he had made a mistake. Through the half-open door of the strong-room he saw that the intruders were well inside the second compartment, and he realized that the filing sound he had heard had been caused by the cutting of the electric alarm. The safe itself, with the lock of whose ingenuity the Hargreaves had been so proud, and of whose absolute impene-trability they had boasted, was wide open, and before it two men were standing.

They carried dark lanterns and were evidently masked, but Sir Arthur fancied there was something oddly familiar about one of them as he watched them peering into the safe. Nearer to the silent watchers, behind among the shadows, a third dark figure was stealing up to them. Suddenly, before Sir Arthur had formulated his plan of action, one of the men bending over the safe turned. Arthur barely suppressed an exclamation of consternation, for in his hand he held the famous Blue Diamond; his comrades and he gazed at it with a murmur of satisfaction, and while their attention was thus occupied Jenkins leaned towards his master.

"I will pull the door to and lock them in, Sir Arthur."

He dashed forward and caught the door, but the contingency had been thought of and guarded against by the burglars: the door did not yield—it was fastened back.

The sound Jenkins made had reached the ears of the men in the inner room; they turned, and with a snarl like a wild cat at bay one of them sprang forward.

Pistol in hand, Sir Arthur advanced.

"It is all over!" he cried. "Put the Blue Diamond back in its case!" he commanded.

The man upon whom his eyes were fixed—the one holding the Blue Diamond—hesitated and made a backward motion.

"Lay the case in the safe and hold up your hands!" Arthur's clear imperious tone rang through the little chamber, and sullenly his opponent obeyed.

Arthur made a step or two forward, his pistol still pointed.

"Now unfasten this door!" But he was reckoning without his host. As he came into the room, keeping his eyes fixed on the man whom he took to be the leader, the other, standing farther in the safe, raised his hand; simultaneously a loud shriek rang through the room and echoed through the house, and the veiled figure which had been creeping behind sprang forward right before Arthur. There was a flash, a report. Arthur had a vision of a loved, familiar face; then, as the smoke cleared away and the men rushed in, they saw that he was standing upright apparently unhurt, but with a dazed, horror-stricken look on his white face, while at his feet lay a huddled-up heap, all undistinguishable, brown, save for one long tress of golden hair that caught the light of the lantern.

Gazing at it with distended eyes, Sir Arthur stooped in a slow, benumbed fashion, but before he could reach it the man who had fired, dropping his pistol, rushed past him, and pushing him backwards threw himself beside the prostrate form on the floor.

"Oh, Hilda, Hilda! Speak to me, Hilda!" he cried.

Chapter Twenty-Two

THE CRY and the shot had roused the house; the loud clanging of the alarm-bell could be heard above the tumult; the grooms and stable-men admitted by the women rushed to their master's assistance and one of the burglars was soon overpowered.

Meanwhile Arthur, whose energy, whose very senses, appeared for the time to be paralysed, still leaned against the wall, where the force of the burglar's impact had sent him, his eyes fixed in a terrible, incredulous stare upon the form lying upon the ground. Jenkins and one of the footmen had secured the other man, and then Jenkins turned to the one who, oblivious of everything apparently but the quiet form over which he was bending, was holding a white hand to his lips, and still beseeching in hoarse, broken accents:

"Hilda! Hilda! Speak to me!"

Jenkins gave one glance at the pale face from which the hood had fallen back, at the golden hair, then with a horrified start he turned to his master.

"Sir Arthur, do you see as it is—"

"Hush!" Sir Arthur broke in fiercely. "Don't say it! It is not true! It is only a dreadful mistake. It—it can't be, Jenkins, you know—"

"Begging your pardon, Sir Arthur, I can't see as there can be any mistake," Jenkins said stolidly. "I could take my oath that it is—"

He was interrupted by the tramp of feet along the passage. Superintendent Stokes, accompanied by his men, roused by the alarm-bell, had arrived on the scene.

The superintendent instantly took command of the situation; one of the intruders was still held between the first footman and a groom. With a wave of his hand the superintendent ordered him into safer custody. Then he went forward and surveyed the other couple without manifesting any surprise.

"What in the world is all this about?"

Mr. Gore stood in the passage, peering over the shoulders of the crowd surrounding the strong-room door. Hearing his voice, the bystanders made way for him, and he advanced somewhat gingerly.

"What is the matter, Arthur? An attempt to steal the Blue Diamond, I suppose? Why don't you speak, boy?" Then in a different tone as Arthur turned his dull, heavy eyes upon him and apparently tried to answer, for his lips moved though no words were audible, "You are ill—wounded?"

Sir Arthur shook his head.

"No," he said in a rough, broken tone, evidently only with difficulty made articulate. "No, I was saved. She —she saved me!"

His uncle's gaze travelled farther; then he went forward, uttered a quick exclamation of astonishment, and, straightening himself, looked at the superintendent.

"Surely that is the girl without a memory? What was she doing down here?"

"That has got to be found out, sir," replied the superintendent. "But," with a significant glance round, "I dare say I could make a pretty good guess at it. I can't say as I'm much surprised, though I hardly thought matters were quite as bad as this. Hist! She is recovering," as there was a faint flutter of the white eyelids. "And, just in the nick of time, here is Dr. Grieve. Your work is here, doctor."

"I thought it might be! I was driving home from Overdeen when I heard the alarm-bell." The doctor bustled in and put Mr. Gore unceremoniously aside. "One moment, my dear sir, you must leave the patient to me, please," with a keen glance at the masked man who was evidently unwilling to obey him. "At once, please!" the doctor went on. "I can see that there is no time to be lost."

With a silent gesture of despair the man moved aside and was instantly secured by the police. He made no resistance as they snapped the handcuffs on his wrists, but, as if hardly conscious what they were doing, stood motionless, the bright dark eyes, which were all that could be seen beneath the mask, fixed on the doctor as he went about his ghastly task with professional precision.

Presently, shaking his head, Dr. Grieve turned round.

"She will get better, doctor?"

For a moment Dr. Grieve looked up in surprise, not recognizing the hoarse, changed tones as Sir Arthur's.

Then as he saw the young man's haggard face he understood.

"I am not all-powerful, Sir Arthur," he said gravely. "And nothing but a miracle could save this poor girl now. She has been shot right through the lungs and there is internal haemorrhage; she may, in fact she will probably have a conscious interval, but it is only a question of a very short time."

He knelt down and contrived to force a few drops of some stimulant between the pallid lips, and in a few moments there was a little fluttering gasp and the deep-blue eyes opened once more.

"Hilda!" The handcuffed man sprang forward, dragging his guardians with him. "Hilda, you must live —it cannot be that I have killed you—I who love you so! For my sake, Hilda!"

With a faint flickering smile the girl looked into his face. She made a little imperative gesture, and he tore off his mask "That is better," she said faintly. "I—I am going to die, Jim."

Then her eyes wandered restlessly away from him, round the curious little room, at the pitying faces; then she said softly:

"Arthur!"

The young man kneeled down beside her, too bewildered yet to grasp the meaning of the situation thoroughly; his mind seemed only capable of retaining the one impression, the stupendous fact that Hilda was dying.

The girl turned her head a little towards him.

"Now—you understand, and I can only say—forgive!"

"Ah, no, I understand nothing," Arthur said, his breath coming in great gasps, "except that you have given your life for mine! Ah, Hilda—"

The girl's eyelids flickered.

"It wasn't—just that," she whispered; "it was for Jim. I am glad you were not hurt—you were very kind to me. But just now my time is short and I want it all for some one else. You will understand everything, some day, and perhaps then, if you have not forgotten, you will—forgive."

"Forgive!" Arthur repeated in the same bewildered accents. "Hilda, I can only—"

"For deceiving you," the weak accents went on. "Don't you see that this—this was why I came to the Manor? Why I drew you on to care for me? It was not love really—it was only a sort of fascination."

She paused and struggled for breath. Dr. Grieve held a glass of some restorative to her lips, and with an effort she spoke again.

"When it's all over, when I am—away, and you know how it all was, you will soon forget me and be far happier without me. I seem to see it all"—closing her eyes for a moment—"but you will keep the diamond necklace, and I think I am rather glad it is so, for I am weary of it all, and you have been very good to me. Now—now I have but a few minutes left, and I only want—Jim!"

A look of ineffable joy transfigured the dying face, a look of trembling ecstatic joy which Arthur had never seen. She turned her head away and stretched out her weak hands to the man who, on the other side, was bending over her in unutterable anguish.

"Only you, now, Jim!" she whispered. "Take me in your arms, dear; I want to forget it all, the weariness and the fret, and only remember that we are together again —you and I."

The man held out his manacled hands with a pitiful gesture.

"For her sake I give you my word of honour I will not attempt to get away," he said.

The men to whom he was handcuffed glanced inquiringly at Superintendent Stokes, and receiving his nod of assent speedily released him. The man then knelt down and took the dying girl in his arms. As if by common consent all the others drew back to the outer doorway, but those standing nearest caught the broken accents.

"Ah, Hilda, my darling, my own! I have killed you, though for your sake I would have laid down my life!" and there was the sound of a man's deep sob.

The girl tried to put her arms round his neck and failed.—'

"Ah, Jim dear, don't do that! The time is so short and I want to say—to tell you that it was not your fault. I threw myself in the way, for I saw you meant to shoot him, and he was pointing at you, I thought, but now I am—afraid—afraid of what may happen. But they—they ought not to do much to a man who, by accident, shoots his own wife."

As the last words left her lips there was a low sigh, almost a moan, Hilda glanced round restlessly.

"So this is the end, Jim! The great *coup* has turned out a failure after all. We weren't brought up to think honesty the best policy; but if I could have my time over again I would do differently I think."

"Oh, don't, don't!" the man broke in passionately. "Hilda, my heart is breaking! It has been my fault, all of it. Forgive me, darling—tell me once more that you forgive me!"

Hilda put up one hand to the dark face so near hers.

"There is nothing to forgive, Jim. If there were, a woman forgives anything—to the man she loves. All that is gone, Jim—only our love remains," drawing his head down.

Dr. Grieve looked at the superintendent.

"She may last an hour or two, or she may go any minute," he said, "but she will probably not recover consciousness again. You had better clear these people away—they are only blocking up the air and doing no good," with a nod towards the crowd outside the door.

But as the superintendent turned and vigorously supported Dr. Grieve's views they began to disperse.

Mr. Gore, who turned away with the others, felt his arm caught from behind.

"Uncle Robert!" It was Mavis's voice; her face looked white and frightened. "What has happened? Arthur told us to stay upstairs, Dorothy and I—and we did for a long time; but when we heard the scream and the people running about we came down. What is it?"

"A determined attempt to steal the Blue Diamond, I should say," her uncle replied grimly, "one that pretty nearly succeeded too."

"But, Uncle Robert"—Mavis's voice sank very low, and she trembled from head to foot—"who was it on the ground? It looked like, but it could not be, Hilda!"

Mr. Gore put his arm under his niece's and led her back to her room.

"Don't you see, child, I was right all along. That poor thing lying there was an impostor, in league with these burglars. It was she—there can't be the least doubt of it—who admitted them to the house; and it is quite evident that she had contrived to worm the secret of the lock out of Arthur."

Mavis put up her hand to her head.

"I mean that she came purposely," he corrected, running his hand through his white hair and ruffling it up until it stood on end. "Heavens, Mavis, is it possible you don't see how it is now? The girl was one of a gang of burglars who had planned a great stroke of business—no less a thing in fact, than to get possession of the Blue Diamond; and this woman was sent here to worm herself into Arthur's confidence—I dare say they saw he was just the sort of young fool to do anything for a pretty face—and finally admit the rest of the party."

Mavis interrupted him with a cry of pain.

"Oh, I can't believe it, Uncle Robert, I can't believe it! Hilda—"

"You will have to believe facts, I suppose," snapped her uncle. "Now some one has got to break the news to your mother, Mavis, and it seems to me that you are the proper person."

"Yes, yes. I will go at once. Dorothy is with her now," faltered Mavis. "Uncle Robert, do you mean that she hadn't lost her memory at all?"

"Lost her memory! Certainly she hadn't. That was merely a pretext for getting into the house and stopping there. I dare say she had seen the idea in some novel or other that put it into her head. Very likely she knew the sort of people she had to deal with. If I had been here she would have found it a difficult matter. But what is the matter here—what is all this noise about?"

They had reached the long corridor leading to Lady Laura's room when their progress was arrested by a little group. Mrs. Parkyns and Dorothy were bending over a shaking, sobbing figure in the window-seat. With a throb of surprise Mavis recognized her maid. She paused.

"Why, Minnie, what is wrong?" she asked.

Dorothy looked up.

"Oh, Mavis, she is so upset! She thinks—"

"It isn't thinking, Miss Dorothy," Minnie broke out vehemently. "I am sure. I saw his face quite plain."

Mavis glanced at Dorothy.

"What does she mean? Whom has she seen?"

Dorothy's face was very pale; great tears were standing in her eyes.

"She thinks that the—the burglar—the one who tried to shoot Arthur—is Gregory, Arthur's orchid man, you know, and—"

"So he is, so he is!" wailed Minnie. "There is no mistake, Miss Dorothy. Oh, what a fool I have been! What a fool—and worse! It will be the death of me, Miss Mavis! I couldn't live and face it."

"Minnie, what is the use of talking like that?" Mavis said wearily. "You will have to put up with it if it is so; but I can't think—"

She paused and revolved matters in her mind; of the man bending over Hilda she had caught only the most cursory glimpse; still, she had a vague feeling that in some sense his appearance had not been unfamiliar.

After a moment's bewilderment Mr. Gore stepped forward.

"The girl is right enough!" he said excitedly. "I had the queerest feeling all the while that I had seen the fellow somewhere before, though I couldn't locate him; but Arthur would have me go to look at the orchids yesterday, and this was the man who took us round."

"Oh, it was Jim Gregory, safe enough, sir!" Minnie said, looking up with dry, tearless eyes and twitching lips. "Why was I ever born?" with another burst of sobbing.

"Come, come, my good girl," he said, "you won't do a bit of good by distressing yourself like that! You are not the only person who has been made a fool of over this business—you can console yourself by thinking that you are in just the same boat with a good many more!"

"Ah, if that was all, sir!" Minnie gasped. "But—"

"Yes, sir," Mrs. Parkyns said severely—the events of the night had left her usually comely face unwontedly pale—"Minnie, finding as she had a key as fitted the door, has been meeting her young man in the conservatory when the family was at dinner."

"What! Do you mean to say that she let him in to-night?"

"Oh, no, sir, no! She had nothing to do with that," the house-keeper interposed. "It was before that."

"Is Mr. Gore here? Could I speak to him a moment?" The interruption came from Superintendent Stokes, who had suddenly appeared at the end of the passage.

Mr. Gore bustled forward.

"Certainly! What can I do for you?" he said.

"Well, Sir Arthur is upset by all this, and it is no use asking him anything. There ought to be a magistrate here. I have taken the liberty of sending a dog-cart over for Squire Lewis."

"Quite right, superintendent, quite right! To take that poor thing's depositions, I conclude?" Mr. Gore said, lowering his voice.

The superintendent shook his head.

"No, it is too late for that, sir. She passed away a few minutes ago."

"What dead? Well, well, poor thing!" the other said, looking very much shocked. "It seems terribly sudden. Well, it isn't for us who have never known her temptations to judge her. If she sinned she has suffered for it, poor girl."

"Just so, sir," the superintendent acquiesced respectfully. "If you could leave the ladies for a moment, sir, I could explain."

Mr. Gore moved aside with him, and Mavis went on.

"I must go to my mother," she said. "Try to control yourself, Minnie. We shall all be wiser another time."

"Yes, Miss Mavis!" But Minnie's face was not any less woebegone—the shadow of a terrible fear still lay in her eyes.

Dorothy followed her cousin and slid her hand into hers.

"Mavis, did you hear the police officer say that Hilda was—dead?"

Mavis shuddered.

"Yes, I heard! But, Dorothy, I think I must be dazed. I don't seem to care about anything—to be surprised at anything."

Dorothy's soft brown eyes were full of tears.

"It is all so dreadful! I cannot help thinking of her. Only a few hours ago she was as well as any of us, and now—and it is so terrible for him—poor Arthur!"

Chapter Twenty-Three

"HE IS asking for you, Arthur, and he has but a short time to live. They have taken him into Jenkins' room."

"Why?" Sir Arthur was sitting in his study, his head laid on his clasped arms on the writing-table. The face he raised as Garth Davenant entered was haggard and lined, there were dark circles round his eyes, and his mouth twitched convulsively.

Garth laid his hand on his arm.

"He must have taken the poison before she died, Arthur. It—it has taken rapid effect since, and Dr. Grieve says his hours are numbered."

Arthur looked at him with dull, lack-lustre eyes.

"He was Gregory, you know, Garth—the best man I ever had for orchids," he said in a monotonous tone.

"Yes, yes, I know. We have all been blind, old chap. I must confess I thought—"

"And he was Hilda's husband," Arthur went on as if he did not hear. "As I have been sitting here, Garth, that one phrase, 'Hilda's husband' has been beating into my brain with ceaseless, senseless iteration." His face worked painfully.

The compassion in Garth's eyes grew and deepened, but his voice was studiedly cold when he spoke.

"Hilda's husband," he repeated steadily. "But there is much else to be told, Arthur, much that she wished you to know. Won't you come and hear it?"

For a moment Arthur hesitated, but the stronger will of the other man conquered, and he rose.

Garth put his arm through his and led him, walking with the halting, uncertain step of extreme old age, to a room where another act of the tragedy was being played out.

On the threshold Arthur hesitated; the narrow pallet bed had been drawn out to the middle of the room to suit the doctor's convenience, and at a little table behind the bed Mr. Lewis, looking watchful and alert with his papers before him, sat waiting to write. Dr. Grieve was there, and Mr. Mainwaring, Mr. Pauncefort, the Davenants' solicitor, and his own. Superintendent Stokes placed a chair for Sir Arthur. The young man's gaze, after wandering round the room restlessly, had come back to the bed. He started incredulously as he saw the drawn ashen face, in which the only living things seemed to be the bright, black eyes that darted round incessantly, as he heard the heavy, laboured breathing.

The sick man was trying to raise himself in bed; his finger was pointing at his late employer.

"I am glad you have come, because I must tell you —must make you understand that it wasn't her fault. The blame of it was all mine; she did not want to come, but I made her. I had thought it all out—it seemed too good a chance to be missed—and she would do anything for me."

Sir Arthur shivered a little, but he did not speak. The thought struck him that Gregory's tone was strangely altered—that his accent was now undeniably that of a gentleman, a man of education.

"It is pretty well over with me now," the voice that was at once so familiar and so strange went on. "Well, it was the only way, and I'm not sorry now that I took it, for I shall see her again soon. It is, as she said, that no one else shall be punished for what I did that I must speak. But perhaps if I tell you how it was with Hilda from the beginning you will understand better. Her father had been a man of good birth who broke his wife's heart—she died when their only child was born. He was turned out of the Army, and finally sentenced to a long period of imprisonment for fraud. Hilda never knew the meaning of the word home. In her childhood she was neglected and half-starved, beaten and sworn at when her father had bad luck, and left to do what she could when things went well with him.

"Later on as she grew up he realized that her beauty was a valuable asset, and then no expense was spared on the girl. The best masters were given her for accomplishments, she had carte blanche with her dress. When I first saw her twelve years ago she was eighteen, and a veritable angel of loveliness, with her fair face and wealth of golden hair. Her father was using her as a decoy for his gambling tables. I was then, as I have been for years, a gambler, a black-leg, a thief, one shunned by every honest man. I had believed my heart to be as hard as a millstone, but I suppose there was a weak spot left, and I fell desperately in love with Hilda St. Leger, as she was called then. Doctor, you must make my strength last out for what I have to say, please."

He drank eagerly from the glass Dr. Grieve held to his lips, and then sank back with a sigh of relief.

"That is better. That wasn't strange, perhaps, but the queerest thing was that she fell in love with me. Her father did not make any objection; already he and I had been partners in many a doubtful deed and I fancy he saw that the girl would still be useful to him. For a little while after we were married I tried to keep straight for her sake, but the world is slow to believe in repentance or amendment, and I went back to my old courses. My father-in-law and I entered into a partnership, and for a time all went well.

"Then, in an evil hour, we thought of the great Blue Diamond of the Hargreaves; in his younger days my father-in-law had known the Hargreaves—it must have been a likeness to him that Lady

Laura saw in Hilda—and from that moment our whole thoughts were given up to planning how we could best make it our own, and at last my father-in-law evolved a scheme that we ultimately adopted. Before we put the plan into execution, however, my father-in-law was run over by a motor-omnibus and fatally injured. There were others in the scheme then, and we had to go on. It was while going to see her father in the hospital that Hilda was met by Nurse Marston, and thus recognized by her when she came here."

"I don't see that all this is to any purpose," said Sir Arthur. "It is extremely painful to me to have to listen to it, and I should prefer her name kept out of it as much as possible."

"Don't I tell you this is her wish, not mine?" the dying man retorted. "It was her wish that you should hear how Nurse Marston died; or rather she made me promise to make it clear that the man whose name has been widely connected with the mystery, Mr. Garth Davenant, had nothing to do with it. There didn't seem to me to be any satisfactory way of doing it but this, so I took it."

Again he paused; the Doctor held something to his lips. He drew himself up.

"That is putting new life into me, doctor. Well, our plans prospered beyond our expectations. Hilda had been established here more readily than I could have conceived possible. I had been fortunate enough to obtain the situation in the orchid-houses. A couple of my associates had been installed as my assistants. It only remained for Hilda to make herself sufficiently attractive to Sir Arthur to obtain from him the secret of the lock, and the game was ours.

"Just as we had reached this conclusion everything was knocked on the head by the sudden appearance of Nurse Marston on the scene. When I learned from Minnie Spencer, in the housekeeper's room that night, that Nurse Marston had recognized Hilda and asked for an interview with Lady Laura I knew that there was only one slender chance between us and ruin—and that was to get hold of the nurse before she saw Lady Laura. In order to gain my purpose I had been making love to Minnie Spencer for some time, and two or three times I had persuaded her to unlock the conservatory door and come and have a little chat with me while the family were at dinner.

"That night I delayed her longer than usual, so that she had no time to fasten it after me, and I was thus able to get in later on. I stood in the conservatory waiting, and as Nurse Marston came into the small library by one door I opened the other. She started back, but I was prepared for her. I threw a chloroformed cloth over her head and seized her in my arms. Mind you, I did not intend any real harm to her—I simply meant to have her taken care of until the diamonds were ours and we were safely out of the country, and then she might have come back and said what she liked. If she had listened to me when I told her so she might have been alive now, but she struggled and fought like a wild cat. Once she got her head out of the cloth and screamed. You have heard cries spoken of. I rammed the cloth closer and closer to prevent her being heard, and carried her on through the shrubbery. At first, when I noticed how quietly she was lying in my arms, I thought it was only the chloroform taking effect, but when I was a safe distance from the house, and had met my confederate, we stopped to look. I found to my horror that it was all over with her—she was dead!"

"Ah, I thought that was how it was!" Superintendent Stokes remarked as he drew a long breath.

"We tried to restore her, but it was no use, and I had to realize that I had killed her without intending it, and was a murderer in fact if not in intention. Bad as I was, I had hitherto drawn the line at breaking the Sixth Commandment, and for a time I was utterly aghast. Then the question of concealing the body presented itself to me, and I recollected the Lover's Oak. Accident had revealed it to me some time before the fact that it was hollow, and I had several times thought that it might be a suitable place in which to conceal some of our booty—for, needless to say, we did not intend to content ourselves with merely the Blue Diamond; we should have levied toll on the plate as well. It now struck me that the body would be safer there than anywhere else. I hadn't reckoned for the vengeance of Heaven, you see!

"I think that is all. If in the servants' hall or elsewhere I have appeared to foster the suspicion against Mr. Garth Davenant it has been merely as a cover to our own designs for the time being, and with no desire to injure him eventually."

Superintendent Stokes looked at his notebook.

"The tobacco-pouch?" he said.

The dark eyes opened once more and looked even faintly amused.

"I must have dropped it. Minnie worked it for me, after the pattern of that given by her mistress to Mr. Garth Davenant. She must have gone into the room and recognized it, and, fearing it might get me into trouble, annexed it. In the same way, remembering the conservatory door had been left open, when she came to look for Nurse Marston she bolted it, and thus fostered the idea that she might still be in the house. But I fancy Minnie has had her suspicions of me lately."

"Hilda did not know!"

It was Sir Arthur's voice, husky and strained; it was more an assertion than a question, but Gregory chose to answer it.

"She had no idea at the time or till long afterwards. But naturally she could not help connecting me with the disappearance when she heard of it. Since the body was discovered she could not help knowing, and I fear—I fear it has made her very miserable— my poor Hilda!"

"Mrs. Leparge?" the superintendent interpolated tentatively.

"Well, you cannot expect me to inculpate my friends. It was difficult for me to see Hilda, and notes were dangerous. Mrs. Leparge brought a message."

"I see; I surmised that," the superintendent assented slowly. "Well, I think that is all clear—all the mystery is plain enough now."

The unnaturally bright eyes gazed round.

"Then my task is over."

"This paper must be signed and witnessed," Mr. Lewis interpolated hurriedly. "I will read it over to you."

It was a somewhat lengthy document and Mr. Lewis was a slow reader, so that this process took time.

When the document was brought to the dying man he scrawled his signature and then pushed the paper away from him almost convulsively, and fell back.

Like one in a dream Sir Arthur suffered Garth to lead him away. His uncle joined Mr. Pauncefort and Mr. Lewis as they stood in the passage outside. Thither Superintendent Stokes followed them after giving a few directions to his two subordinates, whom he left in the room. Mr. Gore turned to him at once.

"I was not prepared for this, superintendent—I was not indeed. I knew Mr. Garth Davenant had nothing to do with the murder, as some of these wiseacres have suggested, but I did think the poor thing had gone outside of her own free will to meet some one, and been the victim of foul play. I never dreamt that such a thing as this could happen in a respectable house. That little hussy who admitted the fellow—I hope she will get some punishment," vindictively.

"I think she has had her punishment," the superintendent said a little indulgently as he remembered pretty Minnie's changed appearance. "Though she would have spared us some trouble if she would have spoken out from the first. But I think the girl was terrified, and she had no idea how bad things were really. It was some words I overheard between her and Mr. Jim Gregory that put me on the right track though."

"What! You suspected!" ejaculated Mr. Gore.

"I was pretty nearly certain," said the superintendent slowly, "but I hadn't much proof, and it was no use speaking out too soon, and letting our birds escape."

"I understood that you suspected Mr. Garth Davenant; I am sure my nephew informed me so."

"I was inclined to do so at first," the superintendent acknowledged frankly, "and I was a fool for my pains, as I soon found out.

I made it my business to inquire into Mr. Garth Davenant's movements and—well, in short, I came to the conclusion that whoever was guilty I must look elsewhere for the murderer."

"But what on earth—" Mr. Gore was unable apparently to get over his astonishment.

"Well, some little time ago I began to suspect the young lady was not quite truthful."

"I should think so indeed. One would have thought anybody but an idiot would have seen that," wrathfully interpolated Mr. Gore.

"You don't suppose that if I hadn't had a pretty good suspicion how the land lay here," the superintendent went on, unheeding the interruption, "that Mr. Garth Davenant would have remained at liberty so long. No, no! In an ordinary case, with the evidence against him apparently so strong, he would have been arrested before now and brought up before the magistrates. There has been blame thrown upon me because he hasn't. But I knew he had nothing to do with it, and I had got my eye on the right men. Mr. Jim Gregory and his associates would have found themselves in a trap when they walked outside."

"You don't mean that you were watching?"

Mr. Gore's opinion of the superintendent's intelligence went up by leaps and bounds.

Superintendent Stokes smiled a little.

"Certainly we were, sir. Otherwise we shouldn't have been on the spot when the alarm-bell rang. Yes, Sir Arthur's getting up when he did cost that girl's life; but, well, when all is said I dare say it is best for her as it is."

"Much the best," Mr. Gore echoed, rubbing his forehead.

Chapter Twenty-Four

"THERE IS Minnie Spencer, off to her mother's. Miss Mavis has made her go. I heard her tell Mrs. Parkyn's she should. They say Minnie is afraid to put her head out of doors, she is that frightened of seeing Nurse Marston's ghost—and no wonder, I say. I am sure in her place I should be ashamed of showing my face in the streets after being made such a fool of." Lizzie, the smart under-housemaid, giggled and glanced coquettishly at Tom Greyson—if rumour spoke true she would be in no wise averse to consoling the good-looking young gamekeeper.

Greyson did not smile back; he was looking away from the smiling prettiness of the girl confronting him down the avenue, where in the distance he could see a moving black speck—a speck that was Minnie Spencer.

"She wouldn't go in the shrubbery, not if it was ever so," Lizzie went on, with a swift upturned glance at the young man's absent face. "Last night she scared us all, rushing out of the still-room, and saying as she had seen Nurse Marston in the bushes outside. I wouldn't have her conscience, that I wouldn't, not for the world! They say as her ladyship was all for dismissing her, but Miss Mavis wouldn't hear of it. She knew it would be difficult for Minnie to get another place—it isn't every mistress as would give a girl like her a chance."

"Ah, another chance! That is what many of us would like in this life," observed Greyson. "But I must be off," and with a curt nod of farewell he moved away.

Lizzie Prentice looked after him resentfully.

"Pretty sort of boor he is! I shouldn't wonder if, after all, Minnie was well rid of him," she muttered to herself as she turned back to the house.

All unconscious of the compliments that she was bestowing upon him, Tom Greyson strode across the park and through the Home Wood to his cottage.

He found the key hanging upon the nail and let himself in; the woman who looked after his cottage had gone home, but his tea stood ready for him on the round table, a bright fire burned on the hearth. It was a cheerful and homelike interior, but Greyson's face was dull and heavy as he threw himself down in his easy chair and whistled his dog to his knee. Presently he rose, and not without a certain awkwardness, yet with the air of a man who is accustomed to waiting upon himself, reached down his caddy and made himself a cup of tea.

He sat stirring it for some minutes, while his eyes wandered to a rocking-chair that stood by the window —how well he remembered buying it! Minnie always had a fancy for a rocking-chair, and he had saved up a long time for it, determined to get the best of its kind, and he had planned that it should stand just there. That ornamental work-table too! He had stinted himself for weeks so that Minnie might not miss her pretty things, and he had often pictured to himself the time when he should see her there, busy with her bits of work. That was before Jim Gregory had come on the scene with his false face and lying words; Tom clenched his fist suggestively as he thought of him, but eventually he roused himself with a shake and gulped down his tea. Then, without a look at the goodly pile of scones and the appetizing slice of ham waiting for him, he rose and reached down his hat, banging the door behind him with a firmness which betokened some resolution taken.

Outside the night was fast drawing in; there was a touch of frost on the grass, it felt crisp to his feet, and yet in the distance there was a faint suggestion of mist that warned him that the month of fogs was not yet over. Greyson took the turning that brought him out in Lockford Street and then slackened his steps and looked about him absently.

Presently he caught sight of a little figure hurrying along the narrow, cobble-paved path. The girl would have passed without looking up, but Greyson placed himself in her way.

"Good evening, Minnie! You are in a hurry."

She looked up with a start.

"Yes. I—I must get back. I didn't mean to be so late, but mother kept me, and now it is nearly dark."

She tried to hurry by him, but Greyson turned with her, accommodating his long strides to her fleeting steps.

"I have to speak to Mrs. Parkyns about the game that's ordered," he observed, "so, if I shan't be in your way, Minnie, I will just walk up with you."

Minnie's face flushed; some of the scared look died out of her eyes.

"You are only doing it out of kindness, Tom, but thank you very much, I'll take it as it's meant, for I'm frightened to death at the thought of going up the avenue and through the shrubbery by myself."

"I thought that was about how it was," Greyson said gruffly as they turned in at the gates.

They did not talk much as they walked up the long avenue. Once Minnie looked up at him.

"Miss Mavis gave me till it was time to dress, but I should have been back before this only Widow Jackson was in at mother's and I had to stop till she had gone before I could talk with mother. Widow Jackson had so many questions to ask. It upset me a bit."

"They all have," the man assented. "A lot of clacking idiots."

He relapsed into silence again. Only too well did he realize much of the painful nature of the questioning to which Minnie would be subjected. Not in Lockford only was she an object of interest. The murder of Nurse Marston and the subsequent suicide and confession of her assassin had aroused the public in no ordinary way, and Minnie, as having been deluded into an engagement with the murderer, could not hope to escape observation, by no means of a charitable nature. The girl had paid a heavy price for her fickleness and folly, and Greyson's heart ached as he saw how thin her cheeks had become and the pathetic droop of her eyes and mouth.

"I saw Miss Mavis driving with Mr. Garth Davenant," he said after a while. "I think they were going over to Overdeen. I hear it is to be put in order for the wedding at once."

"Yes," said Minnie apathetically. "But Sir Arthur says he shan't be at it," she added. "He is going away as soon as he can. He don't feel in touch with weddings and no more do I," with an irrepressible sob.

"Now, Minnie, don't take on like that," Greyson said awkwardly.

"Isn't it enough to make me?" the girl sobbed. "I tell you, Tom Greyson, all this has gone nigh to kill me. Often and often I wish they had took me off to prison, as I thought they was going to when the superintendent told me it was all found out. I tell you the truth, though I was frightened pretty nearly out of my senses about that conservatory door, the thought that he had"—she paused and caught her breath—"killed her never entered my head; I thought he knew something about it, and I have taxed him with it times without number; but he told me he hadn't, and one always wants to believe the people one—loves."

There was a moment's silence, then Greyson said heavily:

"Ah, that is right enough."

Minnie smothered a sob with her handkerchief; then, as Greyson walked on with his eyes steadily fixed before him, his cap pulled over his eyes, she suddenly clutched his arm.

"Tom! Tom! She is there again! Oh, I wish I was dead and out of this!"

"What on earth do you mean, Minnie?"

Greyson stared at her, an odd little thrill passing through him as he felt her hand grasping him so tightly.

"There! There!" Minnie almost pulled him round and pointed. "It—don't you see as it is Nurse Marston?" she gasped.

Straining his eyes through the mist, and in spite of the overhanging branches, Greyson fancied he caught sight of a shadowy figure, a glimpse of a fluttering cloak, the gleam of a white apron. He started forward.

"Wait a minute, Minnie, I will—"

The girl caught at him with a cry of terror.

"You aren't going to leave me, Tom! I daren't stop here by myself—I should die of terror! Tom! Tom!"—her hands tightening as he still showed symptoms of wishing to escape—"I can't let you—"

"Don't you see that I must find out what it is, Minnie?" he remonstrated. "I should catch her up in a minute."

Minnie drew a deep sobbing breath.

"I know well enough what it is. It is Nurse Marston walking again. I was in hopes now that she would rest, but it seems—"

"Come, come, Minnie," the man reproved, though his eyes looked puzzled, "you have nothing to fear from that poor thing; and I don't believe as she would come back to frighten folk. I'll just take you back to the house, and then—"

With an effort Minnie grew calmer.

"Thank you very much, Tom!" she said humbly. "Perhaps you would not mention it to them indoors as she had appeared to me again. They would all say as it is no more than I deserve, and that's right enough. Indeed, I sometimes think that my punishment is more than I can bear."

She drew her hand from his arm as she spoke, feeling a tiny pang as she reflected that a year ago he would not have let it go so easily.

At the entrance to the stable-yard he paused.

"You will be all right now, Minnie. I have made up my mind to find out what that thing is. Maybe I'll come and see Mrs. Parkyns later."

Minnie stood still and watched his tall form striding away, her eyes filling with tears.

"Oh, what a fool I've been! What a fool!" was her unspoken reflection as she turned indoors.

Meanwhile Greyson, as he quickly made his way back to the shrubbery, was feeling distinctly puzzled. Hitherto he had set down the stories of the appearance of Nurse Marston's apparition as merely hysterical fancies; but to-day, momentary as had been his vision, his own eyes had convinced him that they had at least some foundation in fact, and he was unable, as he mentally phrased it, to see daylight in the matter.

He looked about him carefully in the shrubbery, but no sign of any intruder could he see. He was giving up the search in despair when, on turning down a side path to go back to the Manor, he saw a figure in a nurse's bonnet and cloak standing with her back towards him.

He came to a sudden stop, his heart beating faster, then he stole quickly and silently forward; the damp grass deadened any sound of his footsteps, and the figure still remained silent, motionless, until he was within a few paces, then with a weary sigh it moved away.

With a quick breath he sprang after it and caught it in his arms, his grasp tightening as the first moment of contact showed him that this was no spirit or wraith, but real flesh and blood—flesh and blood, moreover, that was not inclined to take capture meekly and was capable of offering decided resistance.

"Well, really," a brisk matter-of-fact voice said, "what is the meaning of this? What sort of conduct do you call it, Tom Greyson?"

Greyson's grasp relaxed, his arms dropped.

"Miss Gidden!" he ejaculated in amazement, certain conjectures flitting hazily through his mind.

"Certainly it is Miss Gidden!" that lady assured him tartly. "What did you take me for, Tom Greyson, that you should think proper to pounce upon me in that fashion? Not for poor Mary Marston's ghost, I presume, like those other people?"

Greyson took off his cap and rubbed his forehead as he stared at her.

"Then you are the ghost that has been frightening people?" he said slowly. "I can hardly believe—"

"I am," the lady avowed freely. "At least, I suppose I am," she corrected. "I know when I have been taking a walk up here or in the Home Wood anyone who meets me usually throws up his or her hands wildly and rushes away."

Greyson could not take his gaze from her.

"Why could you not speak out before and put an end to all this fright?"

"Why should I?" Nurse Gidden said as she shrugged her shoulders. "I had no intention of alarming people; if their consciences pricked them and frightened them nearly to death when they saw me, was I called upon to set them at rest? Minnie Spencer, I suppose, or that wretched girl, Hilda? I tell you, Tom Greyson, I couldn't make it out at first when I saw folk run away from the sight of me. I was staying down here for my holidays as you know, and I don't as a rule wear uniform then. Still, when I go out in the dusk I fancy it is a sort of protection, and I used to come up here through the Home Wood and across the park sometimes of an evening, thinking of Mary and wondering where she could be. I felt sure from the finding of the notebook that the clue to her disappearance must lie between the Home Coppice and the Manor, and I used to fancy that if I looked perhaps I might find something that would help me—little thinking how near she was to me all that time, poor thing! Mr. Greyson"—striking her hands together passionately—"I loved Mary Marston. She was my greatest friend; there seems to me to be something unutterably cruel in her death."

"Ah, it was a terrible thing!" Greyson assented, his face looking gloomy and preoccupied.

"Well, we must leave it at that," said Nurse Gidden. "And, anyhow, I must be getting back, for I am only in Lockford for the day. Poor Mrs. Marston is not long for this world, and I want to be with her as much as I can. Still, I felt I must just come up here once more. Down here they must have gone and across there to the Home Wood. I can see it all in my own mind. Good night to you, Tom Greyson!" and with a curt nod she took her departure.

Greyson walked back to the Manor; when his business with Mrs. Parkyns was done, he asked hesitatingly if he could see Minnie Spencer. Mrs. Parkyns looked at him doubtfully.

"Well, you can, for she will be down from dressing Miss Mavis in a minute; but do you think you are wise, Greyson? Still, if the girl has done wrong she has suffered for it, and you know your own business best, both of you, I suppose."

"Well, I have got a bit of news for Minnie as I think she will be pleased to hear," Greyson went on steadily, "if so be as you would give me the opportunity of telling her, Mrs. Parkyns, m'm."

The housekeeper was pleased with this appeal to her importance.

"Certainly! Certainly!" she said affably. "You wait here, Greyson; I'll send her to you. And as for your news, I dare say we shall all be hearing it before long." She opened the door with as near an approach to a wink as her dignity would permit. "Here she is! Minnie, here is some one as is anxious to have a word with you. Come in, my girl; there is no call for you to look so frightened."

She pushed the girl into the room and shut the door.

Minnie glanced up timidly.

"Tom! What is it? Have you seen—"

Greyson took her cold hand in his.

"I have come to tell you that I have laid the ghost for you, Minnie! 'Twas naught but Miss Gidden, Nurse Marston's friend; I caught her in the shrubbery."

The quick colour flushed Minnie's face.

"Oh, Tom! Are you sure?"

"Ay, there is no doubt about it, my lass! She owned up to it herself as you had run away from her, believing her to be Nurse Marston. So there is no more cause for you to be scared. She won't trouble you again."

"No!" The tears sprang up in Minnie's eyes and rolled down her cheeks; wrenching her hand from Greyson's, she drew out her handkerchief. "Oh, I shall never, never forgive myself!" she sobbed. "Thank you so much for finding it out and telling me, Tom!"

Greyson drew near and laid his rough hand almost timidly on her shaking shoulder.

"Come, come, Minnie! It is no good crying over what is past. You'll be wiser in the future. You know as if there is anything you want doing you have only to tell me. You can trust your old playmate, can't you, Minnie?"

"Yes, yes!" the girl whispered, her sobs almost choking her. "You—you have always been good to me, Tom."

Greyson's blue eyes grew dim as he bent over her.

"It is early days yet, Minnie, and I hadn't meant to speak so soon; but some time, dear, don't you think you could bring yourself to forget the past and let me take care of you? I would be very patient if you would give me one word of hope, Minnie."

For one moment Minnie glanced up, her tears checked by her surprise.

"Oh, Tom, you don't mean—It is like you to think of it, Tom. But don't you see I am not deserving of such goodness—now?"

Emboldened, Greyson ventured to put an arm lightly round her waist.

"Don't talk about goodness, Minnie," he said gruffly. "Don't you know you are the girl I have always wanted? Tell me that some day—"

Minnie had turned to him and laid her head on his shoulder with a little weary sob.

"Oh, Tom, Tom, you have been so good to me, and I am so tired!"

Chapter Twenty-Five

MAVIS was sitting in the morning-room, her favourite chair drawn up to the window, her work and books lying untouched before her as she gazed absently down the avenue. The girl was looking pale and tired. The events of the past few months had tried her sorely; the revelations of Hilda's duplicity and her terrible death, as well as the discovery of Nurse Marston's body and the suspicion which for a time had been attached to Garth Davenant—all these had had their effect upon her. She was unable to rouse herself to take an ordinary bridal interest in her trousseau, for preparations were now going on apace, and before Christmas she and Garth would be married.

Her white cheeks and general languor had aroused Garth's anxiety in no slight degree, and he had insisted upon a speedy wedding, after which he meant to carry off his bride to the Riviera, where later on Lady Laura and Dorothy would join them.

Sir Arthur, unable to bear the comments excited both in the Press and throughout the country by the recent proceedings at Hargreave Manor, had, as soon as the double inquest was over, betaken himself to the Rocky Mountains in search of big game, and incidentally, it was hoped, forgetfulness, and the Manor was to be left to the combined care of Mrs. Parkyns and Jenkins.

The sound of wheels in the avenue roused Mavis from her abstraction at last, and a faint tinge of colour crept into her cheeks as she recognized Garth Davenant driving his two-seater. As she leaned forward it struck her that he was looking graver and sterner, that his mouth was set in new lines, and she glanced up quickly as the door opened.

Garth came across and took her hands in his.

"How are you this morning, sweetheart? I am glad to see the roses are coming back a little to these pale cheeks."

"How is it that you are at the Court again?" Mavis questioned. "I thought you were in London."

"I had to come down this morning," Garth said gravely, "to bring my father and mother some news."

"News!" Mavis repeated wistfully. "Not—not bad news, I hope, Garth?"

He put his arm round her reassuringly.

"It is sad news, dearest; but I really think and hope that for him as well as for my poor mother and father it is the best news we could hope to hear. My brother Walter is dead."

"Dead!" Mavis echoed, her eyes filling with tears. "Oh, Garth, your poor mother, poor Lady Davenant!"

"It has been a terrible blow for her," Garth assented. "But I think in time she will come to see that it is for the best. It will at least mean to her the cessation of the ever-haunting anxiety which has been gradually wearing her health and strength away. While to poor Walter—Mavis, have you ever thought what a life his must have been, tortured by an abiding remorse, as I know he was, haunted by the constant fear of capture and the felon's dock? Better, far better, had it been for him had he boldly stood his ground at the time and taken his punishment, whatever it might have been. Ah, Mavis, you never saw him, but when I remember the big brother of whom I used to be so proud when I was a boy, and then think of last night, the contrast seems too dreadful!"

Mavis softly laid her hand on his in silent sympathy, and presently he went on:

"I was able to be with him at the last—it did not matter then. Before he was always afraid that my movements were watched. But he sent for me."

Mavis looked bewildered.

"Was he in England then? I thought—I fancied that he never came back, that he was safer abroad?"

"He died in a mean little lodging in one of the dingy streets at the back of the Strand," Garth said. "For years Walter had been in the habit of paying periodical visits to England, visits which used to keep us in a constant state of anxiety, and since illness overtook him—an illness I verily believe brought on by the constant state of ferment and unrest in which he lived—the yearning for his own country seemed to grow stronger, his visits became longer and more frequent, and our anxiety consequently increased."

"Poor, poor fellow!" Mavis whispered as she wiped away her gathering tears. "And poor Garth!" with a swift glance at the man's half-averted face.

"Yes, it has not been a pleasant thing to have hanging over one! I wonder now whether you guess why I met Nurse Marston in Exeter, Mavis?"

The girl looked at him in surprise.

"You do not mean—?"

"Walter had come over," Garth proceeded. "He was staying in Exeter in a poor quarter of the town, and he was taken ill; it was impossible to procure proper nursing and attention for him there without attracting suspicion, and I hit upon the idea of asking Nurse Marston to come over and see what really was the matter with him and if she could do anything. Once before she had nursed him in London, and several times when my mother had seen him he was in hiding at the Marston's cottage. Mrs. Marston nursed him, you know, and both she and Mary were devoted to him; but when Mary and I got to his lodging we found that something had made him fear that he was being followed, and that, ill as he was, he had managed to get away. So Mary came back the same day, and was thus, unfortunately, at liberty when a nurse was wanted at the Manor."

He paused to note how Mavis received this information. She looked at him reproachfully.

"You could let Nurse Marston know that your brother was in England, and yet you would not trust me, Garth! I think I—"

"It was not my own secret, dearest," Garth said slowly. "Such tremendous issues for all of us were involved that I dare not risk letting a single unnecessary person into the secret. One unguarded word might have aroused suspicion, and until Walter was safe out of England I dare not speak. Besides, even if I had been at liberty to tell you, Mavis, I should have hesitated to add another anxiety to those which were already weighing heavily upon you. Must I confess it"—a tender smile dawning in his eyes—"the thought that you would trust me, were taking my bare word, was very sweet to me. It was that thought that kept me silent. Mavis, you will not turn against me now?"

There was a moment's pause; Mavis bravely struggled against the feeling that Garth ought to have confided in her and overcame it. She looked up in his face with a smile.

"You were quite right, Garth."

Garth's arms drew her to his breast, his lips were pressed passionately to hers.

"My own darling who trusted me! There shall be no secrets between us in the future, please Heaven. Ah, Mavis, I wonder if you can guess how I am counting the days and hours until the glad time comes when we shall be together—alone—just you and I, Mavis!"

"Perhaps I can," Mavis whispered softly, drawing his dark head down to hers, "because—perhaps I shall be glad too, Garth!"

Overdeen Priory was looking its best as the rays of the setting sun fell athwart its glories of Virginia creeper and canariensis, turning them to vivid gold and glowing scarlet; the old grey walls and the mullioned windows peeping out from the wealth of blossom and vegetation gave the requisite touch of softness and shadow. Out on the lawn, beneath one of the wide-spreading cedars, a dainty tea-equipage was set on a wicker-table, while several inviting-looking basket-chairs were standing round. By the tea-table two ladies were sitting, their soft white dresses forming an extremely cool and pleasant contrast with the green sward around.

Very peaceful and homelike the scene looked, Garth Davenant thought as he came out of the library with his small, white-coated son on his shoulder and crossed the pleasant lawn to his wife and her cousin.

"It is impossible to do any work with this fellow, Mavis," he called out. "I meant to look over that brief of Fletcher-Heatons, but not a line have I read. Master Noel was passing and nothing would serve but that he must come in."

"I think Noel is getting spoilt," said Mavis. She held out her arms; the baby chuckled with delight as his father tossed him to and fro and his mother tried to catch him.

Two years of marriage had altered Mavis but little; her figure had grown rather more matronly, her face was a trifle paler, her expression had gained in sweetness and strength; otherwise she was just the same simple, gentle-natured girl whom Garth Davenant had wooed and won in those spring days at Lockford.

Far more change was there apparent in her cousin Dorothy, though for the moment she was smiling at little Noel in almost her old light-hearted fashion. The feathery hair was still tossed lightly back and curled over the small head, but there was a look of settled sadness about the brown eyes, a misty, far-away expression as though Dorothy's actual life was lived not in the present but the past—an expression that appeared to be curiously in contrast with the small, purposeful mouth.

"The picture of Mavis, isn't he?" Garth said as, after giving him a final toss in the air, he deposited him in his mother's arms and turned to Dorothy.

"He is very like her," she agreed. "But sometimes he reminds me—there is such a look of Arthur."

Some of the gaiety died out of Garth's face.

"I know; I have often seen it," he assented, looking absently at the fair-haired baby while his thoughts went back to the young man who for the past two years and a half had been a wanderer on the face of the earth.

For, in spite of his mother's and sister's entreaties, Arthur had steadily refused to come home. Lady Laura heard from him irregularly, sometimes two or three times close together, hurried scrawls little more than accounts of dangers passed, and making a few inquiries about those at home. Then would come long intervals of silence, periods of waiting that wrung the hearts of the women-folk who loved him and prayed daily for his return.

Of that past tragedy at Lockford Manor there remained but little trace, save in Lady Laura's whitening locks and in the absence from Hargreave of its master.

Up in the churchyard on the hill Mrs. Marston slept by the side of the daughter for whom she had mourned so passionately, and the stone above them testified to the respect and esteem of the Davenants for their faithful friends and servants.

Sometimes when Mavis was staying at the Manor she would steal up in the dusk of the evening to the old churchyard, and, standing beside the white marble cross which bore but the one word "Hilda," would drop a tear as she remembered the wayward loveliness of the woman who had assuredly, if she had sinned deeply, loved much, and had suffered much.

Dorothy was often with Lady Laura; it seemed as if Mavis, in going to Overdeen, had left her place for her cousin. But of late a new element had crept into Dorothy's life—an old governess of hers, having inherited a large fortune when it was too late for her to make a personal use of it, had devoted it and herself to the founding of a large crèche. There most of her time was spent, and there Dorothy had visited, with the result that of late the love of the little children had crept into Dorothy's heart, and, to the dismay of Lady Laura, she had definitely announced her intention of spending at least half of the year at the Home.

With all her sweetness Dorothy could be obstinate when she chose, and her aunt's remonstrances had not moved her from the position she had taken up. She was willing to spend part of her time at the Manor, but she frequently declared that her real home, her interest, would be in the crèche.

It was very seldom that she mentioned the cousin who had once meant so much in her life. Incessantly as the name was on Lady Laura's lips, it rarely left Dorothy's, and to-day was almost the first time since Arthur's departure that Garth had heard that name from her.

After a pause he went on, being now very glad that the long silence was broken:

"Lady Laura has not heard from him lately, has she?"

"Not for over three months," Dorothy said dreamily. "He was in Afghanistan then, and spoke of perhaps making his way into Tibet. She is getting very anxious about him."

"He ought to come home," Garth said gravely. "That there would be a certain amount of unpleasantness to be faced, I grant, but a man has no right to shirk his responsibilities in such a fashion."

He watched Mavis for a moment as she busied herself with the tea-things; then the sound of a car in the avenue caught his ear. He leaned forward.

"It is your mother, I believe, Mavis."

"Mother!" Mavis repeated in some surprise. "Why, mother was going to the Lewises! I don't think—"

"I feel sure it is the car from the Manor," Garth repeated. "Perhaps it is some message from Lady Laura."

Mavis turned.

"No! It is mother! She has seen us—she is coming across to us. But who is with her?" She moved a few paces forward; then something familiar in the tall figure following Lady Laura struck her. She paused, and then she cried, "Garth, Dorothy, it is not—it cannot be— Arthur!"

Garth sprang to his feet.

"It is, though!" he cried excitedly.

Lady Laura's face was quivering all over with excitement, tears and smiles seemed equally near.

"Do you see whom I have brought you, Mavis? Yes, he has come home at last."

"Why didn't you let us know?" Garth inquired as Mavis ran to her brother. "We would have come over."

"I did not know myself," Lady Laura explained, her eyes growing dim as she watched the brother and sister." A letter he sent to tell me must have miscarried, so that I had not the least idea until he walked in. He had to hire a car to bring him up. However he is here, and that is the main thing."

"Quite!" Mavis assented as she drew back and surveyed her brother at arm's length. "But here is a young man to whom you have not yet been introduced—your nephew—and Dorothy. You have not forgotten her?

"No, I have not forgotten Dorothy," Sir Arthur said as he held out his hand. "What is this I hear about you, Dorothy, that you want to join a sisterhood or something?"

"Not exactly." The girl laughed, though her eyes did not meet his. "But now that you have come home Aunt Laura will not mind and I shall be quite free."

"Are you perfectly certain that my mother's consent was all that was wanting?" Sir Arthur asked as his attention was claimed by his small nephew.

Lady Laura was easily persuaded to stay for dinner; her pride in her newly-recovered son was very evident.

Mavis and Garth too vied with one another in showing their joy at having this dearly-loved brother with them again. Only Dorothy felt somewhat left out in the cold as the evening progressed. After his first greeting Arthur never spoke to her save when courtesy made it imperative. It even seemed to Dorothy that during dinner he avoided looking in her direction, and she rose from the table with the feeling that the old pleasant, cousinly relationship was broken for ever, and that there was nothing to replace it.

"Now to-night you are to come up very soon—you are not to sit smoking for ever so long," Mavis paused at the door to say to her husband. "We cannot spare Arthur—mother and I."

In the drawing-room Lady Laura and Mavis settled themselves in one of the big settees for a comfortable talk about Arthur, and his wanderings; Dorothy joined them for a few minutes, but presently, feeling out of everything and unsettled, she wandered absently through the open French window and walked slowly along into the scented twilight beyond.

She strolled away up the grassy paths to the quaint little old-fashioned garden which Mavis called her own, and sat down beside the fountain. Somehow Arthur's return had made her realize far more vividly than his absence had done how entirely outside his life she stood, and, despite her courage, tears gathered in her eyes as she felt a strange unaccustomed sense of loneliness.

She hardly knew how long she had been there when she caught the sound of footsteps and saw a tiny speck of light advancing towards her. She sat still; surely whoever it was would not notice her, and would pass by, but her white gown made a patch of light across the dull grass, and the steps came straight towards her.

"Dorothy!" Arthur's voice said softly as he threw away his cigar. "Here you are! I was looking for you."

He stood gazing at her in admiration.

"For me!" the girl echoed as she sprang to her feet. "Does Aunt Laura want me? I will go at once." She moved forward.

Arthur laid his hand on her arm.

"My mother is quite happy talking to Mavis. I am not her messenger. No. I want you for myself, Dorothy. Can't you stay and talk to me a little while?" as the girl seemed disposed to hurry away. "Aren't you going to tell me that you are glad to see me back again?"

"I am glad you have come back," the girl murmured, twisting her hands together nervously. "But I must not stay out, Arthur. I have letters to write, and—"

"Can't they wait a few minutes?" Arthur inquired reproachfully. "You were sitting quietly enough just now when I came up, Dorothy; and I must tell you why I came home."

"Aunt Laura wanted you—we felt sure you would know that," Dorothy said confusedly.

Arthur still retained his hold on her arm, and almost before she had realized that they were turning away from the house he had guided her into a side path.

"I don't think my mother's wishes had much to do with my return," he went on. "I am ashamed to say that I had in no way realized how my continued absence was wounding her. My resolution was formed when I received a letter from her with certain news." He paused and looked earnestly at her.

Dorothy turned away her head.

"You don't ask me what the letter contained," Arthur went on after a moment. "It told me that you were proposing to take up work in a home in East London. When I heard that it struck me that it was time to come back if a hope daily growing stronger in my heart was ever to become a reality. So I am here, Dorothy, to say that I cannot spare you—to ask you to come to the Manor and take care of my mother and me. We want you, Dorothy, more than the crèche does. Will you come? That is the question I have journeyed six thousand miles to put to you. Will you at least give me one word of hope?"

Dorothy drew her arm from his—her trembling was so excessive that he could not but notice it.

"Oh, Arthur, you do not realize—you have not thought—"

"Haven't I?" he interrupted, a touch of passion in his voice. "What else do you imagine has been in my mind through the long days and nights that I have been away from you? I could not come before to you. I made a terrible mistake, Dorothy. Tell me that it is not too late to rectify it!"

"You have forgotten," Dorothy began slowly, almost beneath her breath.

"May I tell you how I feel, Dorothy—that for a time I was deluded: I followed a chimera, but all the while I must have felt that the reality was here. Do not tell me that the awakening has come too late, child. Give me one word of hope that some day you may let me teach you also to forget the past, to give the present to me."

"You are sure?" Dorothy's voice quivered with emotion. "Arthur, I—"

Arthur ventured to catch her trembling hands in his.

"Sure—certain, Dorothy! Will you—"

His arm went round her, his fair head was bent over her beautiful brown hair.

"I—I—think I am sure too," the girl whispered.

THE END

Lightning Source UK Ltd.
Milton Keynes UK
UKOW06f1125080416

271844UK00001B/27/P

9 781911 095255